SHADOW OF THE ASH
JAMES FRENDO

Dedicated to my grandfather.

Grief fuels creativity.

If you or someone you know is struggling, please reach out to the following resource:

United States and Canadian Suicide and Crisis Hotline: 988

CONTENTS

CHAPTER ONE

G runting in exertion as he cut away the thick vines ahead of him,
Scout Commander Zayid grumbled quietly as he swatted yet
another insect off of his neck. What possibly could have inspired the
Estyrian military command to want to attack a jungle city was beyond
him, but that type of information was above his pay grade by a significant degree. Stopping for a moment to sip from his waterskin, Zayid
glanced behind at the twenty men following in his trail. Nineteen of
them he'd known since he first joined the army, but the twentieth man
was a new face.

Foremost amongst his group were Sahura and Mosegi, his left-
and right-hand man respectively. Following behind them were Heru,
Sarapi, Arta, and Hathmon, the most combat-oriented of the bunch.
Ani and Nofre were joking around with Nezeb and Sabak, the scout
group's reconnaissance experts, while the twins Mharo and Mhuro
argued about who was the older brother. The cook, Khonsu, was idly
scanning for herbs as their medic, Sephis, kept him on the trail. At the
back of the line of men, the alchemists Nophi and Senuf compared
notes with each other as the trio of troublemakers, Nuru, Kheres, and
Ra-Kep, earned their titles by goofing off in the foliage.

Trailing behind, almost out of sight, was Amon. While Zayid and his men had been working together for several years, Amon had been placed with them by order of the upper echelons of military command without explanation. Orders were orders and Zayid didn't ask why he was supposed to come along, but something told him not to trust Amon. Perhaps it was the way he carried himself, or the highly controlled tone of voice he had, but the commander didn't want to let him out of his sight.

Once he was done with his drink, Zayid turned back towards the jungle and hefted his blade up once more to cut away vines in his path. From what his map told him, Zayid knew that he would be coming up on the outskirts of the city soon enough. It didn't help that the damnable jungle canopy was too thick to let in much light, and that not every predator was wise enough to stay clear of them. "I wonder," he mused inwardly, "if we could just wander the jungle for a few weeks and tell the higher ups we never found it?"

A shrill cry of surprise pierced the quiet ambience of the jungle, the entire group drawing their weapons as they turned in its direction. The trio burst out of the foliage, panting heavily as Zayid angrily pushed his way through the line to get to them. He crossed his arms and glared at each of the three, letting them catch their breath before speaking. "Would one of you care to enlighten me as to why the three of you are screaming bloody murder in the jungle? Or, for that matter, why you broke off from the group in the first place?"

Kheres and Nuru, still bent over trying to catch their breath, weakly raised their arms in the direction they came from. Ra-Kep stepped forward, heaving from exertion as he spoke. "I... saw something we ird... in the trees," he said between gulps of air, "went to go check it out...you've got to see this, commander."

Zayid rolled his eyes and, one by one, slapped each of them hard on the back of the head.

"The fact that the three of you made it past childhood is a miracle by the strictest standards. You should know better by now not to wander off, especially without letting anyone know. Now, what could you have possibly seen that warranted that reaction?"

Nuru cleared his throat and spoke up, looking at Zayid with a shockingly uncharacteristic seriousness. "We were walking along, and the air seemed to change. The shadows got a little darker, the jungle just went... silent. Then out of nowhere, we found this big red tree thing. We thought it was some monster that came to kill us, and ran back as fast as we could."

Out of the corner of his eye, Zayid saw Amon's head snap up at the mention of a strange red tree in the forest. After a moment's consideration, he spun the trio around and shoved them forwards. "Well then! If there's a tree scary enough to frighten the three of you into fleeing, then that's a tree I want to see. Lead the way!"

Stumbling forwards, the trio began retracing their steps as the others followed cautiously behind. After a mere minute, that unnatural change could be felt; it was as though they had stepped into another world, identical yet intrinsically altered in some fashion. Zayid shivered softly as he stepped into this strange area, an instinctive revulsion welling up in his stomach. Still he continued onwards, his sense of duty overpowering his feelings of unsettlement.

Soon the scout group entered a shaded grove, thick water sloshing around their ankles as they filed in. The normally talkative bunch were silent with the exception of uneasy murmurs, all eyes locked onto the center of the grove. A great willow tree stood menacingly, the normally wispy hanging branches frozen into metallic daggers. It was as though a great vat of molten metal had been dumped atop it, solidifying into a twisted mockery of the tree. What little sunlight pierced the canopy above glinted off of the maroon metal, like a hundred glowing eyes across its form.

After a few moments of silence Zayid cleared his throat, drawing the attention of his men. "Well, I can't poke fun at you three anymore, if I had stumbled across this I'd have damn near soiled myself. Anyone have any ideas what that thing is? Senuf, Nophi, any insights would be appreciated."

The alchemists merely nodded their heads, dumbstruck as to what could have caused this. The group slowly drew nearer, stopping a few feet from the base of the willow. Nophi stepped closer, tapping the metal lightly with the tip of his dagger. Motioning for Senuf to assist him, he slowly began to scrape off thin layers of an ash-like power into a glass vial. "We've never seen anything like this, but we'll take some samples. This may be the same metal we were sent to look for, but how it got this far from Sosias is beyond us."

As the alchemists went about their business, the others warily looked at the strange tree and the surrounding grove. Zayid sent Sahura and Mosegi to check the perimeter while they waited, the remaining sixteen men talking amongst themselves in hushed tones. Zayid kept an eye on everything and everyone, gauging the mental condition of his men by their interactions. Once again, Amon was acting just strange enough to draw his attention, barely participating in conversation and always keeping his eyes on the tree. He hadn't even reacted when he saw it for the first time, simply staring at it with his constant unusual calmness.

Ra-Kep left the group as the alchemists finished, staring into the dullish red metal as he approached the tree. After a moment he kicked the trunk, snorting in petty triumph as he did. "Stupid tree," he muttered before turning away to return to his friends. He froze as a sharp crack could be heard from the metal formation behind him, slowly turning along with everyone else to look.

A small crack in the place Ra-Kep had kicked soon began to spread, encircling the entire tree's trunk. Then, as the now-separated base and trunk balanced precariously, the weight of the metal-laden branches pulled the tree to the ground away from the group. When it did, the metal shell's interior was exposed; a thick, black, rotten sludge poured forth, the tree within having decayed to an unnatural degree. In the sludge, dark worm-like creatures thrashed and squirmed in the suden light, and an odor of incomparable vileness caused the entire group to gag or vomit outright.

Then, before the entire group was incapacitated with voiding their stomachs, Amon burst forwards. With the collar of his tunic pulled up over his mouth and nose, he swung his blade at the jagged metal edge of the fallen tree. In a shower of sparks, the sludge caught fire almost immediately. Amon stepped back and watched as the abominable slime was consumed by flame, the worm-things screeching as thick black smoke poured from every opening. Zayid and his men watched in silence as they recovered, the smoke burning away the disgusting scent and its source.

Amon sheathed his blade and turned back to the group, all of whom were staring at him in either shock or awe. Zayid simply gazed upon him in disbelief, unsure whether to thank him or treat him with even further suspicion for dealing with the strange goop so easily. He quietly walked towards Amon until they were but a foot apart, a scrutinizing glare cast by Zayid looking the man up and down. "Where exactly did you say you were transferred from?"

Amon stared back incredulously, blinking a few times in surprise before answering. "The 32nd Infantry division, on orders from my commanding officer. Why do you ask?"

"Why do I ask? We just found a metal tree, which you didn't bat an eye at, and when it started oozing black slime you seemed to already know just what would work in destroying it! Either you're just lucky and act without thinking, or there's something you're not telling us. Frankly, I don't know which is more dangerous to the safety of my men and the integrity of this mission." Zayid snapped, tired of feeling left out of the loop on an aspect of his own mission. The other scouts were all waiting to hear what was going on, their own curiosities surfacing.

Amon sighed and rubbed the back of his neck, looking at Zayid with an expression of both awkwardness and confusion. "Wait, so you weren't told why I was put in the group? Wow, uh... four years ago, the Ishtar incident. Some sorcerer's experiment got out of hand, so the 18th, 26th, and 32nd Infantry divisions were dispatched to clean up the mess. Spent nearly eight months dealing with the craziest shit under the sun, learned that if something doesn't seem right you should apply fire immediately."

Zayid felt realization and a small amount of shame wash over him; every Estyrian soldier had heard the rumors and stories about the Ishtar incident, and how some of the things the infantrymen had to do left them changed men. He patted Amon on the shoulder apologetically with a sigh of his own. "No, they didn't tell me. I should have figured it out on my own, it makes sense. I'm sorry for bringing it up."

Amon shrugged it off, a thin smile on his face. "It is what it is, intel gets lost in the chain of command all the time." He turned back to the tree, most of the smoke having cleared away by now. When it had fallen over, some other trees had been knocked over by the metal branches. Beyond those fallen trees, a large open area was lit by sunlight brighter than what was normally found under the jungle canopy.

Zayid furrowed his brow in concern, slowly walking towards the opening in the thick trees. "A field would have been on the map... Come on everyone, form up. This could be important to take note of, and I'm not going to have my head on the block if we miss something that damns us later."

The scout group quickly crossed the grove, going over the fallen trees and up an incline. Once they reached the top of the incline, every man simply stopped and stared in shock at what lay beyond. Zayid took a step forward and blinked, unsure if he could trust what his eyes were telling him. "By the shining scales of Stygirius," he murmured, "what the hell happened here?"

Before them, a series of jagged ravines carved through the earth like cracks in pottery. Dozens of feet deep, the land near these crevasses seemed devoid of life. What trees still stood on that shattered land were black and twisted, dead remnants of the once untouched jungles. That same maroon metal was present in great splotches, having bubbled over the sides of the ravines and pooled in large quantities before solidifying. The skeletons of various animals were littered haphazardly upon the ground, half-sunken into the metal or leaving scorched bones where they had burned to death.

In the far distance, the amount of land torn apart seemed to increase. Reddish metal in great concentrations could be seen, light reflecting off of their surfaces. Large sections of stone jutted up from the wasteland, displaced by the earth's movements. In that distant area, nothing remotely resembling a jungle stood. All that remained was the by-product of some disastrous calamity.

All heads swung towards Amon, expecting him to have some insight into what had happened here. It took him a moment to notice the expectant looks, but he shook his head. "Listen, I don't know what you all think I went through, but this is on a whole different scale.

Ishtar was the work of one careless sorcerer, this..." He shook his head again, trying to think of anything he could compare to this. "This is beyond human abilities."

Silence laid undisturbed upon the group for some time as they gazed out at the broken land, each person lost in their own thoughts. Eventually Zayid broke the silence, gathering the attention of the twenty men around him. "Listen up! This... destruction is just a sign we're on the right track. From what I can see, the wastes lead in the same direction we were already going, so we're going to stay on the jungle's edge and follow it to Sosias. Any questions?"

Sephis slowly began to raise his hand, but Khonsu quickly slapped it down. A quiet chuckle rose up from the group as Sephis rubbed his hand, comedically exaggerating how much it hurt. With a smile on his face, Zayid did a quick headcount before turning toward the treeline. "Okay, let's get moving! And if you see the trio wandering off again, leave them."

The three troublemakers paled before beginning their hike, sticking close to Zayid rather than lingering behind again. The others followed in his wake, never leaving the jungle but staying close to the treeline. Hours passed as the scout group traversed the edges of the wasteland, the sun slowly sinking as the day ran on. The unnerving effect that the strangely ruined lands had upon them all lessened with time, and surely enough of the chatter of conversation returned to help distract them on their journey.

As dusk settled upon the land, the scout group came upon a ridge. Zayid gave the order to ascend, sending the men grumbling as they walked up to the summit. Another hushed silence fell over the group, both shock and relief stunning them all as they looked towards the wastes. A red sun was falling towards the horizon, streaks of orange scattered across the clouds as the vast wasteland glimmered softly with great stretches of that red steel. At the horizon's edge, the silhouette of vast ruins stood out against the sinking sun - Sosias was finally within reach.

Zayid planted his sword in the dirt, quickly assessing the area. Though the ridge was bare, it was not afflicted in the same manner as the wasteland. The jungle was only a few dozen feet downhill, and a small stream was but a few minutes walk away. With a smile he clapped his hands loudly, drawing the attention of the others. "Okay boys, packs down! We're setting up camp here, we leave for the city at dawn!"

A collective sigh of relief was exhaled by the men as they slipped their leather travel packs from their backs, unpacking bedrolls and retrieving hatchets for firewood. Amidst all the commotion, Amon stood at the edge of the ridge and stared out at the distant city. His brow was furrowed in an expression of concern, watching the outlines of the broken walls as though they were going to move. Zayid slowly walked up beside him, staring out at the city as well. Both men felt it, an instinct deep inside which called for their immediate retreat. They were staring into the clutches of hell itself, and it waited patiently for their arrival.

After a few minutes, Amon quietly posed a question to Zayid. "Do you think we'll make it out of there? I mean, it might just be the fear in me talking, for all we know it could be perfectly safe, but..." He trailed off, swallowing audibly. "This feels so different from Ishtar, so much bigger."

Zayid simply stared ahead, his eyes locked onto the center of the waste. "I couldn't say. We're a group of armed men trained in stealth and reconnaissance, but we very well may be walking into a trap. Perhaps we'll be able to fight our way out of it, or maybe it'll kill us before we know what happened. All I know is that I'm not leaving a man behind who can be saved, and that I'm either going home to a medal or not at all."

Amon chuckled and looked over at Zayid, seeing the man in a new light. "A medal, hm? I didn't take you for a glory hound, commander."

"Oh, I'm not doing this for the glory, it's worthless to me. I'm doing this to show my daughter that her old man's not useless after all. Maybe even get her forgiveness one day." Zayid smiled sadly and patted Amon on the shoulder, turning back towards the camp. "Come, lets get set up for the night. Tomorrow's going to be a tough day for all of us, and I need my beauty sleep."

Amon turned and watched the commander go, leaving him with more questions than answers. The beginnings of a proper camp were starting to take shape, the frameworks of makeshift tents gathered around a half-built campfire. After glancing back at the setting sun, Amon joined the others in their preparations. Tomorrow would begin their journey across the wasteland. Tomorrow, the fallen nation of Sosias would be intruded upon by the Estyrians once more.

CHAPTER TWO

Some time had passed since sunset, and soon the only lights were the pale glow of the moon and the crackling campfire's burning glow. The scout company were either gathered around the campfire or on watch, quietly chatting amongst themselves as they ate from their rations and the smoked meat they'd made during the trek through the jungle. Zayid, Hathmon, and Artam stood at the edges of the camp, staring down the slope of the ridge lest some jungle cat sneak in unseen and drag someone into the trees as an evening meal. The rest were telling stories, making jokes, and having as good a time as they could.

Khonsu had just finished his much-adored knife juggling, a trick which brought endless entertainment to his comrades, causing a well deserved round of applause to rise from the seated men. Suddenly, Nuru stood from his seat and walked around the circle of log seats to sit down beside Amon. The more attentive people grew quiet and stared, watching the interaction between the two lest Nuru earn his title of troublemaker. The mischievous man smiled and took a bite from his dried boar, chewing with a thoughtful expression for a moment. Then he swallowed, wrapped his arm around Amon, and pulled him close. "So! Amon, buddy, what was Ishtar like? You've got to have a few stories-"

Nuru's sentence was cut short by a yelp of surprise as a large dagger suddenly embedded itself into the wood just below his groin. Across the campfire, Khonsu picked up another dagger and wiggled it menacingly. The cook leaned over and whispered into the ear of Sephis, who nodded and glared at Nuru. "Khonsu says to not be rude, and that the next dagger won't be a warning if you keep it up."

Nuru gingerly removed his arm from Amon, who was quite obviously trying his best not to laugh at the nearly-neutered man, and scooted a few feet away. The rest chuckled softly, amused by the antics and subsequent consequences that he got up to. Amon let out a soft sigh, patting the scout on the shoulder. "You're fine, I won't hold it against ya. Honestly, until today I was wondering why no one had asked sooner."

A few moments passed in silence before Amon sighed once more, louder this time. "Okay, how many of you want to hear about the Ishtar incident?"

A chorus of confirmations rose up from every other seated man. Amon shook his head softly and leaned forwards, staring into the fire. "Fine, fine. But you'll all be disappointed in the end, disappointed or horrified. We didn't do anything spectacular there, you know. Now, where to begin..."

"It was, as you all know, about four years ago. A sorcerer's project had gone awry, and we were sent to clean up. Before any of you ask, I don't know who the sorcerer was or what the project was, that information's above my paygrade. We spent the first six months or so just guarding a single location, a sandstone cave filled with a strange liquid. It was smooth and black, and I swear to Stygirius you could see distant stars sparkling in the inky blackness. It was as though someone had tried to bottle the night sky, and spilled it into this cave for safe keeping."

"The reason we were guarding it was that things crawled out of it every few days, beasts that defy description. They were easy enough to handle, stab them and either burn them or push them back in, but don't let them touch you is what we were told. May the gods help the man who lets a person either fall into or get dragged into the pool though, and may they give peace to that poor soul. That stuff changed people. Humans went in and what came out was only human-shaped half of the time, twisted and changed like they'd been given to some demented cosmic sculptor. Elongated or fused limbs bent at impossible angles, rotting scales that covered the flesh which sloughed off to reveal writhing bones, any and every horror imaginable."

"Now, if that was all that happened there, you'd never have heard about Ishtar. Those first six months were the easy part, the last two weren't as fun. See, the liquid was supposed to stay in the cave. To be fair, it did, we just didn't know that the cave also led to the oasis by the village of Ishtar. Long story short, by the time we realized it had gotten into their water supply things had already taken a turn for the worse. Villagers started to slowly change, becoming feverish as their bodies were transformed over days in front of our eyes. Often-times, it was too much for them to handle and they seemed to die. When the people we thought to be dead started crawling out of the mass graves, we got new orders."

"The 18th and 32nd divisions were sent to handle the situation. Two months we spent watching close to a hundred and fifty men, women, and children lose their bodies to mutation. We tried burning the dead when they first died, but when they started moving again all they did was scream. We shepherded them into the biggest building in town, but they never stopped that gods-damned screaming. Eventually one of the men had enough, took a torch to the place. By the time we got there, it was too late. The inferno had caused the building to crumble, and all we could do was watch as their twisted bodies writhed in agony."

"That's where we learned that fire, if hot enough, solves most problems. The people inside were burned to ash, and we were told by someone high up on the chain of command to cut our losses and do the same to the rest of the village. Within a week, Ishtar and all of its residents were ash, and we were sent back to our garrisons like nothing ever happened." Amon looked away from the fire, wiping a tear from the corner of his eye. He looked up at the rest of the men, noticing that it had grown oddly silent.

The other members of the scout company were staring at him, their faces etched with a mixture of pity, horror, and disgust. The silence was unbroken for a few solid minutes as the men absorbed and processed this information, a few members retreating to the ridge's edge to retch out of sight. Amon sat and rubbed his hands together awkwardly, head hung low as he contemplated just how big of a mistake this may have been. "I uh... I told you that the story wasn't anything spectacular."

The various members of the company stared blankly into the fire or off into oblivion, trying to get a handle on their emotional states after being told of the tragedy at Ishtar. Realization had struck them with force, all of the various times foot soldiers had been reprimanded for talking about Ishtar and inquiries about the events being shut down suddenly made sense. Amon waited a few seconds longer before rising to his feet, deciding that sitting with the others would likely only make the situation worse. He only got a few steps before someone had grabbed his hand, preventing him from leaving. He turned to see who had stopped him, gazing upon Nezeb and the sympathetic smile on his face.

"I'm sorry that you had to go through that, Amon. But I'm happy you made it out, and I'm sure that whatever happens won't be anything like what happened in Ishtar." Nezeb gently pulled the confused infantryman back to the circle around the campfire, seating Amon down beside him and Sabak.

The rest of the men nodded in agreement, offering their silent sympathies to Amon for his traumatic experiences. Nuru cleared his throat and wrung his hands, the context of Amon's hesitancy made painfully clear and a wave of guilt washed over him. He stood and walked over to Amon, falling to one knee before the man with his head held low. "I... I'm sorry for making you talk about what happened. Please forgive me for my stupidity."

Amon stared at him for a few moments, the silence stretching on longer and longer. A bead of nervous sweat dripped down Nuru's face, unsure whether or not to move from his position. The tension rose only a few more seconds before Amon began to chuckle, patting Nuru on the shoulder and motioning for him to stand. "All is forgiven, Nuru. I can't blame a man for ignorance to a truth purposefully kept from him. I can however say that I got an apology from you, something famously rare if I've heard correctly."

Across the circle, Kheres spat out the dried meat he had been chewing on and guffawed loudly at Nuru, pointing at him and heaving in laughter. That same laughter spread throughout the group, everyone laughing with rather than at Nuru. He couldn't help but softly chuckle, returning to a seat with a smile on his face. Soon the laughter died down, the mood once again lightened throughout the camp.

Amon grabbed a stick and began to poke at the fire, a charred log collapsing and sending a spray of sparks into the air as the embers below flared. He looked out at the comrades around him, seeing how the conversations and merriment resumed almost immediately. Turning to Nezeb, he gently patted the scout on the shoulder and leaned in close. "So, I've spilled my guts to everyone here, but I've no idea how the lot of you got into the military or even into this unit. Have any stories?"

Nezeb turned to him with interest, smiling widely as he did. "Ah, curious about the rest of us, hm? I suppose it'd only be fair. Now, you've got to promise that whatever is told on this mission stays between the lot of us, alright?" He waited until Amon had nodded in agreement before continuing, elbowing Sabak in the ribs playfully. "Me and Sabak have been friends since childhood, thick as thieves as it were. Quite literally, too. We stole a few dozen loaves of bread from the village baker over the years, but nothing serious. Anywho, a visiting army captain saw us running through the streets, jumping over barrels and dodging through crowds of people. He immediately had us brought to him, offered us a life of glory in the military as scouts."

Sabak butted in with a grin, cutting off Nezeb's next sentence. "What he didn't know was that we were actually running from the local poacher, who had been selling his meat in some back alleys. Thankfully, the only thing he was really afraid of was the military, so he decided to leave the issue lest they investigate his business. Anywho, we accepted his offer and got an express ticket into the scout corps. Our favorite commander Zayid was the first to look at us, but passed us over on the first selection."

Nezeb rolled his eyes and shoved Sabak's head back, sending his friend rolling backwards over the log. "That's what you get for interrupting. Anywho, a few weeks in, we got pretty hungry. So we snuck out one night to the officer's pantry, managed to get past the guards and all the way into the pantry before we were caught. Who caught us, you might ask? None other than commander Zayid, who had also been stuffing his face with an illicit midnight snack. We were expecting to get our hides beaten off of us, but instead he gave us a key to the pantry and offered to get us into his scout company as long as we made sure to cut him in on the pantry raids."

Amon arched an eyebrow at the story, glancing over his shoulder as the fastidious and professional commander of the scouting company with a look of incredulity. "Wait, so HE was sneaking into the pantry after hours? I can't believe it, I'd have bet a year's salary that he was one of the most straight-edge officers I've ever met." He shook his head and began to chuckle, the mental image of a shocked-looking Zayid stuffing his face with fresh bread forming in his mind's eye. "I take it you've been supplying him with food ever since?"

Sabak playfully smacked Nezeb on the back of the head, answering while his friend glared at him. "Yup. Because of us, we're one of the best-fed scout companies in the entire military. If anything I'd say we normally eat like a bunch of officers, but when there's a big meeting that requires even Zayid's attendance we grab as much as we can carry and feast like kings while the officer's mess hall is unguarded."

Mharo leaned in, curious as to what the trio were talking about. "Hey, are you guys sharing stories of how you got into the company? Sweet! I love hearing the one about Zayid in the pantry."

Amon chuckled and nodded, motioning the twins over. "What about you two? How did the two of you end up in this group? Seems like everyone here has a story, and it's only fair that I get to know them now that I'm working with you."

Mharo got up and grabbed Mhuro by the arm, pulling him over as the two thieving scouts scooted out of the way to make room for the twins. "Well, where to start... I suppose we could just start at the beginning. We had a fairly average childhood, farm boys by an oasis plot. We helped run it until we came of age, then decided together to join the military. In basic training we tested unusually high on in-combat co-operation, so we initially were supposed to go to more advanced training to become higher-ranking warriors."

Mharo stopped to take a breath, and Mhuro picked up where he was in the story without missing a beat. "However, commander Zayid saw something in us that the rest didn't. Mharo and I had created a sort of private language for the two of us, so we could talk without having someone else read it. He convinced his superiors that we'd be excellent in sending encoded messages, especially since no one else can understand our little language. A few bribes and some sweet talking later, we ended up here."

Amon nodded with an impressed smile, looking at the twins in a newfound light. "So you two are the communications experts, then. Makes sense, I can't tell you how useful it is as an infantryman to know that your intelligence hasn't been intercepted and tampered with. Shame about the road not taken though, I've heard that some of those mage-guards live like nobility even on the warfront."

The twins shrugged in unison, smiling widely at Amon. "It is what it is, no point in regretting what might or might not have been. Though living like nobles doesn't sound too bad, I'm sure that our parents would appreciate the money we could send home at that level of status."

Amon looked around the campfire for a few moments, wondering who to ask about next. His gaze fell upon Khonsu and Sephis, and he began to wave them over. The pair walked around the campfire to the gathering of men, joining the little circle forming on that side of the fire. Nuru stood and went back to his friends on the far side of the camp, making room for the two of them to sit on the log. Amon smiled at the cook and his companion, eyeing the sheathed knives on Khonsu's belt idly. "You're a pretty good aim with those. Thanks for the intervention earlier."

Khonsu nodded with a smile and leaned over, whispering into Sephis's ear. Sephis smiled and scooted forwards, drawing Amon's attention. "He says thank you, and don't worry about it. One of these days he's going to miss, and on that day he'll have spared the world from the possibility of Nuru having children."

The small group of them collectively chuckled, sharing a laugh at the absurdity of the prospect. Amon looked at Khonsu curiously, debating internally on whether or not to ask. "So... if it's not a sensitive topic, why don't you speak? I've noticed you whispering into Sephis's ear whenever you have something to say, but I've never heard you say anything yourself."

Khonsu and Sephis looked at each other and nodded, looking back at Amon with nonchalant smiles. "I've told this story enough times to know it by heart, so I've got it. Eight or so years back, when Khonsu was still a fresh recruit, he saw an officer accepting bribes to let some people desert. He went to report it to his officer, but the officer in question had seen him leaving. He was cornered as he was leaving, and had his throat cut for trying to stop the traitor."

Khonso lifted his beard and raised his chin to reveal a thin white line stretching from one side of his neck to the other, causing Amon's eyes to widen in shock as Sephis continued. "Well, lucky for this big lug, I was an apprentice to a medic situated nearby. I found him just as they left, and managed to apply bandages to his neck quick enough to slow the bleeding til I could get a properly trained medic. He nearly didn't make it, but the cut was mostly shallow and we kept someone nearby at all times. A week later, he managed to whisper to our chief medic what happened and the traitorous officer was executed."

Sorely impressed, Amon gazed upon Khonsu with a newfound respect. "But what about his voice? Why can't he speak?"

"The knife didn't hit any major arteries, but it did manage to damage his vocal cords. He can only speak in a whisper now, and seeing as I saved him I've been helping him ever since. He didn't even want to go back to his regiment without me, and seeing as the infantry didn't want to carry around someone useless in a fight like me we were sent to the scouts." Sephis finished the story with a smile, leaning against Khonsu.

Amon was about to say something in return when Zayid suddenly walked into the ring of logs, clapping his hands to get everyone's attention. "Okay, enough chatting. Go to bed, you'll need the rest if we want to cross the wastes in good time. I'll see you all in the morning, and I'll wake up whoever's covering the second shift of the watch in an hour or two."

The men around the campfire grumbled as they went to their tents and bedrolls, and Khonsu shrugged as he got up to leave as well. Sephis stood with him and stretched, yawning as he waved goodbye to Amon and the rest. "Good night you guys, sleep well."

Amon sat and watched as everyone else went to bed, a little confused as to why the conversation had ended as suddenly as it did. He turned to look at Zayid, and found Zayid looking back. They stared at each other for a moment before the commander winked and chuckled, throwing a nearby bucket of water onto the fire before turning away to go back to his post. "Good night, Amon."

CHAPTER THREE

At the crack of dawn, the camp was awoken by the sound of metal striking metal over and over again. Khonsu stood beside Commander Zayid with a playful grin, a large iron pot in one hand and an iron ladle in the other. Over and over he struck them together until the entire scout company was awake, peering out of their tents with barely opened eyes and minor irritation etched onto their waking faces. Zayid rested his hand on Khonsu's shoulder to signal the cook to stop, stepping forward to bring everyone's attention to him as Khonsu packed up his kit. "Alright everyone, you know what day it is! No point trying to stay in bed, I won't let a single one of you get a wink more than I've already given you. Up!"

With grumbles of annoyance and a few people begging for just a few more minutes of sleep, the scout group was up and packing up their sleeping arrangements within a few moments. Sunlight had barely began to rise above the treeline by the time that the entire camp had been packed up, the campfire completely snuffed out and its ashes pushed a dozen feet down the ridge before being buried in an earthy hole. Amon had just barely gotten his stuff together when he got up and walked to the gathering, staring in wonder at the environment that had been seemingly untouched by their presence. He walked up to Kheres, the closest person, and waited until a break in the conversation to insert a question. "Sorry to interrupt, but I need to ask. How did you guys just erase every sign of a camp being here, and why haven't we done this sooner?"

Kheres, who was munching on an apple, turned to him and looked thoughtfully off into the distance. "Ah, right," he said in between chewing and taking another bite, "you're not a proper scout. In order to make sure that whoever we're scouting doesn't know we're here, we have a system for pretty much everything when it comes to covering our tracks. Leave no trace, don't mark the land, sleep on rock faces so there aren't any flattened grasses that might indicate a camp, the works. Once the target's on the horizon we get into this train of thought, so you'll probably be seeing a more serious side of us from here on out."

Ra-kep butted in, pushing a yelping Kheres aside so he could be heard better. "It's all been fun and games so far, but now that we're here we need to be professional. Quiet and orderly this, timely reports that, yadda yadda yadda." Ra-kep began to goose-step for comedic effect, changing the inflection of his voice to sound more like Zayid. He only got a few steps before he turned around on his heel and found himself face to face with the Commander, his voice trailing off as the blood drained from his face.

Commander Zayid squinted at Ra-kep, scrutinizing him intensely. The other two of the troublemakers tiptoed away to the other side of the group, putting some distance between them and the Commander while Amon chose to stay and watch. After a few seconds Zayid grabbed Ra-kep by the shoulders and adjusted his posture, forcefully straightening his back and putting his hands firmly by his sides. He slapped the scout on the rump and sent him off goose-stepping again while shouting verbal commands, the terrified Ra-kep trying to maintain his adjusted posture and follow the orders.

"Left! Right! Left! Right! Keep them feet up in the air at waist height with each step, I don't want to see a single bend in those knees boy! If you're going to do impressions of me during a formal military ceremonial march, you're damn well going to do it right!" Zayid shouted with the ferocity of a drill instructor, the coy smile on his face revealing the sheer joy he was getting from the entire situation. The rest of the scout company had turned to watch as well, laughing quietly amongst themselves at the ridiculousness of it all.

After a few minutes of the goose-stepping, Zayid waved his hand and dismissed Ra-kep. He turned to Amon with a smile as Ra-kep ran back to his friend, motioning for the infantryman to walk with him as the company began to move down the ridge and towards the wastes. "Don't mind those three, they're tricksters and more than a bit stupid by any sense of the word, but they do wonders for morale. Not to mention the chaos they can create and get away with if given an outlet, like an enemy encampment or a particularly rude nobleman's caravan. Are you excited to finally arrive at Sosias?"

Amon thought for a few seconds before responding, carefully choosing his words. "I'm happy to perform my duties to Estyria, and if that means going to Sosias then I have no complaints. If I may speak freely however, I'm not particularly excited about entering a wasteland of unknown origin where all of our maps show a jungle used to be. I'm also not looking forward to entering a city where the Estyrian military lost the most men in a single campaign I can remember, especially one where victory was supposed to be all but assured."

Commander Zayid threw back his head and guffawed loudly, clearly amused by the answer. "Well said, my friend, well said! If I'm being totally honest, I agree with you wholeheartedly. Even as officers, the majority of us only have bare bones information on the siege a year ago. All we're told is to discourage talking about it amongst our men, and that's as much as the higher-ups will tell us. The extent of the wasteland's spread I'm sure they'll want to hear about, and it's unfortunately up to us to see whether or not it's passable."

"Speaking of which, Nuru! Kheres! Ra-kep! Front and center, stat!" Zayid shouted, walking up towards the edge of the wasteland. Like a jagged line, there seemed to be a sharp cutoff between the untainted jungles and the harsh, barren soil of the wasteland. The trio of troublemakers immediately lined up in front of him, standing at attention. He looked them each in the face, staring intently into their eyes for a few seconds. Then, without warning, he shoved the three of them across the line.

The trio fell on their asses onto the dusty ground with yelps of surprise, staring up at their commander in confusion. Zayid sighed and crossed his arms, turning around to look at the scout company. "Okay everyone, entering the wasteland doesn't kill you instantly. Let's get moving, we're burning daylight!"

Forming up in rows of three, the men arranged themselves into formation and waited for Commander Zayid to start walking. He situated himself at the head, with Sahura and Mosegi flanking him on either side, and Amon was pulled in beside Sephis and Khonsu. As soon as the trio had dusted themselves off and walked to the back of the formation, grumbling as they went, Commander Zayid let out a sharp whistle and the formation started forwards. As each individual crossed over the border of the jungle into the dead wastes, they felt the same sensation run up their spines. A feeling of hesitation, revulsion, and fear washed over them, but the scout company pushed through and began the long march to the city.

The short hours of the morning passed in relative peace, the sun slowly climbing higher into the sky as the scout company made their way into the barren plains. The march had been wholly uneventful, simply a long walk through gray and dusty dirt on their way to a distant destination. However, as the sun began to near its apex, the true scarification of the land became abundantly clear. The first time they had come across one of the great ravines, Scout Commander Zayid had ordered a full stop and went to investigate himself. Though nothing lurked within them, he came back somehow shaken. His left- and right-hand men took him aside and asked what was the matter, but he had simply shaken his head and ordered the march to resume.

As the scout company passed the ravine, they were given a good look at what had shaken Zayid so badly. The ravine was deep enough that even at midday it was pitch black at the lowest depths, a bottom to the cracks in the earth not visible to the human eye. All along its walls were flows of solidified red metal, the same type that they had encountered before. Skeletons could be seen jutting out of the deposits, the flowing molten metal carrying the dead down to the depths of hell. With this ill omen in mind, the normal conversations which were held in order to pass time on the march grew quiet and grim.

The great chasms and rifts in the ground grew more and more common as they went further and further into the accursed lands, growing longer and beginning to connect with each other like the arcs of a lightning bolt spreading in many directions. The red metal began to be more and more prevalent on their path, the memories of what the material did to the tree still fresh on the minds of the scout company. Any time which they had to cross over a large deposit which either bridged a gap or simply was the quickest route through the wastes, they did so in great haste and extremely reluctantly.

When the company found a large stone outcropping jutting from the earth, they sheltered under it to refresh and eat their midday meal. Khonsu began to prepare food for the group as the others found somewhere relatively clean to sit, large rocks bereft of dust being a luxury seat which only the lucky found. Out of the heat and able to give their aching legs some time to rest, lively conversation once again sprung up amongst the scout company. Zayid had Sahura and Mosegi seated by him, his map of the area fully unfurled as the three of them did their best to try and document the changes in the landscape with a stick of charcoal. Amon had seated himself by Khonsu and Sephis, finding that their company was far more enjoyable than that of the rowdy bunch scattered around.

Sephis had spent the last few minutes teaching him how to properly suture a wound closed with a basic needle and thread, something which could be incredibly useful upon his return to the 32nd Infantry division. He just finished pulling the threads closed on a practice suture done on a piece of his pork jerky, receiving a nod of approval from Sephis, when he looked over at the group's impromptu medic. "So, we were cut off last night before we got a chance to finish. Would you mind telling me about everyone else?"

Sephis nodded and smiled, reaching across with a pair of shears to snip the string he'd given to Amon. "Sure, it'd be no problem. Talking while working is always more fun, and while we chat I can show you how to actually tie off a suture so it doesn't just open up again. Who'd you like to start with?" He said, leaning across to where Amon sat to show him up close the proper knot to use.

Amon watched the medic go to work with great interest, internally memorizing the style of knot that Sephis was tying and doing his best to follow along with the steps. "Hmm, lets see... How about the quartet of warriors you guys have? I didn't think that a scout company would actively have people whose primary skill set is fighting." Once Sephis was done with his knot, he began to fiddle with the strings of his own stitches to try and recreate it.

Sephis leaned back and chuckled, recalling the details of the story within his mind. "Haru, Sarapi, Arta, and Hathmon, our resident fighters. They're not particularly good scouts, but they fill a different niche that Zayid wanted to have in the company. If we're ever sent on a long-term scouting mission, then the Commander has us set up a temporary base of operations til the mission's over. They're supposed to be the guards of that sort of base, but otherwise they're mostly here to make sure we won't get slaughtered if we actually do get found."

Amon nodded his head, accepting the logic of the decision. He'd managed to get the knot nearly tied, but just as he was pulling the ends of the strings apart to tighten it the entire thing split apart into two somewhat twisted threads. He hung his head in defeat, grinning despite himself as he heard Sephis begin to laugh quietly. "I'll give it to you, these are harder to do right than I would have otherwise thought. Where did I go wrong?"

Sephis leaned forwards and watched as Amon went through the process again, sticking his finger into the strings halfway through the process. "There. You crossed them over each other, but you didn't actually wrap one around the other. If you don't, the entire thing just unravels." He took the string in question from Amon's hand and slowly slipped the end through the hole made by the crossing strings. He handed it back and watched with delight as Amon finished the process, pulling the strings taut and finding that every other step had gone right.

"Well well well, it seems that either my eyesight isn't as good as I thought or my memory isn't, because I didn't see that the first time." Amon lifted the pork jerky up to eye level, inspecting the suture and smiling with inward pride. "You know, there was a time in my life where I would have bet money that my hands weren't near steady enough to do this. But turns out that steadiness isn't the issue, it's just making sure that you don't put in the needle too deep or too shallow."

Sephis snorted, taking the needle back from Amon and wiping it off with a rag before resting it in a bowl of boiling water. "That's certainly one way of looking at it. Though if all you needed was to know where to put a needle, I imagine every soldier in every army would be a trained field medic. Unfortunately for the rest of you, there is a lot more that I would have to spend weeks teaching you before you fully understood the scope of our jobs. Now, who's next on your quest to know everyone at least a little bit?"

Amon looked around the shade, trying to figure out who would be the most interesting to hear about. His gaze fell upon the pair of alchemists, and he pointed them out to Sephis. "Those two, Nophi and Senuf. They're alchemists, I thought that they were a fairly rare sight in the military. How did you get them to join?"

Sephis nodded and smiled, glancing over at them. "Good question. To be honest, I don't quite know myself. How they were recruited into this company, your guess is as good as mine; if I had to put money on it, I'd say that they're either still in training and saw this as a good opportunity to discover new herbs or they heard about the places this scout company gets sent and thought it'd be interesting. Commander Zayid always manages to get us the weirdest assignments."

Amon gazed over at the pair, who'd set up some equipment on a flat rock and were actively performing tests on the residue they'd gotten from the tree as well as the dust on the ground. A small puff of smoke had come out of the funnel of the alembic flask, which seemed to amaze the pair of alchemists to no end. He chuckled as they began scribbling furiously into their notebooks, flipping through a large book which must have weighed as much as a standard soldier's pack on its own. "It seems to me that this scout company has every-thing one could possibly ask for in a proper military deployment, but surprisingly few dedicated scouts. Why is that?"

Sephis shrugged, pointing over his shoulder towards the Com-mander. "It's Zayid's choice who is put in his company for the most part, and apparently this ongoing project of his has some of the high command interested. He's got this idea of a new type of military division, units made up of a few people of every specialty we can think of under one banner. He told me about it before, said the goal is to create a team of people who can insert themselves into any scenario and have enough versatility to accomplish any goal with some degree of success. Now, most people would call him a nutjob, but you can't lie about results. This company has managed to pull off some crazy stuff, but those are stories which I'd need far longer to explain in detail."

Amon thought this over for a moment or two, considering the benefits and downsides of having a group of various military pro-fessions working as a unit. While they may not be the best equipped to do one specific thing, a military unit like what Zayid had put together here would be highly adaptable to the situation. He stared over Sephis's shoulder at the Commander, watching as he scribbled out landmarks onto the map. "What's the story with Zayid anyways?

I know he has a daughter who he's not on the best of terms with, but otherwise he's a mystery to me."

Sephis turned and looked as well, sighing as he gazed upon his superior. "That's a story I don't feel comfortable telling. If you're that curious, ask him yourself one of these days. In the meantime, is there anyone else you'd like to know about?"

Amon shook his head, standing up and stretching his legs. "I think that's good for now, we should save some topics for the rest of the trip so we don't go mad." He turned around and looked out at the wastes, the vast grayish-brown plains of soil and earth stretching on for as far as the eye could see. The shimmering pools of solidified metal sparkled in the sunlight, providing a strange sense of menace despite their apparent mundanity. In the far distance, the ruins of Sosias stood tall amidst the crags of rock and shattered ground, the center of the devastation.

Amon's eyes seemed to gravitate towards the city as he observed the vast desolation before him, squinting slightly as a soft gust of wind blew some dust into his eyes. He began to wipe it away before stopping, looking around and seeing a wind begin to pick up. The first wind they had felt since arriving at the edges of the wasteland, the first wind they had seen since their camp had been set up last night. Others in the group noticed it too, standing up and walking to the edge of the shade while using their hands to block the dust from hitting their faces. In the distant city, a great gray cloud began to whip up around the city's edge.

Amon felt a hand on his shoulder and instinctively stepped aside, letting Commander Zayid through to the front. The company watched as the winds picked up speed, whirling faster and faster around the city. The effects were far lesser this far away, but the strange sight of a whirling funnel of ash and dust enveloping the city wasn't diminished by distance in the least. As the particles which had previously blanketed the city were lifted forcefully into the air, a quiet gasp ran through the group as the maroon steel which they had so strongly avoided became visible. It appeared as though a great amount of the buildings they could see were encased in it, and the reflective glare of sunlight off of the metal seemed to cast reddish rays of light into the whirlwind.

For a few moments, it seemed as though the faint memory of a great column of fire could be seen against the pale blue sky, an imprint of an inferno long since ended. As abruptly as it had started, the wind ceased blowing without warning. The great cloud of ash and dust slowly drifted back down onto the ruins of Sosias, blanketing the city once more. There was a silence which fell upon them, one which was so absolute that even the breath of a mouse could be heard. After a few moments, that silence was broken by the hushed whisper of Khonsu's voice. "What the fuck was that?"

CHAPTER FOUR

O nce the shock of seeing the strange wind had worn off, Zayid turned towards Sahura and Mosegi and motioned for them to bring over the map. Scribbling onto the page with his stick of charcoal, he drew a whirlwind figure above the city and wrote 'strange weather patterns' beside it. The others continued to stare at the city, as if expecting another unnatural occurrence to tear up the sky and instill fear into their very hearts. But no such event came, and the tension of waiting slowly drained as the shattered wasteland seemed to return to the mockery of normalcy it had previously. Most heads turned towards Amon as though he could provide an answer, but his head was turned towards the alchemists and their impromptu workshop.

He made his way through the group until he stood in front of the pair, both of whom had been staring slack-jawed at the city even now. Once his body obstructed their line of sight, Nophi and Senuf snapped back to attention and looked up at Amon in surprise. He looked down at them with a scrutinizing gaze, staring into their eyes for a few seconds each before his stare wandered over to their equipment. "I saw your little experiment, saw the puff of smoke it created from that flask. Did that have anything to do with what we just saw, or mere coincidence?"

The two alchemists looked at each other in surprise, the possibility of such a thing happening not having crossed their minds. Without a word they dove back towards the book, flipping rapidly through the pages as they searched for a record of a comparable situation. They replied without even bothering to look at him, too consumed by their search for understanding to tear their gaze from the book for even a second. "We don't know, but we'll look. If we did do it, we're going to need to try and recreate it to learn the extent of our ability to alter the weather with these materials. If we didn't, then it may have been a coincidence."

Zayid approached Amon and the alchemists, looking over at them and arching an eyebrow towards Amon. When all he received was a shrug, Zayid sighed and whistled loudly to gather everyone's attention. "I hope everyone enjoyed that little display, but break time is over. Strange whirlwind or not, we're going to the city and I plan on getting there before nightfall. Get your gear together, I want to get back on the march in ten minutes!"

The grumbling of nearly two dozen people who didn't want to leave the shade could be heard all around Zayid, paired with a general trepidation towards entering the city that could be almost tangibly felt in the air. Khonsu packed up his cookware again as Sephis slipped his needle and twine back into his medic satchel, and the alchemists reluctantly closed the book and began to seal and put away their various flasks and tools. Zayid took one last look at the map, making sure he hadn't made any false corrections, before rolling it back up and tucking it into his pack. Within minutes, everyone had taken up their marching formation and was ready to go. Zayid took one final look at the jungle in the distance, the safety of the green canopy an attractive possibility compared to the city of death before him, but he forced himself to turn away and start the march.

The closer the scout company grew to the ruins of Sosias, the rougher the terrain became. The cracks and crevices which they'd previously been able to avoid became more and more frequent, and the ground seemed to be almost entirely covered in the strange maroon metal beneath the dust which coated everything in sight. More and more often did the large spires of crag-rock which seemed to have been pushed up out of the ground appear, the splitting of the earth in some places compressing it powerfully in others. Midday came and passed, the sun slowly beginning a downwards slide towards the horizon. The ruins became clearer as the scout company approached, the intact buildings - and the sheer scope of destruction wrought on those not intact - becoming more defined.

The walls of Sosias had been brought low, a few towering spires of scorched black stone and red metal standing where the walls had been strongest. The rest of the great wall had been shattered, large fragments of the once-proud barrier scattered around the city's out-skirts. Large jagged spikes of metal were often embedded in larger sections of the wall, pierced through by these darts as though they'd been launched at great speeds. As the company approached the border of those walls, they found that the base of the wall and the open area near what had once been the treeline was covered in piles of bones, burned clean or encased in metal. Such corpses were unidentifiable, and no one dared get close enough to see whether or not they were Estyrian or Sosian.

As they approached the city, Commander Zayid ordered the for-mation to come to a halt. He stepped forwards alone, slowly walking forwards until he reached the edge of Sosias. A small hill of rubble marked where the wall had once stood, and he cautiously ascended it before looking around. As far as the eye could see, the clay and mud huts of the former slums were all but decimated, not a single structure standing that had been in this ring. All that remained were the broken husks of countless homes, shattered remnants of walls peaking above the thick ash which seemed to coat the ground in an endless blanket. He slowly descended the other side, stumbling as he stepped off the rocks and found that his foot sunk into the ash almost all the way up to his shin.

Turning around, he shouted back to the scout company which the pile of rocks had obscured. "All right, it's safe to come over. Formation is no longer needed, climb over and spread out. Watch your step, the ash is deeper than it looks."

One by one, the men came over the pile and looked around in a mix of awe and horror at the ruins of the outer ring. The company began to spread out, their attention drawn to various places of interest both near and far. Before anyone wandered off too far, Zayid whistled and had everyone come back to form a circle around him. Once Zayid was happy that he had the company's attention, he pulled out two rolled up maps and handed one of them to Sahura. "Okay, listen up. We've got some objectives to fulfill, and I've got a plan to do just that."

"We're going to split into two groups, one to begin an evaluation of the red metal deposits of the city and one to find an appropriate place to set up as a base until we depart. Sahura and Mosegi will be leading the group to evaluate the city's remaining spoils, and I'll be looking for an appropriate place to set up a base of operations. Amon, Senuf, Mhuro, Sarapi, Arta, Sabak, Nuru, Khonsu, and Sephis - you're with me. The rest of you are going on the evaluation team. We'll meet up back here by the time the sun begins to dip below the horizon, and then we'll move to the FOB from there. Any questions?"

Amon raised his hand, and once he got the nod from Zayid he cleared his throat. "This is more of a request than a question, but if no one minds, could you make sure to pick up any Estyrian insignias or banners you see? We may not be able to identify the bodies, but if we can bring home flags or anything that signifies the dead as ours, then we can finally give the families of the men in those units some peace."

Zayid nodded, a melancholy smile on his face. "Good idea, Amon. New objective to add to the list! If any of you see something that was once ours, collect it and bring it back to camp! Don't get yourselves hurt or killed over it, but if you can manage it then you'll be giving peace of mind to grieving widows."

Everyone nodded or said something in agreement to this, and Zayid clapped his hands together. "Excellent! Now let's get moving, there's only so many hours in the day and I do not want to have to chase the lot of you down in the darkness." With that the scout company split into two, one going straight into the city as the other ventured off around the ring.

Zayid led his group straight through the outer ring, trudging through the ash towards the center of the city. The large pyramid at the center of Sosias towered above the rest of the city, split nearly in two yet still managing to have a sense of presence to it that was nigh inescapable. He'd had his map open since they started their trek towards the interior, smaller than the area map he'd been scribbling on earlier yet far more detailed even at a glance. He stopped suddenly, causing Amon to nearly stumble into him before tugging the infantryman closer and showing him the map. "Tell me, does this look like the angle we came in from?"

Amon looked at it closely, his eyes widening as he gazed upon the intricately drawn map. It was a map of the city, drawn back in its height. Every road and path could be seen, the separate buildings in the inner rings able to be picked out amongst the many around them. Zayid's finger was pointing to an intersection in the slums, a crooked crossroads near the wall. Amon squinted and leaned in closer, inspecting the shape and order of the buildings up and down the roads on the map. He straightened his posture and looked around, noting the ruins around them and trying to match them with what was on the map.

After a few moments he leaned back down and looked closely at the map again, squinting as he tried to overlay the map onto the visible ruins in his mind. He reached out and pointed to a fork in the road a few streets over, tapping on it a few times. "If I had to say, I think we're here. Which means," he said as he traced his finger up the road towards the water separating the rings, "we should be going southwest if we want to head inwards. There is a mountain off to the side if we follow the ring around a bit, but I'm not sure what it would even have that's worth the effort."

Zayid nodded and rolled the map back up, tucking it into his satchel before setting off again on their altered course towards the interior. The group followed behind, hands on their weapons lest something pop out of them. It was nearly a half hour before they got to the edge of the slums, the grayish ash growing darker as they approached the bank of what used to be a river. The canal where water used to flow was empty, instead coated in a gray-black sludge which coated the countless mostly-decomposed bodies seated at the bottom. Though white bone poked through the slime in dozens of places, leathery skin treated by intense heat was stretched over some few torsos and skulls. The group recoiled in disgust as they happened upon it, feeling revulsion and the urge to vomit well up in their stomachs.

None succumbed to the urge like they had when the tree had fallen over, but none wanted to risk getting closer lest their stomachs fail them again. It was Amon who pushed himself to give the horrid trench a second glance, looking left and right. As far as the eye could see, there were no bridges or ways to get across the canal. All that could be seen was rocky outcroppings, places where bridges might have once been. "That's the only way across I can see. Are... are we going to have to go through that to move forward?"

Sephis was the first to speak up, gently putting his hand on Amon's shoulder and pulling him away from the canal. "I really don't think it's a good idea to go wading in the strange gray slime filled with corpses to get across. Isn't there some other way we could get rid of the slime, like burning the stuff? I really don't want to have to go through that, and Stygirius only knows what would happen if we got it on our clothes or our skin."

A quick glance at the faces of the others in the group showed similar hesitation towards sending anyone into the dried up canal, and Amon couldn't deny that the prospect of going in himself felt like a mental punch to the gut. From the back of the group, Nuru stuck his head up to put in his thoughts on the matter. "Hey, it's just more horrible slime close to that weird red metal. What are the chances that lighting it on fire will get rid of it all? It'd definitely make getting across easier."

Zayid sighed and crossed his arms, clearly torn. "Let's put it to a vote. Whoever wants to go into the sludge canal, raise your left hand. If you think that burning it is a better idea, raise your right hand."

There was not a single left hand raised amongst all ten of the men, and thus the decision was made unanimously. Amon pulled a torch from his back and lit it, holding it above the canal. He closed his eyes and muttered a soft prayer to Stygirius under his breath, begging not to have something worse result of this action, before dropping it. Much like the tree, the goop caught fire almost immediately and spread in a roaring blaze down both sides of the canal, lighting the entire outer ring's river bed aflame. Amon took a few steps back as the fire blazed brightly, a wave of heat bursting out and driving him away from the lip of the canal. He raised a hand to his face, the explosive spread of the fire causing him to try and block the light before he saw something unusual.

As he and the other nine members of the company watched it burn, one by one their gazes lifted from the fire to the smoke rising above it. Through the noxious smoke, a different view of the city could be seen as though they were looking through a veil. They saw the city of Sosias as it had been during the calamity, a raging inferno unlike any other. The crackling and popping of the fire as bones cracked and burst from the heat coincided with the snapping of oak timbers as the buildings before them collapsed, sending a wave of sparks out in all directions. Instinctively the group took a step back, looking away for but a moment as they shielded their eyes from the sparks. When they looked back, the smoke had risen too far to peer through the veil and the fire had burnt itself out.

Zayid stared across the canal, seeing the ruins of charred or utterly shattered wooden buildings burnt out long ago and reflecting on the fact he had seen how they'd gotten that way in the first place. Wordlessly he walked over to Senuf and spun him around, digging through his pack and pulling out some items. He righted the alchemist to face him and shoved a journal and a pen into his hands, leaning in close and staring directly into his eyes. "You are going to walk and write. By the time we regroup, I want at least three theories ready for presentation as to what it is exactly that we're seeing. I don't know what is going on, but by the heads of Stygirius I better have a few good ideas."

Senuf paled and wilted back a little, shrinking under the sudden pressure to perform as well as the intensity in Zayid's eyes. He was clearly confused himself, stumbling over his words as he tried to logically explain what he'd just witnessed. "I-I-I don't know Commander, there's so many possibilities and variables to consider. Is the phenomenon magical or natural in nature, what triggers it, is the trigger alchemical or natural or magical, so on and so forth. I'd have to take notes, run repeat experiments, replicate the process to see if it produces the same result, consult the book-"

The alchemist was cut off by Zayid as he clamped a hand over his mouth, taking a deep breath and calming himself before speaking. "Senuf, I need you to listen to me. I know you want to do all of this, but we're in the middle of what is still considered enemy territory. The city is in far more ruins than a normal siege should produce, the ground itself is scarred and tainted, and now we're seeing things in fire and smoke. I don't expect you to give me a solid answer, I just need you to get a hold of yourself and theorize. Can you do that for me?"

Senuf slowly nodded his head, his widened eyes slowly relaxing as he pulled himself out of the hyperactive train of thought he'd been stuck on. Zayid removed the hand covering his mouth, and he inhaled deeply as his full ability to breathe was restored. He opened the journal and flipped to a blank page, beginning to scribble with his head firmly down. Now that he had a task to focus on, Senuf visibly relaxed as his training kicked in and he began to document both phantom images with as much detail as he could remember.

With Senuf calmed and put to work, Zayid turned towards the rest of the group. They had been talking amongst themselves quietly, sharing their own thoughts on the whole situation amongst themselves. Only Amon had been watching his handling of the alchemist, nodding in approval towards the way he'd focused Senuf on a task to avert his attention. Zayid whistled loudly, calling the attention of his subordinates. "Alright, we're going across the canal now that it's been burnt out. Keep your eyes open for anything strange, and if you see movement call it out. Amon, walk with Senuf - he'll be distracted for the time being, and I really don't want to have him walk into a pit."

The group got ready to move again, adjusting their packs on their backs before walking up to the edge of the canal. The entire canal had been purged of the horrid sludge as far as the eye could see, burnt away without a trace. One by one they carefully descended the slope, careful not to touch any exposed skin against the heated stone, and ascended the other side. The nigh-demolished slums were behind them now, and the burnt-out hollow shells of the trade district were all that could be seen on their path ahead.

CHAPTER FIVE

Where the wastelands and the slums had been eerily silent, with the exceptions of the scout company's voices and footsteps, the trade district had an ever-present distant noise in the background. From any given direction, one could hear the sound of creaking timber straining under its own weight, robbed of strength by the fires that had torn through the district long ago. The slightest touch could cause any of the smaller or more damaged buildings to collapse, the precariously balanced structures collapsing inwards in a cloud of ash and wooden fragments. Nails which had once held boards together had melted in the inferno, the hinges and locks of doors melded into solid objects unable to be moved or manipulated. Not a single structure was spared from the flames, and though some were far more intact than others it wouldn't have taken much effort to bring a large building down.

Ash coated the streets, the walls, the rooftops that remained - everything in sight was covered in it, ankle deep in the shallowest of places. To walk through it was like trodding through fresh fallen snow, providing just enough resistance with each step to be noticeable. Wherever they went, a trail of numerous footsteps was left in their path, unable to be concealed without further disturbing the surrounding layer. Their voices seemed muffled in the district, as though the ash was eating away at the edges of their words. The slowly falling sun cast shadows which only slanted further as the day went on, the gaps in the wooden frames of the buildings above them creating strange figures from the darkness which startled the scouts to no end.

Amon walked beside Senuf as he'd been instructed to, gently guiding the alchemist away from wandering off the path with a hand on his shoulder. He was fairly impressed with the man's ability to focus on writing and block out any awareness of his surroundings, even if that meant Amon had to steer him away from walking right into a sharpened timber which would have impaled him. Thankfully Sephis and Khonsu had chosen to keep him company, falling back a few steps so they could converse on their walk. Unlike their prior conversations however, there had been no comedy thus far. The desolation of the district, and the brief glimpse into the raging fires which had consumed it, seemed to siphon away the joy and happiness in their hearts.

Amon looked around as he walked, watching the sunlight filter through the charred and blackened support beams of the buildings above. He took a moment to imagine the city before all of this happened, observing in his mind's eye the thousands of people who must have walked these very streets every day. He smiled softly, a vague longing welling up in his heart, before he was shaken out of his imagination by a hand on his shoulder. He flinched visibly, his head snapping around to look at who had touched him. Sephis gazed at him with a concerned expression, cocking his head to the left as he noticed the bewilderment on Amon's face.

"You alright, Amon? You didn't answer my question, and you seemed to be somewhere else for a minute there." Sephis slowed his pace, looking at Khonsu for a moment and motioning for him to watch Senuf as they spoke. Once they'd fallen behind just enough to get a bit of conversational privacy, he spoke up again. "It's this place, isn't it? It's messing with our heads, making us distracted when we'd normally be focused."

Amon merely nodded, the disorientation taking a few moments to wear off. He blinked a few times to clear his eyes, reaching up to wipe a stray tear that had been welling up in the corner of his eye. "I'm fine, I was... I was imagining what this place would have been like before the siege. Whatever we did here, it destroyed so much more than just the city itself. It's like there's something missing, something I just can't put my finger on."

A sharp whistle rang out through the air, getting the attention of both men. They ran through the ash, following the trail of san-dal-prints to rejoin the group as fast as they could. They found the other eight men standing at the entrance to a large open area, frozen in place as they looked inwards. Amon and Sephis slowed their pace as they approached, walking up to stand beside their comrades. Amon split off from Sephis, walking up to the front of the group and stop-ping once he was behind Zayid. "Commander, what did we stop for... oh."

Amon's voice trailed off as he followed the Commander's line of sight forwards, staring across the square at the large mass of red metal which sat in place. What he'd initially thought were strange formations rising from the ground were revealed to be bodies, frozen in death and entombed in the metal. Men and women alike, armed and unarmed, were turned into morbid statues, the metal having bonded to their skin while they died. Slowly the group began to walk through the square, taking care not to touch any of the statues as they traversed the perversely displayed mass grave. Though none of the encased bod-ies seemed to have any sharp edges or dangerous features, the thought of touching one of them simply felt wrong at an instinctive level.

In complete silence they slowly worked their way through the courtyard, their eyes locked onto the statues with both horror and a strange sense of intrigue. Zayid led the line, his footsteps marking a path through the courtyard that the others followed as closely as possible. Near halfway through, the Commander stopped dead in his tracks and turned to closely inspect a particular set of statues. His gaze took in every detail it could on the petrified victims, and his breath caught in his throat as he came to a realization. The coating of steel must have been thin upon the poor souls when they had died, because he could make out a shocking amount of detail.

The man on the left had his shoulders under the man on the right, trying to help him flee from whatever caused the wave of molten death to wash over them. Their faces were frozen in petrified agony, the pain of the metal burning their flesh as it washed over them clear on their expressions. In his free hand, the man on the left held a sword - not just any sword, one of the serpentine blades standard in the Estyrian army. His chestplate clearly had the symbol of Estyria etched above the heart, and though the other man wore the clothes of a Sosian commoner he still chose to try and save him. This knowledge floated in Zayid's mind freely, countless possibilities as to why he'd done this popped into his head before he looked away, trying to regain his focus on the matters at hand.

The others had taken this time to look around as well, coming to similar conclusions as they saw both Sosians and Estyrians fleeing at the same time. Sabak seemed the most confused, looking around from statue to statue as though one of them would hold the key to understanding. "Why," he uttered softly, "are they fleeing? I thought the army had been sent in to besiege Sosias, so why are there soldiers aiding the civilians in the city?"

Zayid turned towards him, a grim look on his face. "That's what they told me. Hell, finding the missing shock forces was one of our objectives after securing the city, but I think we just found out what happened to them. It doesn't matter though, we still need to find a place to set up camp, and I don't like the prospects of bunking with these poor bastards. Lets get a move on, we can discuss it when we've got somewhere to sleep."

Sighing in collective agreement, the scouts got ready to move and continued on after Zayid. Once they left the square, they followed one of the main roads all the way through the trade district. The closer they got to the ring, the more and more corpses they found along the way - unlike the market square however, they were not statues. A large wave of the red metal had flooded through the streets, and the only way to tell that anyone had been caught in it was the desperate hands, arms, and heads poking out of the otherwise smooth surface. As the number of limbs sticking out increased, it only seemed to make sense that the number of bodies below them were far greater.

By the time that they had reached the edge of the trade district, the entire group seemed to be affected by a deep, sullen mood. Though they were soldiers, trained to fight and kill for their nation, the natural empathy of human beings still tugged at their hearts as they began to understand the true scope of death that this city contained. Arriving at the next emptied canal was a great relief to them, for spending even a few moments more amongst the burnt husks felt like an eternity. Unlike the previous canal, this one was devoid of any unnatural oozes or residues. It was filled with that same maroon metal which seemed to touch everything in the ruined land, both the city and the wastes around it.

Beyond the canal, the noble district's towering stone buildings stood tall despite the damage inflicted upon them, large cracks in the walls or spikes of metal piercing through to their interiors. Zayid smiled, pulling out his map again and beginning to inspect the middle ring. With the streets mostly unblocked and the buildings somewhat recognizable, traversing this ring would be far easier than trying to navigate the slums or the trade district. He began to jog forwards, approaching the border between districts with a smile on his face. "Come on, we're getting close!"

The other nine men followed behind without complaint, happy just to get out of the oppressively bleak district. While the rest kept pace behind Zayid, Amon ran a bit faster than the rest to catch up with the commander. "Getting close? Close to what exactly?"

Zayid was about to respond before he tripped over, falling to the cobblestones with a loud crash and a groan. Sephis ran up to check on him, but by the time he got there Zayid had already sat up and began rubbing his arm. "Stupid roads, what the hell did I trip over?" He said, pulling himself to his feet. The entire group stopped a few feet away, watching as he kicked away at the ash until something solid could be seen.

From below the ash, an iron chestplate of Sosian make was unearthed. Shock briefly flashed into existence on Zayid's face before it was overtaken by a grim expression, a line of thought coming to light in his mind which could change their understanding of the Sosian calamity. "All of you, help me clear off this part of the road. I have a hunch, and I'm very much hoping to prove it wrong." Then Zayid crouched down, using his hands as scoops to push the ash aside.

His subordinates did as they were told, working as a group to clear away the ash. The more of the ground was revealed, the more sets of Sosian armor and weapons were unearthed from below the ash which coated everything. Once a few square feet had been cleared off, a grim picture was revealed; the Sosians, a normally peaceful people, had been forced to fight some great foe. The owners of these suits of armor had been incinerated where they stood, their bodies crumbling to ash as their armor and weapons were warped and dented by the force of whatever had slaughtered their people. Zayid sat back and sighed, resting his head on the palm of his ash-covered hand.

"Whatever did this to the Sosians, it wasn't us. I can't think of a single force in this world that can destroy people so... horrifically. Not just killing them, ripping them apart in a single fell stroke." Zayid's voice was monotone and bleak, his demeanor shaken by the realization that this destruction was beyond the normal capabilities of warfare.

The group fell quiet once more, Zayid's words hitting them with an almost physical force. A few among them began praying silently, for both the peace of the dead and for their own salvation from whatever did this. Amon leaned back, staring up at the sky aimlessly - the emotions roiling inside of him defied explanation or classification, but he felt like just sitting here despairing over what had occurred would only worsen it. He pulled himself to his feet and dusted off his clothes, beginning to walk down the road without a destination in mind. The others turned to watch him go, the confusion his actions created in them snapping them out of their collective despair.

Arta stood and ran up behind him, grabbing Amon by the arm to stop him from going any further. Amon stopped and turned towards the scout, an eyebrow raised questioningly. The others got up and walked over as Arta grabbed him, the instinct to stay as a group motivating them all into motion. "Where the hell," Arta asked with an interrogative tone, "are you going? Last I checked, you've got no map and no way to tell where this road even leads."

Amon shrugged, tugging his arm out of Arta's grasp. "Honestly, I don't know where I was going. I just didn't think that sitting in the dirt when we've got a base to set up is very productive. I get it, this entire city is a monument to death, but I've got a job to do."

Amon turned and began walking again, leaving the others standing and watching him go. It was Khonsu who made the first move, whispering into Sephis's ear before going after Amon as well. Sephis turned to everyone else and shrugged, joining the other two as they walked down the road. "Khonsu says that Amon's right, and I think he's got a point. Let's find somewhere to sleep, we can feel sad later."

Zayid began to chuckle, pulling out his map and jogging up to join the trio. The others followed behind quickly, motivated by the idea of sleeping more than anything else. Following the map to the place he had previously been heading to, Zayid took point once more and led the scout group further into the noble district. The sun was getting lower and lower in the sky, but Zayid was confident that he could get to his destination in time. After some wrong turns were corrected, Zayid looked to his left and erupted into joyous laughter before running through a set of gates.

Chasing their commander, the nine men followed closely behind to find themselves in front of a large building. Commander Zayid was standing at the top of a set of stairs, pointing up to the Estyrian emblem carved above an open doorway with one hand and spreading his other arm wide in invitation. "We've made it! I would like to welcome you all to the Estyrian embassy, our new base of operations for the time being! Now get your asses in here, we need to start setting up."

One by one, the men went past Zayid and entered the hall of the embassy, spreading out and checking the building for damage or anything of interest. As Mhuro went to enter, Zayid laid a hand on his shoulder and pulled him aside. He looked up at the sun, squinting as he did, before he handed Mhuro the map. "I need you to run back to the rendezvous point and lead the other team here. Can I trust you to do that for me?"

Mhuro nodded and took the map, turning around and setting off at a sprint back down the road towards the slums. Zayid watched him go, silently wishing the twin luck on his journey, before entering the halls of the embassy himself. The entrance area was large, a set of stairs on both the left and right sides of the room leading up to a second floor which had a balcony overlooking the hall. The scouts were ducking in and out of rooms, clearing them for use or closing the doors on the ones that had major damage in them. He smiled and watched them work for a few moments before idly looking around, something nagging him in the back of his mind. He snapped his fingers and spun around, looking at the large doorway once more. "Where the hell are those doors?"

Over the next few hours, the embassy was transformed from a decrepit stone building amongst many into a functioning base for military operations. The secondary group had been brought to the embassy safely by Mhuro, as per Commander Zayid's request. Before anything else was to be done, the issue of reattaching the doors to their hinges was of utmost importance. They'd been found flung away from the doorway by some unknown force, and though it had taken the combined efforts of twelve men they managed to drag them back to the entrance before lifting them back onto the hinges. After securing the building, the scout company spent the twilight hours moving the rubble found throughout the building to the courtyard, using the large pieces of stone to erect barriers for the sake of defense.

Afterwards, as the sun finally dipped fully below the horizon, the scout company was finally allowed to relax. Khonsu had carried a supply of firewood and water with him from the jungle, and had begun the process of making a stew with chunks of salted meat and some herbs he had picked a day or two prior. The ambassadorial offices had been repurposed into barracks due to the presence of a fireplace in each room, and the records office on the second floor had been completely emptied in order to convert it into a proverbial war room. While the rest of the scout company were happily enjoying their supper, Zayid had Sahura and Mosegi delivering their report of what they found.

CHAPTER SIX

"I'm sorry, you'll have to excuse me. There is a *what*?"

Zayid sat at the long table which he'd repurposed into a desk, staring with incredulity at his subordinates. A large map of the city had been unfurled across it, with some loose scribblings about the status of the districts and their contents drawn on each area they'd been in. Mosegi and Sahura stood awkwardly on the other side, trying to properly explain what they had seen on the other side of the city. Sahura opened his mouth to speak but stopped when Zayid raised his hand, looking down to stare at the map with intensity.

Zayid extended his hand out towards Sahura, a stick of charcoal in his grasp. "Take it. Draw it. I'm not sure I'll quite understand it however many times you say it, so just... show me."

Sahura gingerly took the stick of charcoal and leaned over the table, pulling out his own map to have something to reference. He began to draw and speak, making a large and thick line from the city center to beyond the northern wall. "We circled north around the city, trying to map out the slums before moving inwards. After a certain point, we found an area where that red metal seemed to jut out of the ground like spikes. We moved past them without much effort, but these rows of spikes just seemed to grow more and more frequent as we moved inwards."

A large solid line had been drawn and filled in, allowing Sahura to move on to the surrounding area. He began to draw the spikes in their enormity, row after row of them radiating out from the line like the by-products of a blast wave. "Once we'd passed the spikes, we found that the city - even up to the pyramid itself - had been reduced to literal dust in a certain area. The borders between the rings blurred as we found ourselves on an open plain, without even the foundations of a structure in sight." He continued drawing, marking diagonal lines over a certain area around the thick line to signify the desolation.

With the alterations done he put down the charcoal, setting it aside and gazing upon the finished map. A full quarter of the city had been flattened fully, every building or hill flattened by whatever had caused the wastelands to come into being. He sighed, reaching over and pointing his finger to the large black line. "And this is the center of it all. Strangest ravine I have ever seen, absolutely coated with that red metal on every inch of the walls. It's a straight drop down, too - almost looks like someone took the biggest sword ever made and just slammed it into the ground."

Zayid groaned under his breath and began to rub the bridge of his nose, the stress building up to create an extremely unpleasant headache. "So, if I'm finally getting this right, there's a giant crevasse in the middle of the city which goes from the center to outside the walls. Everything around it has been reduced to dust, and further away from it the weird metal has formed a sort of... line of spikes around the radius of it. And this strange ravine of yours is full of the red metal, so you didn't just mark it down as a potential mining spot because..?"

Both Sahura and Mosegi seemed to be at a loss for words, trying to figure out how to explain what they'd seen but struggling with describing it. Mosegi picked up the stick of charcoal and leaned over the table, drawing an x beside the ravine. "When we went here, something happened. It's hard to explain, but I suppose the closest thing would be the whirlwind over the city that happened before we got past the walls. I tossed a torch down to see how far it would fall, and when it disappeared from sight without hitting the bottom we all heard something above us. All anyone caught was a glimpse of a bright orange light, and then it disappeared."

Zayid stewed on this for a moment, taking the charcoal stick back from Mosegi and drawing an x on the canal between the slums and trade district. "There was a strange substance, somewhat like the stuff in the tree, that was filling the canal. We burned it, and in the smoke we saw the city aflame. This trend of finding strange visions and unnatural occurrences is not a welcome surprise, and I think we should all be on guard. If this place can affect our eyes, who's to say it can't make us hear things that aren't there or put thoughts into our heads? If you see someone acting strange, we'll head back here immediately."

"Regardless of this shitshow of an operation, you two did good today. You are dismissed, go get some food in your bellies. Oh, and send in the alchemists if you don't mind." Zayid said, leaning back in his chair. He watched the two men leave, smiling softly as they left the room and closed the door behind them. Even in strange circumstances such as these, those two would always be dependable in Zayid's eyes.

A few minutes later Nophi and Senuf walked into the command center, carrying both their journals and a faint smell of smoke. They stood in front of the table as Zayid motioned them over, pulling up some chairs and sitting opposite the commander at the map table. Senuf cleared his throat as he placed his journal onto the table, opening it up to the notes he'd been writing during their trek. "Good evening

Commander Zayid. I take it you're wanting to ask about the theories we came up with about the strange visions we've been experiencing?"

Zayid smiled and nodded, switching his gaze from one face to the other. "Indeed I am. I've also had an idea which may help solidify our understanding of what's going on, but I'll wait until you're done to speak more on that. Please, you have my full attention."

"Well, so far we've got a few ongoing theories. Once the company was reunited we shared notes and compiled information into the most likely possibilities. First is the theory that the summoning of the avatar of Khigstus left behind some sort of hallucinogenic residue, and whenever one of these events occurs it is because we have inhaled this residue. The red metal could be the culprit, though that would require further testing. This theory does have the downside of having to label the whirlwind as a natural phenomenon, which we both agree is unlikely." Nophi spoke quickly, his eyes locked to the page as though he was running through a list of pre-written points to go over.

Senuf was more animated when he spoke, the ideas roiling in his mind clearly motivating excitement within him. "Our second theory is that the siege of Sosias had an unknown variable that is magical in nature, and what we're seeing is actually residual images of the fall itself. This would explain all three of the visual phenomena we've encountered, and it also means that there are likely more we could find across the city to piece together what actually happened. All we'd need to do is find a common catalyst for these events and then keep it with us, so if we stumble across one it'll appear."

The alchemists looked to each other and smiled, clearly proud of their work. Zayid nodded as they finished explaining, and there was a silence in the room for a minute or two. Nophi and Senuf waited expectantly as the seconds passed, unsure why Zayid wasn't saying anything. Eventually he leaned forwards, a questioning expression on his face. "So what's the third theory? I know you two better than to believe for a second you'd only settle on two options, you always have at least one more idea which is more unlikely but explains everything well."

The duo looked at eachother uncomfortably, shifting in their seats before Nophi decided to respond. "This one is a stretch, even for us. It would explain everything, but it'd also mean that we'd likely have to abandon the mission should it prove true. Anything in this city would be contaminated, and we could only bring back what we originally took with us."

Zayid leaned forwards, both concerned and highly interested. He knew that these two were likely the smartest amongst them, and that Nophi would not say such a thing unless he was absolutely sure. "That possibility, no matter how small, is something that could endanger all of our lives. Tell me this theory, and we'll move forwards from there with all of the knowledge we have available."

Senuf gulped softly, looking around the room as though he expected to see some eavesdropper listening in. He leaned across the table towards Zayid, speaking only in hushed whispers. "The third possibility is that somehow the Sosians angered their god, and angered it enough that it smote them in spite. That might have been why it seemingly destroyed both our forces and the defending Sosian army. I'm not a priest or a sorcerer, but it stands to reason that if they were faced with destruction the Sosians would try to summon their god, and no one would expect your own god to turn on you. This entire area would be affected by that power, and disturbing the site of a god's vengeance could inspire it to bring down its wrath once more."

Zayid stared back at Senuf, his face a calm mask hiding the tumultuous mess of emotion rolling around inside his head. While the explanation was indeed highly unlikely, the horrific possibilities that such an event opened up were far too vast for him to wrap his head around. After a moment he grabbed both of the alchemists by the arm, tugging them close and making sure they were giving him their absolute attention in this moment. "Speak of this to no one," he said through gritted teeth, "and keep this third theory to yourselves. We're not qualified to even begin dealing with the ramifications of that, and seeing as we're already here I don't want my men to start talking about abandoning the mission."

They nodded quickly, not wanting to invoke Zayid's anger if they could avoid it. He released their arms and stood from his chair, walking around the table and heading for the door. "So far, I've begun to think the catalyst you're looking for is fire, or maybe smoke. You had something puff smoke before the whirlwind started, we lit the canal on fire and saw the vision in the smoke, and you tossed a lit torch down that ravine before you had that glimpse of orange light. Do with that thought what you will, but right now I want you two to show me what else you've been working on."

Zayid swung upon the door and motioned for the alchemists to leave, closing the door behind him as he followed behind. He walked along the second floor's balcony, glancing over the railing down at the rest of his company below. Eating from their bowls of stew and talking amongst themselves, they seemed quite happy. This was the first time since they'd left Estyria that they'd slept somewhere with a roof that wasn't a tarp or leaves. He smiled softly as he walked, sighing as he turned away from the sight to return his attention to the alchemists.

They'd stopped in front of the door that led to their makeshift laboratory, a room which had once been a vault or perhaps a prison of some sort. It was the most structurally sound room in the entire building, and the only one to have a solid iron door. Should one of their experiments go explosively wrong, it was collectively decided that containing the accident would be the best use of the room. Nophi gripped the large iron ring that served as a doorknob and pulled with all of his might, grunting in exertion as he swung the door open and held it so the other two could enter. Once Zayid and Senuf were indoors, Nophi slipped inside and let the door close with a quiet groan.

The laboratory was lit by torchlight, high-set sconces on the walls keeping the flames away from the delicate beakers and flasks set up on the tables below. Two long rectangular tables which ran nearly the length of the room had been painstakingly dragged inside and put beside each other, creating a large flat space for the alchemists to work on. A handful of flasks, crucibles, alembics, and ceramic containers were scattered around the table in various stages of use; around them tools such as handheld bellows used to stoke a small flame or tongs to move heated substances were laid beside their most recent place of use. Some of the things which the company had found on their journeys were in their own containers here, a large pot full of tiny shards of the red metal sat in a corner while the large glass vial with the tree's scrapings was sat amidst several sealed alembics and boiling cucurbits.

Zayid's face contorted into a deep frown of disgust as he immediately pinched his nose, the room being filled with all manners of strange odors and foul scents. Senuf offered him a clean rag to wrap around his mouth and nose, which the commander accepted with gratitude. Once his senses were no longer being assaulted by the unnatural by-products of the alchemist's work, he looked around the table and began to inspect the experiments being run. "Can you run me through what you're doing here? One at a time please, I can only focus on one set of terms I barely understand at once."

Somewhat dejected by having to wait, the alchemists seemed to deflate a little as they turned to each other and tried to decide who would go first. Senuf's half of the laboratory was closer, so he motioned Zayid over and began to try explaining what was going on. "Over here, I've got some of that residue mixed with water in a cucurbit over a candle. When it boils, it'll evaporate up into the alembic and travel down this little tube into a flask which I can use for more experiments." He turned towards the other side of his work area and waved in a general manner. "Over there, I've got the residue running through various processes to see if it reacts with anything. Exposure to flame, blood, tree leaves, the works."

With a smile creeping up onto the corners of his mouth, Senuf leaned over the table and directed Zayid's gaze to a contraption with eight sealed flasks on it. The base of the device had a hand crank on one side, and as Senuf began to crank it quickly the circular top of the contraption spun faster and faster. "Here's what I'm most interested to find out. We were given some reagents by our teachers to identify materials with unusual or even supernatural properties, and each of those flasks has one of the reagents and some of the residue. This will mix them together, and if the reagents react to the substance then we'll have found something that may be quite important."

Zayid watched with an eyebrow raised, his curiosity piqued by Senuf's explanation. For a few minutes there was a period of silence among the three men, the only sound in the room being the soft whirring of the spinning mechanism and the bubbling of alembic flasks. Once an hourglass beside the device ran out, Senuf slowed the mechanism to a stop and rotated his shoulder with a wince. He clapped his hands together twice, Nophi immediately stopping what he was doing and stepping away from his workstation until his back was against the wall. Senuf reached for the nearest flask before stopping and glancing at Zayid with a look of confusion on his face, before he suddenly was struck with realization. "When either of us clap twice, it means move yourself as far away as you can so you won't get hurt if something goes wrong."

Zayid nodded and stepped back, leaning against the wall beside the door as he observed the alchemist slowly unclip the flask from the contraption. Senuf shook the rounded bottom of the flask a few times, the materials inside swirling without any visible change. He sighed and shrugged, setting the flash down on the table. "First flask down, no alchemical mixtures were used in creating the red metal." He continued to unclip and gently swirl the flasks, getting four more without reaction.

On the sixth flask, Senuf reached for the bottle but snatched his hand back with a wince. "Hot! Okay, we've got a hot one, strong positive result on that one." He glanced down at his open journal and scanned the page, looking for what this meant. "Okay, sixth reagent means... hm. It doesn't say, it just instructs the alchemist to unseal the flask and record the smell." Senuf shrugged and retrieved what looked like a long and narrow metal knitting needle, poking a hole in the top of the waxen stopper. A puff of smoke burst from the flask, causing Senuf to double over and begin gagging. "Uuuugh, that's sulfur alright. Gods damn it, that's a strong smell."

Once the smoke dissipated and Senuf could stand without nearly vomiting, he noted the strong smell of sulfur and moved on to the seventh flask. He unclipped it and swirled the flask lightly, sighing softly as it initially yielded no results. He was about to put it down when he saw a soft glimmer of red amidst the black mixture, a dark shade which seemed to absorb almost all of the light it touched. He gulped softly and set that flask down gingerly, a few inches away from the others. "Seventh flask is positive, which means magic of a darker variety was heavily present in whatever put the red metal there."

Senuf slowly turned his attention to the eighth flask, the rounded bottom of the glass container filled with a swirling black mist. Rather than reach for it directly, he grabbed a pair of tongs and moved it from the device as carefully as he could. He set it into a small box, leaving it untouched as he shut the lid and began to make it airtight with a wax seal. "Eighth flask is activated, which means that the residue has a corruptive property. It also means that the gas inside is incredibly lethal, and must be disposed of far from anywhere we plan on going to. This stuff tends to linger for a day or two."

Once he was finished, Senuf looked towards Zayid and wiped the sweat from his brow. "Well! Now we know for certain that we're dealing with some nasty stuff, but that was honestly to be expected. I don't see any of us licking any strange metal trees in the near future though, so we should be fine. Nophi, what have you got?"

Nophi motioned for Zayid to walk around the table to him as he went back to his workstation, allowing Senuf to begin the laborious process of recording the results of his experiments in detail. Unlike the distillation equipment that his partner had set up, most of Nophi's equipment was used for more manual processes. Clasps and clamps held up shards of that red metal he'd gathered from the journey, some shards held submerged in boiling solutions or coated with unknown substances. "From what I can tell, whatever this stuff is it's incredibly strong. It doesn't break, it doesn't bend, it doesn't even melt."

Nophi pointed towards a shard of the metal a few inches long, suspended over a small blueish-white flame coming from a glass bottle. The metal seemed entirely unaffected by it, with no visible changes in shape or appearance. "That's an alchemist's fire glass, the hottest flame we're able to produce. Even steel would begin to twist or at least deform in a minor way after a few seconds of exposure to it, but this stuff is untouched. It doesn't corrode either, which is even stranger.

Almost every metal rusts somehow, but other than gold this is the only one I've seen that doesn't tarnish in some manner."

Zayid grunted softly as he leaned forwards, squinting slightly as he lowered his face to look at the flame and the shard. Nophi tapped on his shoulder to continue on to the next experiment, where a mechanism with a hammer was repeatedly tapping a metal shard halfway embedded into a fist-sized chunk of stone. "This metal also doesn't dull if you have a sharp edge. I set this up when we finished preparing the lab a few hours ago, with this shard fully outside of the rock." Nophi stopped the mechanism and grabbed the stone, slowly using a pair of tongs to pull the shard free from the rock. He held it up to the light, showing the still-sharpened edge of the shard. "I'm fairly certain we couldn't actually mine this stuff even if we tried, unless we managed to make a pick out of it first."

Zayid's eyes widened as he saw with his own eyes the resiliency of the red metal, carefully picking a piece out of the pot which held the rest. He held it close to a torch, watching the firelight reflect off of the maroon surface of the metal. "Very interesting finds you two, very interesting indeed. Is there any chance we could weaponize what you've found? Maybe make a sword of the metal, or produce more of that toxic gas you were talking about?"

Nophi and Senuf looked at each other before looking back at their commander, a little concerned with the idea. "The gas is a flat no, sir. Even a minor accident could kill us all if it were mishandled, and frankly I can think of three people off the bat who'd goof off with it. As for the metal, it's possible. You'd have to find a big enough piece though, and that's unlikely."

Zayid nodded and sighed, swinging his arm in an under-hand motion to toss the shard back into the pot. "Understood. Well, we'll keep looking I suppose. In the meantime, I want this all shut down in the next ten minutes, I don't need some alchemical accident happening while we're asleep. I'll meet you two down on the main floor, you should remember to eat something every now and then."

The commander left the room and the alchemists in it, the sound of fires flickering out and glasses clinking together audible behind him before the door shut. He yanked the rag from his face, taking a deep breath of fresh air as he leaned against the balcony. The pale moonlight filtered through the open gap of the window to his right, the sight of the courtyard and the rest of the district from the second floor bathed in a soft glow. He slowly brought his hand up to the moonlight and opened his palm, the shard of metal he'd mimed returning to the pot gleaming in the pale glow. He wasn't exactly sure why he kept it, but he'd palmed the shard and faked throwing it back almost instinctively. After a few moments, Zayid leaned down and slipped the shard into a small pocket in the leather of his boot. He didn't want to part with it, and something told him that it didn't want him to put it back either.

CHAPTER
SEVEN

On the floor of the entrance hall below, the remaining eighteen members of the scout company happily welcomed Commander Zayid and the alchemists as they descended the stairs, inviting them to sit by the fire and eat as the rest of the company did. Stories of the strange things they had seen in the city were shared, often somewhat different from the truth in order to keep the mood light, as they talked amongst themselves and tried to enjoy their evening amidst the ruins. As the night wound down the stresses and fatigue that the day had set upon them all began to set in, and the alluring prospect of sleeping indoors was at the forefront of the minds of each man. It wasn't long before one by one, the members of the scout company bid their comrades a good night and left the common area to lay themselves down on their bedrolls to sleep.

The last man to leave the common area was Zayid, who watched the fire as it flickered and died. Only when the last flames had died out and all that remained were softly glowing embers did he rise from his seat and leave the entrance hall, quietly entering the room in which he'd set his pack down and laying upon the length of leather and fur that served as a sleeping mat. Wrapping the edges of his bed roll around himself snugly, Zayid rolled onto his side and closed his eyes. Sleep came to him softly, his consciousness slowly drifting off into a dream as his body was given the time it needed to recuperate from the journey. Yet this rest was not peaceful, his nose scrunching up as the smell of acrid smoke permeated his dream.

Zayid sat upright in his bedroll, gasping for breath as he looked around. The world around him seemed to have taken on a reddish tint, and the air was foul with the stench of burning bodies. The room which he'd been sleeping in was entirely empty, lacking any traces of the other three men who'd been bunking in the room along with him. He slowly pulled himself out of the bedroll and walked out of the converted bedchamber, cautiously searching for any trace of the others in the scout company. As he entered the common area of the entrance hall, he saw a handful of people huddling together by where the fire should have been. He approached slowly, and as the sound of his footsteps echoed through the hall they turned to look at him.

Sephis, Khonsu, Mosegi, Nophi, Nofre, and Heru stared at him with wide eyes, shocked to see someone else in this distorted reflection of the place they'd been in before. As they turned to look at him, the thing which they'd been huddling around became visible - Amon's body lay unconscious, shivering slightly as sweat seemed to drench his form. A soft red light shone from the palm of his left hand, and faintly glowing lines of red seemed to illuminate the veins traveling up his arm to the elbow. Sephis was holding his field medic's kit tightly to his chest, his eyes bloodshot and tearing up.

"Commander Zayid? What are you doing here? What's going on?" The medic asked with a quavering voice, clearly terrified and at his wit's end.

"I don't know, I just woke up and everything was different. What happened to Amon?" Zayid responded, quickly closing the distance between him and the others before he knelt beside the commander. He gingerly reached out and laid his hand on Amon's arm, his brow furrowing as he felt the intense heat he was radiating. "What's wrong with his hand, and why's he like this?"

Sephis turned back to Amon and began to wipe away the sweat beading on his forehead with a rag, trying to think of a way to cool the infantryman down. "I-I-I don't know, I j-just woke up and he was out here, shaking and with a fever. I don't know what's making his hand glow, I don't know why or how we're here, or even where here is. I'm just freaking out right now, and I would appreciate some patience!" Sephis's voice ramped up as he went on, the stress of being brought to a strange location and being put under pressure to help his superior rising to a peak as his voice became a shrill screech at the end of his statement.

Zayid flinched back, not expecting the outburst from such a timid person. Khonsu leaned in closer and began to rub Sephis's back, concerned for his friend. Sephis took a few deep breaths and ran a hand over his scalp, taking a moment to try and calm himself. "I'm sorry, you're just as confused as I am. You don't deserve to be yelled at just because I'm not sure what's going on, and shouting won't help the situation."

Zayid nodded and watched in silence as Sephis went about his work, and for a few minutes this was all that the present members of the scout company could do - watch and pray. However, the commander was not content to simply sit here and wait for something to happen. He soon enough rose from the circle of people and began to walk towards the doors, the eyes of the others watching him as he went. Zayid placed a hand on each door and, with a grunt, began to push until they were flung wide. As he did, a wave of heat and incandescent light hit him.

The scout commander stared slack-jawed at the sight outside, a city not yet ruined but in the process of ruination. Thick smoke filled the air above, and great balls of fire fell from the sky with impunity upon the city. Screams echoed throughout the stone streets of the middle ring, and the booming impacts of distant projectiles shook the ground almost constantly. Slowly Zayid walked across the courtyard, leaving the embassy building and approaching the street. As he passed the gates, he turned to his left and stared out at the outer rings of the city.

The trade district was a blazing inferno unlike anything he'd ever seen, undulating flame pulsing orange and red as the sheer heat of the fires distorted the air around it. Waves of the molten metal seemed to slowly pour through each individual street, the outlines of countless people fleeing for their lives disappearing as the maroon steel overtook them. The outer district seemed to be in worse condition, the shattered remnants of countless buildings falling into the crevices opening and spreading which seemed to pour forth that same strange metal. At the watery border between the trade and noble districts, both Sosians and Estyrians alike ran for their lives from the flames and the nigh-pyroclastic flood. The sun, shining dimly through the smoke at its apex in the sky, seemed to be but a reddish ring of light amidst the gaping wound in reality that arced and flexed in the heavens above.

A great cackling laughter seemed to echo through the very air as a massive explosion rocked the earth itself enough to throw Zayid off balance, causing him to stumble and fall to a knee. He turned towards the source of the sound, and his eyes widened in terror as he gazed towards the Grand Temple at the center of Sosias. Perched atop the ruined pyramid, a figure greater than he could fully fathom seemed to flicker just outside of his perception; there was no visible shape or presence he could see, but the columns of smoke and whirling clouds of airborne embers seemed to outline the image of a great burning god. It was not so much a form that he could see in this world turned red, clouded with the ash and smoke that accompanies destruction almost universally, as it was a *presence* that seemed to gaze upon the ruin and laugh.

The entire world trembled as a great arc of flame seemed to form in the skies above the temple, the hand of fate driving it downwards as it split the great pyramid nearly in two. Upon its impact a great explosion erupted from the Grand Temple, a shockwave which seemed to decimate buildings near it and send any loose objects flying at incredible speeds. Zayid raised his arms to cover his head from the blast, but he moved too late. He could feel every last bit of his body, every mote of the man that was Zayid, being torn apart and blown away by the explosion as it continued outwards. The last thing he saw before the scorching blast consumed him was the small mountain on the edge of the city, and the shining light which seemed to emanate from a cave near the summit.

Zayid gasped for breath as his eyes flung open, his hands clawing at his throat for breath as he awoke. He sat up in his bedroll, gingerly rubbing the self-inflicted scratches on his neck as he felt his rapid-ly-beating heart begin to slow to a normal pace. Looking around the room, he saw that Mosegi had woken up in a similar state of panic and that Sahura had been seemingly unaffected. The eyes of the two men locked onto each other, and they both realized at that moment that the dream they had wasn't exclusive to them. Zayid quickly flung the fur covering off of himself and left the room, entering the common area that had been set up.

Khonsu and Sephis sat together beside a newly started fire, the haunted look in their eyes confirming that they too shared in that strange dream. Zayid walked up to them with a look of fear on his face, drawing both of their attention to him. "Did either of you check on Amon? Where's he sleeping?"

The faces of the cook and the medic turned pale as the blood drained from them in realization, and the three of them hurriedly ran to the room where Amon had gone into. They pushed open the door and rushed inside, startling the other three men who'd been sleeping awake. Amon lay upon his bedroll in the corner, similarly in a poor state. His body was caked with sweat, his skin was pallid, and he seemed to shiver every few seconds. The three immediately went to his side, kneeling beside Sephis as he began to inspect Amon with an uncomfortable familiarity.

After a few moments, Sephis grabbed Amon's hand and pulled it into the light, wincing empathetically as he saw the swelling on his palm. A crooked lump had inflated just under his skin, and the veins running up his arm from that hand seemed to be more visible through the skin than usual. "Shit... Khonsu, run back to our room and grab me my medic bag. I don't know what's wrong with him, but I'd bet that this is somehow related seeing as this hand glowed in that gods-damned dream."

Khonsu got back up and sprinted out the door, running to retrieve the field medic's kit as Sephis grabbed a torch off the wall and handed it to Zayid to hold. Pulling a small dagger from his belt, Sephis carefully cut open the swollen lump on Amon's hand. A somewhat congealed blood poured out in a thick, crimson stream from the wound, causing Sephis's brow to furrow in concern. "That's not good. Khonsu, where's that bag?!"

At that moment the cook slid back into the barracks, closely followed by the half dozen others whose attention had been drawn to all the commotion. Khonsu passed the bag to Sephis, who quickly took it and began to rummage through it until he found a pair of iron tweezers. After washing away the strange blood with a waterskin nearby, Sephis slowly drew apart the incision until a small object could be seen. He pulled it out with the tweezers slowly, causing Amon's body to shake and groan in agony as he did, until it finally was free of his flesh.

As soon as the foreign object left his body, the swollen lump on his hand deflated as a blackish-yellow fluid seemed to gush from the open wound until his hand was returned to its normal size. Sephis gagged a little bit as he took a rag and wiped the fluid away, immediately tossing it into the fireplace and shuddering in revulsion. Raising the object up in the light of the torch, all could see that the object which had caused this effect was a sliver of that same red metal which covered most of the city. With a scowl on his face, Sephis rose to his feet and walked over to the fireplace to toss the shard in as well. "If even a sliver of this stuff can cause this effect on someone, I want to get out of here as soon as possible. We're going to have to be careful whenever we touch the red metal, otherwise we might end up like Amon."

As Sephis finished speaking, Amon opened his sleep-crusted eyes and began to blink to clear away what remained, looking around the room at all the people standing over him. "What happened? Why does my hand hurt like a bitch?"

Zayid chuckled and knelt beside Amon, helping him sit up as Sephis went to work bandaging his hand. "You had a bit of a close call there. Somehow a sliver of that red metal got in your hand, and it got infected. You can thank our resident medic here for the quick thinking, he's the one that managed to get it out."

Sephis merely shook his head, dismissing the commander's words. "Anyone could have figured out that the big lump on his hand was the problem, I'm just the first person here to have thought of it. Don't worry about it, it's my job and my duty."

Amon chuckled and smiled, lifting his bandaged hand once Sephis was done with it and curling it into a fist. Rising to his feet, he yawned and wiped some of the cooling sweat from his forehead. "Well, thank you regardless. I had the strangest fever dream, and all of you were in it."

All of those who'd shared the dream of a world turned red, bathed in fire and ruin, silently turned to look at Amon. He stared back at them with a confused expression, the look of a man who'd been left out of the loop. "What? Did I say something wrong? I just had a weird dream is all."

"Did you have a dream of a world bathed in crimson light, thick with the smell of smoke and the screaming of people fleeing for their lives?" Zayid said softly, staring up at the infantryman. Amon whirled around to face him in surprise, opening his mouth to speak but finding that his throat had gone dry. He nodded softly, causing Zayid to sigh in frustration.

"This city is doing things to us. The longer we stay here, the more things we see and the higher chance we have of getting a sliver of that metal in us without realizing until it's too late. Tomorrow morning I want us to go back to the jungle, replenish our supplies and maybe set up a safer camp there. I don't know how the rest of you feel, but I don't want to sleep in this gods-damned city again." Zayid spoke loudly enough to grab everyone's attention, the scout company's members agreeing quickly.

With the crisis averted and the plan to leave the city set out, the scout company prepared for the day and got their plans together. With a base of operations now available to them, the company would split into three groups. The first group would travel through the temple district and go to the Grand Temple of Sosias to explore and recover anything of value inside. The second group, led by Commander Zayid, would be heading back to the outer ring to investigate the small mountain on the outskirts of Sosias. Finally, the third group would stay in and around the embassy, allowing the alchemists to continue their experiments and collecting any intact information that they could recover from nearby buildings.

After the plan had been decided upon and the group's members chosen, Khonsu was the first to bring up the dream that some of them had shared while he prepared their breakfast. One by one each member of the scout company described in as much detail as they could the dream they'd had the previous night. While most of them simply had dreams of home, those who'd met in that strange red-tinted world all seemed to share the same recollection of events.

Once they'd all eaten their fill and finished with exchanging their theories and ideas, the scout company split up into their groups and disembarked. The muffled sound of footsteps echoing through the streets as the first and second group parted ways could be heard from hundreds of feet away, the quiet noise still audible in the dead silence. No wind blew to whistle softly through the ruined buildings. No scavenging vultures circled overhead, waiting for someone to fall and provide them with a meal. The city of Sosias was as silent as the grave, and it did not take kindly to intruders.

CHAPTER EIGHT

The second group had turned northwards when they'd left the embassy, leaving their base-bound comrades behind as Commander Zayid led the march towards the mountain on the city-state's edge. Following closely behind were Sephis and Khonsu, the inseparable duo, chatting with their newest friend Amon. Nezeb and Mhuro walked just behind them, trailed by Nuru. In order to try and ward off catastrophe for any one group, the scout company had split the trio amongst the three groups to try and prevent their collective skill for causing chaos from taking effect. So far the attempt had been successful, with Nuru quietly following along and staying on the path without a word of complaint. The fact that Zayid had started their journey off with stating that he'd leave Nuru behind if he got lost also contributed greatly to the suppression of Nuru's drive to cause mischief.

In order to limit the amount of time spent in the abominable waste of the former trade district, Zayid and the members of the first group had spent nigh on an hour poring over the map of Sosias to find the quickest path available. Their journey through the ring was thankfully short, and within an hour the seven of them had crossed back into the vast ashen slums. From there, all that was left was to follow the slow curve of the wall to the mountain that was their destination. In the dawn's early light they trudged through the ash with boots coated in the white-gray powder, the residue of wrath and ruin sticking to their clothes and to their skin.

In silence they walked for some distance, keeping their heads down and just focusing on walking rather than looking around or talking amongst themselves. The city itself had seemed to have an entropic effect on the mind, slowly breaking down the barriers which stopped a person from losing themselves in their thoughts. Those inclined towards melancholy had become quiet and withdrawn, those of a manic tendency grew agitated and highly energetic. Conversation seemed to be a distant memory in the silence which pervaded the slums, the words of the living unwelcome in this city of the dead.

The mountain had only barely become visible in the distance by the time the sun had stopped touching the distant horizon, fully separating from the distant trees of the jungle. Amon looked up towards the light of day and covered his eyes with one hand, protecting his vision from the bright light as he scoured the sky. "Is it just me, or is it weird that we haven't seen any clouds since we got here? We're supposed to be fairly close to the ocean, and jungles are supposed to get a lot of rain. So why haven't we seen any clouds?"

With the almost supernatural silence broken, the other six members of the second group stopped for a second as their awareness came back to the forefront of their mind. Khonsu stopped dead in his tracks, tilted his head upwards to scan the sky for any trace of a cloud in sight, and then turned his head back to Amon. He shrugged and whispered into Sephis's ear, and Sephis turned to Amon as well. "Khonsu says that there should be clouds, but there aren't. He also thinks that it's weird that a city that must have had a well-made infrastructure has no trace of water. I agree with him, honestly."

The others began to speak up as they resumed their walk, bringing up the various things they'd found subtle yet weird since they'd arrived in the city. With the spell of silence broken at last, the joyous chatter of conversation once again resumed amidst the members of the scout company. The melancholic members of the group were lifted from their depressive slumps, and the manic energy of others was once again tamed into a well-honed focus. The long, trudging slog through a vast sea of ash became an adventure again, and the excitement of finding something new was on the minds of everyone there.

The sun had risen far above the horizon by the time they reached the bottom of the sloped area leading up to the mountain, stopping as Commander Zayid ordered a halt. The mountain sloped upwards sharply a few dozen yards ahead of the group, the slow incline sudden-ly meeting a craggy wall as a spike of stone jutted up from the earth. Large cracks in the rock had spread across the side of the mountain, and the red metal had oozed out of them enough to cover a fair amount of the mountainside before it solidified. Raising a hand to cover his eyes from the sun, Zayid looked up the slope of the small mountain and squinted at the darkness of the cave that sat halfway up the ridge. Grunting softly he turned to his subordinates and lowered his hand, the other six members of his group looking at him expectantly.

"So, seeing as I saw a strange light from this mountain in the shared dream, I'm going to assume that whatever's up there is somehow con-nected to what happened in the city. And seeing as the city is currently in ruins, I'm also going to assume that it's probably nothing good. I'm not going to order any of you to follow me up there, but I need to find out what made that light and if it's a danger to the mission. Is anyone wanting to stay behind?" Zayid asked, fully expecting to ascend the mountain path alone.

Much to his surprise, not a single scout made any move to signal that they wanted to stay down below. He'd been expecting that Nuru and perhaps Mhuro at the very least would want to stay away from the place they'd been led to by a cryptic fever dream, but they too stood with him. With a smile he turned and began to lead the group forwards, ascending the sloping incline up towards the base of the mountain. As they circled around the side of the rocky spire, the group came across a somewhat smoothed path carved into the rock which led up the steep rock face. Looking back towards the city, it was clear that a path of some sort must have once led from the slums up to the mountainside, for the beginning of the trail was directly facing the Grand Temple.

After a moment's hesitation the group of seven began their ascent up the trail, their path occasionally obstructed by large globs of the red metal. Where the path had once been wide enough to allow a horse-drawn cart to easily maneuver upwards, the flowing red metal constricted the safe walking space to a thin area which allowed them to walk in only a single-file line. The walk itself wasn't more than a few minutes of carefully climbing over boulder-sized blobs of the metal and avoiding sliding off of the mountain itself, and soon enough the group arrived at the flat ledge which served as the entrance to the cave. Zayid stood at the top of the path, watching to make sure everyone made it up safely and helping each man over the last wall of red metal. Finally the cave had been reached, and the scout company began to cautiously investigate.

Before anyone could move ahead, Zayid stepped forwards and drew the attention of the six scouts. "Before we go ahead, I want to make sure that we do this right. Most of you will already know how to behave in a potentially hostile environment, but some of you are absent-minded and too curious for your own good." Zayid pointedly stared at Nuru for a few seconds, letting the man squirm under his gaze, before continuing. "Touch nothing. Disturb nothing. Take nothing. Find out what's in here, report back to this ledge when you're done, and we'll decide what to do after that."

Zayid turned and began to walk towards the cave mouth, but froze as he saw something against the wall of coagulated metal. The shape of a body seemed to lean against the wall, seated under one of the red metal flows. Where it should have been encased, the incredibly durable metal had seemingly shattered from internal pressure. Shards of the strange steel lay strewn about its form, and though it seemed to have been scorched black through intense heat, veins of the red metal ran across the figure's surface. Zayid stared at it for a few seconds before turning to his scouts. "That thing," he said as he pointed towards the figure, "we leave for last. Don't ask why, I've just got a hunch."

The six scouts nodded in understanding as they took their time inspecting the figure and the shattered bubble of metal from afar. Once they were done, the scout group split into two handfuls of people. Amon, Mhuro, and Nezeb separated from the others to go up a set of carved stairs to the left of the cave, while Zayid and the rest lit torches and ventured into the darkness. The red metal had draped over a significant amount of the entrance, but there were a few places where a man could step through into the interior with ease. The interior of the cave was hot, moreso the further in they got. To Zayid, it looked as though it had once been a blacksmith's forge; hammers and tongs of various shapes and sizes were strewn about on the floor, and the stone wheel of a grindstone lay on its side near some shattered fragments of long-rotted wood.

Zayid slowly moved towards the back of the cave, feeling the sweat begin to bead on his forehead as the heat rose further and further. When he took his next step, he felt the toe of his boot hit something hard and immobile. Looking down, he grimaced as he saw what looked to be a human body covered in a strange sort of rock. Zayid knelt beside the body and moved his hand towards it, feeling that the heat rose from here as well as the strange rock formation the stone-encased corpse was connected to. Scratching his chin, he pondered the various possibilities that could explain the odd discovery. "Perhaps some sort of magma vent broke open, that would explain the heat and the lack of furnace in this forge."

Somewhere near the cave's entrance, one of the men yelped in shock. Without hesitation, Zayid and the other two drew their weapons and ran over to find out what had happened, torches raised high to cast their illumination across the cave. They found Sephis on the ground, his torch snuffed out on impact with the ground when he leapt back in fright. Khonsu sheathed his dagger and extended a hand towards Sephis, helping the medic to his feet. Seeing that he was okay, Zayid and Nuru sheathed their blades with a soft sigh of relief.

"What happened?" Zayid inquired, drawing Sephis's attention. The medic wordlessly pointed towards the corner of the cave, where the mountainside was cut off from the cave's interior by the red metal. Zayid took a few steps forwards before slowly raising his torch, casting illumination upon the corner that had startled Sephis so badly. A crack in the metal had been created when the figure outside had somehow caused the steel encasing it to explode outwards, allowing one to look at the strange slumped body from within the cave. Just beside the crack, directly opposite the figure, a large shard of the maroon metal was embedded in the cave wall. If a person had looked through the crack without knowing it was there and turned away, they'd end up staring directly into the sharpened spike mere inches from their face.

Zayid chuckled softly and turned back to Sephis, patting the startled medic on the shoulder. "Look around before you lean in to peer through a crack Sephis, you never know what might be waiting for you to turn your back. Otherwise, are you okay?"

Sephis nodded with a faint smile, rubbing his arm softly as he looked away. "Yeah, I'm fine Commander Zayid. Just a little embarrassed that I got scared by a piece of metal is all, nothing my ego won't recover from."

Zayid lifted his torch high and looked around the cave once more, not seeing anything of major import in the light of the flame. He shrugged and began walking back over to the entrance, satisfied that there was nothing left inside for them to discover. The other three followed behind, sticking their torches in the ash to snuff out the fire before striking them against the stone to shake off the powdery residue. He found the other three members of the group waiting there for him, standing in a semi-circle around the figure with their arms crossed or at their sides. Once they noticed the four men leaving the cave, the scout group rejoined.

Amon motioned back towards the stairs which led up and out of sight, looking over his shoulder at the carved steps as he did. "It seems like someone made a home above the cave. Bedrooms, a dining room, a sort of central circular chamber connecting it all to the front door. Fairly standard, if I had to guess I'd say it belonged to whoever had their things in the cave. We found two bodies on the steps, burnt beyond recognition. One of them had a fairly large hole in the skull, so it seems like one was trying to protect the other."

Zayid nodded, leaning to his left to get a glimpse up the stairs. All that he could see was a blackened hand, outstretched in its final moments before the fire consumed its life. "Okay, so with all of that plus the stuff we found in the cave, I think it's fairly obvious this was just the home of some lower class blacksmith. I don't think that's particularly noteworthy on its own, which means the only thing left to figure out is that." He said, turning to the figure slumped over with its back against the wall. He was much closer now, and Zayid could see that what he thought had been scorched and blackened flesh was actually a suit of armor.

Walking over and kneeling down in front of the armor, Zayid peered at the suit with an appraising eye. Blackened as it was and streaked with the same metal that had tainted the landscape thus far, it seemed to be of a fairly high quality. Each component of the suit, from the chestplate to the helmet to the gauntlets, seemed to be inscribed with intricate markings and symbols. The gauntlets were sharp and pointed with each finger, and the helmet had a faceplate which obscured the entire face of the wearer. It was a mask, carved into the likeness of a snarling and wrathful demon. Its eyes were empty and hollow, and only darkness could be seen inside.

Grunting softly, he stood and wiped the ash from his knees. "This is the most intact object I've seen since we arrived in this city. Someone grab the pieces, stuff them in a bag or string them together and carry them. I want it brought back to the embassy, I'm certain it's important in some way."

Khonsu nodded and approached the armor as Commander Zayid walked away, kneeling in front of it and opening his travel pack. The large bag was built for carrying the equipment needed to prepare basic meals, so with a little bit of luck it could fit the armor as well. Khonsu looked at the faceplate of the armor in curiosity, seemingly admiring the craftsmanship before he began to move it. Slowly, carefully, he reached out towards the slumped suit with one hand to pull off the helmet.

Sebhora - Chapter One

Fifteen Months Prior

In the ancient nation of Sosias, where wealth flowed freely and all were united under the banner of great Khigstus, there was a small mountain on the outskirts of the city-state. In and around this mountain a thriving community of artisans and craftsmen had sprung up, and at the base of that mountain a small cave existed. The cave was hot and dry, as a now dormant flow of volcanic magma sat docile in its innermost depths, but at its mouth was a bustling smithy. It belonged to a man named Sebhora, and he loved his work. With a forge lit by the heat of the earth itself, he was a talented smith of iron and steel, hammering both arms and armor into shape as well as tools and household objects like pots and bowls.

From the northern road to Sosias, past the high walls fitted with crenellations and manned by an observant contingent of archers, a man whistled as he sat atop his cart laden with ores and minerals. The clop of his horse's shoes grew louder as the terrain changed from the smoothed dirt roads to the cobbled streets of the city, and curious children ran into the streets by the dozen from their ramshackle homes in the slums to investigate the source of the noise. A small crowd of them followed behind the cart, gasps and cries of wonder abundant within their numbers reaching the driver's ears as they gawked at the man who owned both horse and cart. In the slums of Sorias, it was rare to see someone other than a guard or a landlord displaying such a measure of wealth, and such sights were as much a cause for excitement to the children here as a performance might be to children of the higher classes.

The crowd quickly dispersed as the driver took a turn onto one of the main roads, heading in the direction of one of the bridges which separated the districts and classes. The water was sparkling blue, a source of clean water for both sides that no one dared taint, beneath the stone bridge as the cart's driver passed over from the slums into the trade district. There was an obvious and visible disparity between the two sides, the dirt and grime which seemed to cover every surface of the slums opposed by the comparatively clean wooden buildings which were crammed together to create the bustling hub of trade the district was known to be. The roads were full of people hawking their wares, ranging from fruits and meat to potters and fine silks. Amongst the crowd were the Middle Guard, men dressed in a traditional Sosian garb who ducked and weaved through the seas of people, hunting the pickpockets who flock to such markets.

To avoid lengthening his trip unnecessarily, the driver elected to follow the road around the perimeter of the district and stay clear of the masses further within the district. Within minutes he felt someone jump onto the back of his cart, and as he reached for the sword on his hip he turned to see a boy no older than fifteen reclining atop the ore like a noble upon one of their cushioned couches. The boy held the pose only for a moment before he and the driver broke out into laughter, the boy soon scrambling up to the driver's seat.

"It's been so long, Uncle Chebatli!" The boy exclaimed, hugging the man tightly. "Father said you had to go far, far away to find something for one of his jobs. Did you find what you were looking for? What did you see?"

Chebatli laughed and ruffled the boy's hair, returning the hug happily with one arm while keeping his free hand on the reins. "I did indeed, young Aralin! I rode all the way up the coast to the great port of Krigonia, I saw their tall-masted ships and ate their finest fish. Now I'm back with metal for the forge, and the last thing your father needs to finish that armor."

Aralin excitedly reached back to lift the tarp, trying to get a peak at the material underneath, but found his hand lightly slapped away from the tarp's edge. Wagging his finger playfully, Chebatli tutted softly at his nephew. "No peeking, understand? What's under there is for your father to reveal, and not a second before he's done with it."

Aralin groaned and crossed his arms over his chest, slumping into the wooden seat with a huff. Chebatli chuckled and returned his focus to the road, the two continuing their conversation along the winding roads until they finally arrived at the city's outskirts once more. Arriving at the foot of the mountain - though it could barely be called that, with the great stepped pyramid in the center of Sosias being taller - Aralin leaped off the cart and ran up towards the mouth of the cave which served as the family's home. As Chebatli pulled up to the entrance, he could see his brother Sebhora wiping sweat from his brow as he joined his wife Ixaroatl and his son at the cave's mouth. Happily he pulled the cart to a stop in front of the cave and dismounted, jogging up the slight incline towards the entrance.

The two brothers embraced after weeks of separation, slapping each other on the back and holding each other in joy. Once Chebatli finished with Sebhora, he moved on and kissed Ixaroatl on the cheek while pulling Aralin in for another hug.

"It's good to be home, Seb." Chebatli said, the reunited family all turning to go deeper within. "It's a miracle I made it back without running into bandits or the like, Khigstus himself must have been watching over me." At the mention of the god's name, all four turned towards the great pyramid in the center of Sosias, bowing their heads for a moment in reverence and thanks to the benevolent warrior deity whose statue stood overlooking all.

Turning back towards the cave, Sebhora ushered his wife and child up the carved stairs which led to their home above the forge. "You two go on ahead, I have some things to discuss with Chebatli. Aralin, help your mother prepare supper."

Once the mother and son went upstairs, Sebhora and Chebatli set to work - Sebhora pushed open the large wooden gate which led to the heated forge, and Chebatli unhooked his horse from the cart to lead it to a nearby food trough. With some effort, the brothers took the yoke of the cart and heaved it into the forge, closing the gate behind them so their privacy would be undisturbed.

Jumping back up onto the driver's seat, Chebatli pulled the tarp away from the cart to reveal the vast quantities of rock beneath, most tinged red if a dullish gray vein wasn't already prominent on its surface. "High grade iron ore with an excellent metal content. This haul should keep you topped up for months, but I know you're far more interested in my other cargo." Chebatli said with a smirk, shifting large rocks aside before reaching down until his arm disappeared up to his shoulder. With a grunt and a hard pull, a large locked box was yanked from beneath the mount of ore. Pulling a key from his boot, Chebatli slid it into the lock and turned it thrice before a loud click was heard.

Sebhora gingerly lifted the lid and peered inside, his eyes widening in wonder as he reached in and lifted a small chunk of a silvery, irides- cent material to inspect it in the light of the forge. "Genuine Krigonian Mother-of-Pearl... and in such a great quantity! How in the name of the great protector did you manage to get your hands on this?"

Chebatli chuckled and leaned forward in his seat, resting his el- bows on his knees and looking smugly down at his awestruck broth- er. "Bought it for dirt cheap from an Estyrian trader, the stingy old bastard didn't want to sell at all until I told him he's nowhere near as stubborn as a born and bred, tried and true Sosian merchant. He got quite clammy after that, oddly enough, nearly threw the stuff at me with barely a word in edgewise. One might think that he was trying to get me out of there. Queer fellows, those Estyrians."

Sebhora nodded idly, listening while he took a small piece of the rare material with a pair of forge tongs and placed it in an ore cup. His smile widened as he saw the material slowly melt into a liquid when placed into the forge itself, and when he poured it into a small mold he pumped his fist and let out a whoop of joy at seeing the solidified material retaining its aesthetic properties. "That's it! The last part of the armor! If it weren't Mother-of-Pearl, I don't know what I would have done for an alternative!"

Running up and embracing his brother, Sebhora lifted Chebatli off of the ground and spun him around a few times, both roaring in laughter and joy. When they settled down, Chebatli slapped his brother on the shoulder and guided him towards the door. "No more excuses, okay? Tonight you're going to tell us what you've been work- ing on that requires such secrecy, and why you've been sending me halfway around the world for strange substances."

With a sigh Sebhora raised his hands in defeat. "Fine, fine, but after dinner. I've been preparing all day for your return, and I've worked up an appetite." Throwing open the gate once more, the smith and the merchant ascending the steps to the home carved into the mountain-side.

As they approached the door, the smell of roasting meat wafted through the air from an open window, making both men salivate and quicken their pace to a near run. Aralin opened the door before they even reached the door, the confused but joyous look of a child used to having to fetch his father from the forge but not having to make the trip wide upon his face. Once Aralin let them in and closed the door behind them, they all congregated in the dining room. Low tables were sat in a circle in front of woven mats, all situated around a smoldering fire heating a large pot of stew as well as a haunch of boar roasting over the flame. Ixaroatl was ladling the thick vegetable stew into large bowls before slicing off long strips of meat from the haunch into the bowls with a curved blade, setting the bowls one to a table.

Hungry and tired after a long day, the family sat down to eat around the fire and talk about what was happening in their lives. There were no traditions or prayers before mealtimes in Sosian culture, so all four began to eat heartily the second they sat down. After a few minutes, Ixaroatl pointed her ladle across the circle at Chebatli, swallowing her food before opening her mouth. "So, Cheba, now that you're back home, what are your plans? Going to help around here, or go back to the market district?"

He thought about this for a few moments, idly chewing a trip of boar before answering with the same foodless courtesy he had been provided. "I haven't given it much thought, honestly. Perhaps I could start trying to make some extra money, maybe invest in some good seats for the next Rite of the Codex festival. I remember one year,

Sebhora and I managed to sneak into the temple district for the Rite. It was wonderful."

Sebhora began to chuckle quietly to himself, a knowing smile on his face. "Now now, Aralin just turned fifteen. Let's not spoil it for him, this'll be the first year he'll be able to attend."

Aralin, who had been excited to hear the story in further detail, groaned in disappointment at his father's words. He crossed his arms and glared at Sebhora before turning to Chebatli, a pleading expression on his face. "Oh come on, I've been waiting years and I don't even know what the Rite is! At least give me that much."

Chebatli shrugged in a defeated manner towards Sebhora as though he had no choice in the matter of informing the boy. "He's got a point, Seb. It won't hurt him to have something to look forward to."

Turning to Aralin, he leaned forwards and spoke in a hushed, dramatic tone. "The Rite of the Codex is a ceremony that happens every year. The Grand Prophet of Khigstus brings our holiest relic, the Khigstinian Codex, to the peak of the pyramid in the center of Sosias. The leader of each noble house participates in a ceremonial battle, adorned in beautiful and ornate ceremonial armor, to honor Khigstus. The victor then climbs the pyramid and is blessed by the Grand prophet himself, a passage from the Codex used to imbue them with the might of Khigstus. It's a wondrous sight, honestly. I wonder which house shall prove victorious this year."

Sebhora snorted and washed down his soup with a cup of water, absolute certainty in his voice. "This year, the House of Quetzlipoc shall be victorious."

Raising an eyebrow in surprise, Chebatli leaned forwards and stared across the room at his brother. While bets were often placed and everyone had a favorite house champion, Sebhora wasn't a betting man and neither did he favor House Quetzlipoc. "How're you so certain?"

"Because the day after last year's rite, Lord Quetzlipoc commissioned me to make his armor for this year. That's what I've been sending you around for, materials for that armor. Not only am I being paid handsomely for it, this will put me on the map for other noble houses. And," Sebhora said to his completely stunned family with a smug and victorious smirk, "We've been given front row seats with his house, all four of us."

The room was silent for nearly a minute before it went into a state of ecstatic uproar, no words fitting any of their emotions in that moment. Instead they cheered, shouted, and cried out their pride and gratitude to the heavens as they rushed towards Sebhora from their seats and embraced him in a flurry of energetic happiness. After some time had passed they all calmed down, returning to their seats to finish their meals. There still remained an air of repressed excitement, one that would likely erupt into primal joy again later for each of them.

Ixaroatl was the first to pull herself together enough to form a coherent question, stumbling over her words at first. "Why in the name of Khigstus didn't you tell us sooner? This is amazing news, surely you must have known we all would be supremely proud of you!"

"Well, I didn't want to get anyone's hopes up. If I couldn't get my hands on a large enough supply of amber or Mother-of-Pearl, then I wouldn't have been able to finish the project in time. However, thanks to the diligent efforts of my brother," he said with a wide smile while motioning towards Chebatli, "I will complete a set of armor second only to that of Khigstus himself!"

At this exclamation, Chebatli raised his cup high in a toast to the good news, an action quickly copied by the other three. "To Khigstus, to Sosias, and to the best smith in the whole city, Sebhora!"

The room filled with another round of cheers before everyone drank from their cup, soon after finishing their meals. Each person pushed their table aside and reclined on their mat, relaxing by the warmth of the fire with full bellies and good company. There was a comfortable and peaceful silence that filled the room, with good news on the mind and good food on the stomach there was no need for urgency. Eventually Sebhora spoke up once more, lying flat on his back with his head resting atop his hands. "So, Ixa, what's new with the strange world of politics and the nobility? I know gossip travels quickly through the districts, what caught your interest?"

Ixaroatl laid her forearm over her eyes and groaned in exasperation, the subject of drama and gossip clearly one she'd had her fair share of. "Don't get me started on gossip and maid's tales, I've had about as much as I can stomach. Do you have any idea how many times I had to listen to some handmaiden pour her heart out about how the lady of the house was "so mean" because she didn't say thank you after being served supper?" She sighed loudly, contempt in her tone. "The amount of verbal sewage that I've had to sift through makes the actual information I learn almost not worth the effort. Almost."

Sebhora pulled himself up to a sitting position with a curious smile, knowing from experience the true reason why his wife was complaining. "Well go on then, tell us what you've learned that makes all of these great woes worth your time." Aralin and Chebatli sat up as well, their attention piqued by the exchange.

Not bothering to sit up, Ixaroatl smirked and stretched out her arms. "I heard from a washlady who heard from her sister's best friend, who knows a scullery maid in a noble house she refused to name, that the scullery maid overheard a discussion between her lord and a messenger. Apparently that Estyrian delegation, the ones sent to negotiate a sort of pact of neutrality, tried to swindle the Grand Prophet. They wanted to give us some staff or scepter for the Codex, and completely changed the terms of the treaty. So what did the Grand Prophet do? Kicked them out with a firm boot on their sandy asses!"

The others, who had been listening attentively, broke out into laughter upon hearing of the events - except for Chebatli, who stared into the distance with a somber expression. Aralin was the first to notice, leaning over and gently prodding his shoulder. "You okay Uncle? You look like you just saw a ghost."

This shook Chebatli from his state, and he looked towards Aralin with confusion on his face for a few moments. "Hmm? Oh, yes, I'm fine. Just thinking about what this may mean for the future."

Sehbora and Ixaroatl leaned forwards as well, the serious tone of his ponderings making them slightly worried about what he could mean. Sebhora shifted his weight from one side to another, his eyes going to each face in the room as the general mood suddenly sobered. "What do you mean? Should we be worried about something, Chebatli?"

Chebatli was silent for a bit, opening his mouth to speak but closing it again as he chose his words better a few times. Eventually he sighed, turning from the fire towards the window that faced the city. He stared out at Sosias, houses illuminated by candles and moonlight reflecting off the stark white marble that characterized the temple district and the great pyramid that housed the Codex. The dark yet shiny surface of the iron inlaid upon it as both decoration and support structures seemed to drink the very light itself, giving the center of Sosias an almost ghostly glow. "This place, this paradise in the Khigi jungles where we have lived our entire lives... we have prospered under the blessings of Khigstus, our sins absolved by his Codex and washed away by water every day. He's a warrior god, a protector, but we are not warriors. Our strongest fighters are in the marketplace, not the battlefield."

Everyone nodded in agreement, as it was common knowledge the Sosians were a peaceful people. Aralin spoke up again, cocking his head to the left. "Yes, but why should that make us worry? We're the chosen of Khigstus, under divine protection."

"The Estyrians have three advantages we do not; cunning, cruelty, and capacity. They're a people united by force and by war, who use it to feed their empire. Their cunning means that we should always be wary of them, and of the vassals they puppeteer. They're cruel, which all but guarantees that they'll try to take their revenge in some way. I wouldn't be surprised if the Grand Prophet gets a few assassination attempts in the coming weeks. Thirdly, Estyria is a vast place and its influence is even vaster. Should they choose to go to war with us, I fear they'd have the military capacity to outnumber the entire city's population." Chebatli's voice was quiet and harsh, not listing possibilities but what he obviously believed to be fact. When he finished there was not a sound in the room, save that of the crackling fire.

Suddenly Sebhora reached across the table, picking up Chebatli's cup and raising it to his face. He sniffed it and scowled, his face contorted as though he smelled something foul. "Ixa, I don't know what you put in his drink, but I'll take three."

She began to giggle softly, the laughter slowly spreading through the room and ramping up in volume. Sebhora stood and walked over to his brother, patting him on the back and chuckling. "I get it, the Estyrians are a scary bunch when they don't get their way. I'm just not sure they're willing to risk so much just to take the Codex. They've got their scepter, they should be happy with it. Besides, we're well liked! Sosias has allies and trade agreements everywhere, they're not going to march all the way here unless they plan on bringing all of Galoholme to heel."

Chebatli sighed and began to chuckle at his own words, realizing how sudden that outburst had come and without any provocation. "It appears that my days of travel have upset my mind, it's nothing that a good night's sleep won't solve." The mood lightened once more, cheeriness and joyousness returning to the conversation. Yet in the back of Chebatli's mind those fears tucked themselves away, lying in wait until a time when they could resurface again with greater effect.

The night drew to a close as the moon rose higher into the night sky, gentle illumination filling the city through every open window and doorway. Saying their good nights and snuffing out the fire, Sebhora and Ixaroatl went to their room while Aralin and Chebatli split off to their own separate rooms, painstakingly dug out for them by Sebhora himself.

Sebhora - Chapter Two

Several weeks passed without many things of importance happening, life returning to a state of normality. Each day the family of four rose with the sun and returned home in time for its setting, a large meal at the beginning and end of the day provided by Ixaroatl. News slowly spread of Sebhora's newfound honorable commission, receiving visits from boh neighbors wishing congratulations and nobles curious as to the skill of the supposed diamond-in-the-rough blacksmith.

Sebhora did not waste a day in his duties, taking as few breaks from his work as he could manage. The thin steel frame of armor he had put the final touches on before affixing the plates, not through welding or straps but through small lines of chainmail holding the armor's shape and structural integrity together. Three weeks straight he spent melting the Mother-of-Pearl and slowly coating the exterior of the suit with it, creating a silvery sheen which seemed almost ephemeral in moonlight. The following three weeks were spent layering amber atop the armor in a smooth coat, creating a thick and fiery orange coating which seemed to come alive in daylight.

Ixaroatl kept informed about the goings-on in and out of Sosias through the grapevine of gossip and idle chatter. The Estyrians had not yet sought vengeance as Chebatli had so vehemently thought, but scouts would occasionally disappear into the jungle without a trace. The Grand Prophet made the decision to delay a large-scale investigation into the disappearances, choosing to instead focus on preparing for the upcoming Rites.

Chebatli had slowly grown distant from the others, spending a few nights in a row sleeping elsewhere every few weeks. This sudden shift in behavior disturbed Sebhora, who knew his brother to value nothing higher than family. He was convinced that the Estyrians would come eventually, leading to an argument between the brothers. It was another month and a half before Chebatli returned home and apologized to Sebhora, who embraced his brother and forgave all that needed forgiveness.

Aralin had achieved a great many things in that period of time, learning from his father as well as pursuing his own interests. For many mornings he helped his father in the forge, learning how to properly use the flow of magma through the forge to raise or lower the heat to his liking. His afternoons and evenings were spent training with the Eagle Warrior Cadets, a group of veteran warriors who instructed the next generation of Sosias' military in combat and camaraderie before they were of age to join the city guard or the army. Sebhora and Ixaroatl were proud beyond belief when Aralin was promoted to Scout Leader due to his speed, agility, and skill with a bow. Chebatli gave him a gift the very next day, a brand new longbow and a quiver full of arrows made with the feathers of the elusive Khigi Lightning Hawk, a bird of prey said to fly as fast as lightning.

A little more than fifty days after Chebatli had returned home from Krigonia to the north, Sebhora was hunched over an anvil hard at work. Aralin stood beside him, holding two beautifully carved plates of the armor steading while his father heated a small c-shaped ringlet of iron to glowing white hot. With a delicate pair of small tongs, he lifted the ring and slid the ends into place - first through a similar ring above it and then fed each side through a small hole on each plate. With practiced precision, he squeezed the ends of the ring shut with the tongs and proceeded with a small hammer, tapping it lightly until the seam between the ends was merged together fully. Setting the tools aside, Sebhora held the plates and motioned with a turn of his head for Aralin to fetch some water.

The teenage boy quickly ran to the other side of the workshop, grabbing a waterskin before returning to the anvil. Slowly he poured a trickle of water over the white-hot metal, causing scalding steam to rise as the metal cooled rapidly. Sebhora grimaced as the steam stung his face and eyes but did not move a muscle, this crucial moment too important to make a mistake at this stage of the process. Once the steam cleared and the metal had cooled, he pulled the plates apart softly before tugging much harder, smiling as his previously untested design held against the strain.

Sitting up straight and wiping the sweat from his brow, Sebhora dumped half the remaining water on Aralin's head - much to his initial displeasure - and then emptied the rest onto his own head, cooling them both off. With a broad smile he took the completed chestpiece from the anvil and stood, walking over to the armor stand he'd placed near the entrance of his forge. Setting the chestpiece in place, Sebhora took a step back and gazed upon the fruit of his months of forethought, planning, and labor. Wrapping his arm around Aralin's shoulder and pulling him close, the father and son admired the artistry and the craftsmanship in front of them.

The orange amber adorning the surface of the armor seemed to be alive, incandescent wisps of light shimmering in the firelight. That glow was only made brighter by the milky silver sheen that was layered below the glass-like substance, the reflective nature of Krigonian Mother-of-Pearl heightening the effect. From the crowned helmet which had a face plate sculpted into a serene yet emotionless mask, to the ridged gauntlets designed to catch blades in their grooves, the intricately carved lines in the base steel creating a menacing yet graceful figure from head to toe. It was Sebhora's greatest creation, his magnum opus.

After a few minutes of admiring the statue-esque figure before them, Aralin looked up to his father with a smile on his face. "So what happens now? Do we wait for Lord Quetzlipoc to come? Can I show the armor to some of my friends?"

Sebhora chuckled and looked back at his forge, the large cave a mess from the constant rush from one task to another. Glancing back at the armor for a moment, he sighed and waved his hand dismissively. "Yes, yes, you can go tell your friends and show them the armor, but no touching! In fact, no one within fifteen steps of it, alright? I've got to get this place cleaned up before I go tell the lord that his armor is done. Most noble house's armor is ancestral, you know, their leaders have been training in those suits for long enough to feel like they're more of a second skin than anything else. The Rite is still some months off, so he'll want to start training as soon as possible with it to get that familiarity."

Aralin pumped his fist in the air and let out a whoop of joy, tossing the thick leather smithing gloves aside before running outside through the open gateway. Sebhora watched him go, sprinting down the winding path that led up to the cave until he was out of sight. With a soft sigh, he went to the forge and released the chain holding the volcanic flue open. As the iron barrier slammed shut and the room darkened, he hung the leather apron he wore on a wall peg and went around cleaning up his disorganized smithy. A good half hour passed before he managed to get all the raw materials sorted and his tools put away.

As suspected, Aralin and some of his friends from the Eagle Warrior Cade troop popped in occasionally, gawking with dropped jaws at the spectacle before them. Sebhora was flattered by such a reaction, but much to the boys' disappointment he soon after locked the gate of the forge and went up to the house for a change of clothes. While he owned nothing overly fancy, Sebhora had purchased a modestly nice set of clothes for his dealings with the higher classes of Sosian society.

It was close to what the Sosian equivalent of ten in the morning was when Sebhora left, walking down the trail of the mountain towards the slums. Along the way he stopped by Chebatli's cart, which he'd set up as a sort of mobile general goods store. A nice young couple were walking away with a set of pewter dishes and a large cast iron pot that Sebhora had been trying to sell for a while, smiles on their faces as they passed the blacksmith. Upon hearing the approaching footsteps, Chebatli turned and around and began to speak in a manner designed to draw in new customers. "Hello there, sir- Sebhora, is that you? I didn't recognize you out of your normal clothes!"

The blacksmith chuckled as he stepped up to his brother's cart, looking into the assorted collection of goods being offered. "I was wondering what you'd been spending your days doing. And thank you, I think they look rather nice, don't you?" With a smile and a flourish, Sebhora spun in place to give Chebatli a better view of the clothes he had bought for this very occasion.

"At a glance, I'd have thought you were some minor official from the middle ring, but I think wealth suits you just fine." Chebatli said with a chuckle, glancing his brother up and down. "What's all this for, anyways? You wouldn't get out of your normal clothes for nothing, I've seen you wear them to both weddings and burials."

Leaning in close with a whisper, Sebhora softly said, "I finally finished the armor. I'm on my way to the middle ring to tell Lord Quetzlipoc the news in person."

Chebatli's face lit up as his mind comprehended the words uttered to him, the immense gravity and importance of the situation shocking the silver-tongued trader into silence. After a few seconds Chebatli hugged his brother tightly, pride welling up in his heart for Sebhora's achievement and for the role he had played in making it possible. Soon enough he released Sebhora and patted him on the shoulder, motioning him down the road. "Go on then, the sooner you do it the sooner we can start celebrating!"

With a wide smile and a wave goodbye, Sebhora returned to his journey through the slums. The people living in their crude homes of thatch and dirt automatically moved out of his path, their perception of his status within Sosias changing completely from when he'd walked amongst his friends and neighbors normally. Many recognized him and waved as he passed, and Sebhora always stopped to say hello. By the time he got to the bridge which connected the slums to the trade district, several rumors had already started to spread about a strange highborn man wandering the outer ring and mingling with the common folk.

Stopping at the foot of the bridge, Sebhora looked back upon his home from within the city, the small mountain peaked by a hardened volcanic overflow. Then he turned back towards the center of Sosias, taking in the sight of the sprawling city-state before him. Just across this bridge his whole world would change, the wooden buildings of the trade district leading to the stone of the noble district. Even further beyond his destination, the granite and obsidian obelisks and temples of the temple district were but a precursor to the iron and marble megastructure that was the Grand Temple of Khigstus, the stepped pyramid which overlooked all.

Just as Sebhora was about to take his first step towards a better future for him and his family, the sound of thousands of startled jungle birds squawking and flapping away surrounding the city on all sides. The otherwise cloudless sky was soon filled with countless birds in massive, swarming flocks, and cries of surprise or fear could be heard all throughout Sosias. Then the very earth began to tremble as the sound of hundreds if not thousands of drums were struck in unison, a slow and steady beat being played as the source of the noise spread from one place to surrounding Sosias from every direction. Panic spread throughout the populace as people began to rush to the safety of their homes.

As the beat of the unknown drums slowly began to increase in tempo and became more intricate in its sinister melody, the rapidly emptying streets were filled with the archers of Sosias running to their posts on the great wall which encircled the city. Sebhora had been frozen in place by the sudden events, trying to figure out just what was going on, until he was roughly shoved aside by a soldier making his way to the wall. He fell to the ground in a heap, his shoulder roughly colliding with the cobblestones and causing him to cry out in pain. Groaning, Sebhora rolled onto his back and stared up at the sky, trying to catch his breath.

The drums continued to build their crescendo higher and higher, their tempo rising to a fever pitch until at the climactic moment of the beat, the sound stopped abruptly. There was a complete and utter silence blanketing the city and the surrounding thick jungle, the citizens slowly filtering out of their homes into the streets once more. The archers on the walls looked frantically into the jungles for any sign of movement, an air of anxiety rippling through Sosias. Sebhora pulled himself to his feet and looked around, waiting alongside the entire Sosian people for something - anything - to happen. Much to the regret of everyone who'd had such a thought, it was not five seconds later that something beyond imagining to most of the city did happen.

From the northern jungle, a flaming boulder burst from the canopy and slowly arced across the sky. Every Sosian man, woman, and child's head slowly followed the path of the boulder with terror in their eyes, watching it slowly traverse each ring. It finally came crashing down into the stark white marble of the great pyramid with a resounding boom, leaving a scorched black scar on its otherwise untouched surface. It was then, as dozens of similar fireballs shot forth from the jungles at every angle into the city, and the drums of war once again resumed their frantic beating, that all hell broke loose.

Sebhora - Chapter Three

Terror and panic ran amok in the city on a scale never before seen in the history of their civilization; as the collective screams of the city-state rang out into the air, nobles and commoners alike frantically running from the rain of destruction. While the first boulder was aimed for the Grand Temple, the others fell upon every district indiscriminately. From the slums to the temple district, entire buildings were destroyed - in the outer rings, fires raged into uncontrollable infernos feeding on the wood and thatch of the crude structures.

Sebhora was not shocked to inaction twice, for as soon as the first boulder hit he set off at a sprint back towards his home. The ground rumbled beneath his feet as the first barrage struck the earth, great bouts of flame rising into the air a few streets over as an explosion decimated the area of impact. Using his strength and size to ram his way through the crowd, Sebhora bowled over dozens of people as the need to make sure his wife and son were safe overpowered all other thoughts.

He passed the place where Chebatli had been hawking his wares and stopped dead in his tracks, seeing that the cart and his brother had disappeared without a trace. That moment of dedication saved his life, as merely fifty feet ahead a boulder slammed into the road. The blast threw Sebhora backwards towards a building, knocking the breath from his lungs as he collided with the wall and leaving him gasping for air. He slowly pulled himself to his feet and continued walking, past the burning buildings on either side of the street and over the crater in the road.

Sebhora caught his breath soon after and returned to sprinting once more, leaving the slums behind as the inclined road up the mountain loomed ahead. As Sebhora started the climb, another fireball impacted nearby - above him, the smoking crate on the side of the mountain rained melon-sized chunks of stone down on the path. He dove out of the way beneath a slight overhang on the path, wincing as stray fragments of stone flew at him when the larger rocks shattered on the ground. Once the deadly rain ceased, he crawled out and stood for a moment; looking on in horror, his eyes widened as his world burned around him.

The entirety of the outer rings of Sosias were consumed by the blazing inferno, the thatch roofs of the slums burning like so many calamitous torches. The rough clay walls of those same buildings were hardening rapidly, something that would normally be considered a blessing by the common folk, but the sheer heat of the flames caused entire neighborhoods to crumble and crack. The trade district was in a far worse state - the buildings were all of wood, so rather than the countless small fires that affected the slums it was a singular incandescent and infernal mass. A ring of roiling fire as solid as stone, giving off plumes of black smoke which darkened the sky.

Through the nigh impenetrable wall of smoke, very little was visible. The air itself shimmered with heat and was tinted red as sunlight filtered through the smoke, the only illumination able to be seen from within the inner city was from the glow of fiery death raining down. There seemed to be considerably less fire from the middle ring inwards, but the begging of people desperately seeking salvation as they choked on toxic air was audible even from this distance. The last thing Sebhora saw before he forced himself to look away was a fireball that directly impacted the chest of the statue atop the pyramid, sending it careening down the other side with the screech of tearing metal.

Blinking away tears from the corners of his eyes, Sebhora turned away from the burning carcass of his civilization and resumed his frantic sprint up the trail to his home. The sheer volume of smoke permeating the air was like a thick fog, obstructing his vision and causing him to gasp for breath as he pushed himself harder and harder. Finally Sebhora reached the cave, falling to his hands and knees before beginning to cough and sputter loudly. The cleaner air closer to the ground tasted sweet in comparison to the bitter, tar-like miasma above, but the coughing did not cease.

Sebhora heaved and retched, his body shaking softly as he spat out a dark, congealed, pitch-like substance onto the ground, his lungs finally clear after expelling the smoke which had been sticking in his throat. He heard the creaking of wood ahead of him, and as he weakly raised his head he could see the light from his forge silhouetting a figure standing in the doorway. Within seconds the figure had run out and grabbed Sebhora by the torso, dragging him inside quickly before shutting the gate once more. He lay flat on the floor as he caught his

breath, the surprisingly clean air of the room slowly returning strength
to his body.

Before he had a chance to say anything, Aralin and Ixaroatl ran up
to him from behind, pulling him up to a sitting position and embracing him tightly. Tears of gratitude and joy ran down their ashen faces
in moist lines, and without a word Sebhora wrapped his arms around
both of them and began to cry as well. After a few moments he pulled
his wife and son's heads close and kissed them on their foreheads, relief
filling his mind as he silently thanked Khigstus for keeping his family
safe from harm. Sebhora glanced up towards the doorway, further
relief welling up in his heart as he saw that the figure who'd dragged
him inside was his brother. Chebatli was stuffing wet rags into the
cracks in the doorway between the ceiling and floor, blocking as much
smoke from entering as possible. His gaze wandered to the rest of the
wooden barrier which sealed the cave mouth, noticing the clay which
had been pushed into each and every crevice to try and make the room
airtight.

More than a little impressed by the ingenuity of it all, Sebhora got
to his feet with the help of Aralin and Ixaroatl before walking over
to Chebatli. He gently tapped his brother on the shoulder causing
the man to turn around, before tightly embracing him as well. The
two held each other for but a moment, soon releasing themselves and
stepping back.

Sebhora looked at the three people he cared most about with a
tearful smile, sitting down on a nearby stool. "I'm so happy all of you
are safe. Is anyone hurt? Do you know what's going on out there?"

Chebatli grumbled irritably, stuffing the last of the rags into place
with a rough shove. "It's the Estyrians, no doubt about it. They're
hiding their banners and their men in the jungles, but those drums...
I heard them play once before, at a display of their military might

meant to intimidate a border town into submission. I never forgot that endless, furious drumming, and I had hoped to never hear it again."

Chebatli's hand clenched into a fist which he slammed against the wood, tapping out the next few seconds of the distant rhythm in synchronicity. Suddenly everyone was aware once more of the shaking beat of those great drums, the peace they had found when blissfully allowing the noise to fade into an ambience shattered by the revelation. The room went silent for a time, Sebhora and his kin sitting and hoping - no, praying - that a boulder would not send them to their fiery demise. The only sounds they could hear were the quiet roars of the fires, the booming impacts of the barrage, and the unceasing fury of the drums.

Some hours passed, and still the bombardment of the city continued. Every few minutes a loud boom marked the landing of another boulder into the streets and walls of Sosias, though the occasional quick glance outside revealed that the Estyrians had stopped setting their projectiles on fire. Whether this was to keep the city somewhat intact or if they simply wanted to stop burning potential slaves to death was unknown, but whatever the reason was it was agreed that their intent was not merciful. After those hours of inactivity, hunger began to set in amongst Sebhora and his family. Not having had the time to prepare food for the evening meal, all four soon grew restless and uneasy. Finally Sebhora became too concerned to stand by and wait while his kin slowly starved before his eyes - rising to his feet, he tore the fabric of his shirt and fashioned a crude mask from it. The others grew curious, watching him as he tied the ends of what remained of his shirt together to make a crude sack.

It was when he started walking towards the door that Ixaroatl grabbed his arm, stopping him in place. "Where do you think you're going? All that's out there is fire and death."

Sebhora turned to face her, cupping his wife's cheek with his free hand and leaning in to plant a kiss on her lips. "It will do us no good to become weak from hunger, we must stay strong if we hope to live through this. I'm going to look for food and see if I can learn anything that has changed, you all need to stay here. We're unarmed, after all, and I'd rather risk dying alone than knowing I dragged any of you into harm's way."

Sebhora paused for a moment, lost in thought, before his head snapped towards Aralin with a sparkle in his eye. "If the smoke begins to clear, then you should get to work on changing that. My son, I have taught you almost everything I know. I have faith that you can make something to defend yourself and your mother with, you know how to work the forge as well as I do."

Aralin's eyes widened in surprise at the sudden responsibility laid on his shoulders, clearly not expecting to be allowed to use the forge on his own. He nodded with a smile, wordlessly starting to dig through the various metal molds for something that would work for his plans.

Chebatli chuckled, watching the boy go to work without hesitation. "Like father, like son, as they say. Good luck, Seb, and you better get back in one piece. As bad as the Estyrians are, I shudder to think what your wife would do to them if they killed you."

With a smile on his face and a laugh upon his lips, Sebhora pushed the gate open just enough to slip through and left before it closed again behind him. The thin cloth wrapped around his face to filter out the smoke from his lungs and eyes, Sebhroa kept himself crouched down lightly as he made his way down the mountain trail. The smoke had mostly begun to dissipate, the fires having either burned themselves out or been extinguished by the surviving Sosians.

The sun was halfway down towards setting, the great plumes of smoke that once acted as a curtain covering everything in sight had been blown away by wind. The slums were in shambles, cracked and crumbling huts of clay with their now-empty roofs exposed to the open sky. The walls of the city had been breached in multiple places, each one marked by a field of corpses felled by arrows surrounding the hole and a pile of mutilated bodies at the treeline. None who attempted to flee had survived, and those few groups of people he could see still alive were huddled together, stationary, lest an arrow find their hearts too.

The trade district was a smoldering ruin, its various markets and taverns reduced to ash and dust. What buildings stood mostly hollow shells, ready to be knocked down with but a firm kick. Near the shore fronts however the buildings were still intact, houses and structures alike extinguished and saved by the thousands of people who lay exhausted on the riverbank. The separating lines of water between the rings had once more saved its citizens from doom, as little as that may have mattered in the bigger picture.

Further beyond, the noble and temple districts were damaged but otherwise intact. Stone had proven mostly resilient to flame, though the projectiles themselves caused no small amount of destruction. Those who had suffocated in the smoke lay in the streets, their faces various shades of red and blue in their contorted expressions of desperation and despair. Servants and priests were moving on and blessing the dead, while their grieving kin wept in the streets.

The Grand Temple of Khigstus, once the most beautiful structure in Sosias, was a scarred and battered shadow of its former glory. The once pristine marble of the pyramid was scorched black by the intense heat where the impact craters had created holes on each side, whole sections knocked loose from the pyramid to reveal the iron framework beneath. The decorative iron shapes which adorned the exterior were warped and half-melted, intricate designs and symbols which had stood for many centuries ruined. Atop the pyramid, the bent and torn legs of the statue of Khigstus stood as a solemn reminder of all that had been done to them, complimented by the massive gash down the side that the falling monument had left.

A baleful, red tinge of the sunlight shining through clouds of ash was off-putting, and Sebhora felt numbed to his core by the sheer senseless scale of the slaughter. It was possible a tenth of his civilization had died in the last eight hours, and all Sebhora could push himself to do was to keep moving, to keep surviving, pushing away the pain until safety was assured. He crept through the slums low to the ground, a thick coating of ash layered upon all in sight.

Within minutes he was covered in the stuff, his entire body caked white. When he saw movement, any movement, he laid perfectly still - to anyone not inspecting his immobile form closely, he looked just like any other victim of the fires. It took nearly an hour, but Sebhora found what was once a small farm. The crops were damaged, some simply bursting from the heat alone, but every now and then he found a tuber which had been untouched by the fire.

The red sun was setting by the time Sebhora filled his bag, slowly starting the return journey to his family. The light was dimming rapidly, and the haze of smoke was still present enough to obscure things at a fairly close distance. He had just stood for the first time in hours when footsteps became audible, a group of close to a dozen from the sounds of it. Sebhora knew that he'd disturbed too much of the ash to reasonably play dead, so instead he kept his body hunched over as he began to run as fast as he could. Cries of terror came from the group of survivors which had just entered the fields of the ruined farm, shouting about shadows and ghosts.

Through ruined homes and over blackened bones Sebhora ran, the quickly darkening skies urging him to get home before night fell. It was unlikely the moon would shine upon Sosias tonight, and whatever acts of cruelty or desperation Sosians and Estyrians alike decided to commit would be hidden by the pitch black of a clouded, starless sky. The precious cargo he carried would be able to sustain his family for a few days, and Sebhora could not risk the food falling into anyone else's hands.

Back up the mountain trail he climbed, his legs burning from making his second frantic sprint across a vast ruined slum that day. Caked in ash and carrying a dirty sack, he pushed open the door of the forge and stepped inside. Looking around the room, Sebhora was confused - instead of the warm greeting he was expecting, the kin who he'd been trying to feed were frozen in fear at the mere sight of him. There was a few seconds of tense silence before Sebhora realized what was wrong, and he quickly undid the cloth mask. Tossing it aside, the trio let out a sigh of relief as they realized that the stranger was Sebhora.

Collectively the four of them began to laugh softly as the tension dissipated, Chebatli bringing over a waterskin to help Sebhora clean himself off. Eagerly he poured some onto his head, the ash washing off quickly as rivulets of dirty water began to work their way down his soot-stained form. Once the thick substance had been washed and scrubbed away with some clean rags, Sebhora set down the bag on a table and revealed his illicit harvest to the family. The thought of food invigorated all of them, and Ixaroatl kissed her husband long and passionately as he caught his breath.

"How is it out there?" Chebatli inquired, tilting his head in thought. "Are people okay? Is the city okay?"

Sebhora sighed and leaned over, grimacing inwardly as he forced himself to accurately describe what he had seen. "It is... it's as though someone had dropped the very sun on Sosias. The outer rings are devastated, burnt to ash or terribly damaged. The middle and inner rings haven't fared much better, what they were spared in devastation they paid for in lives. The smoke must have been so thick that they began to choke on the air itself. The pyramid still stands, but it has been damaged and defiled beyond words. The Estyrians brought hell to our doorstep, and forced it upon us."

The room grew quiet and solemn again, Ixaroatl softly beginning to cry beside him. Sebhora pulled her close and held her against his body, comforting his wife in their time of tragedy. Chebatli appeared to be devastated by the news, his eyes hollow and downcast as he stared off into oblivion. Aralin began pacing back and forth, fists clenching and unclenching as anxiety and despair set in for the boy.

Seeking to distract and comfort his son, Sebhora turned his head towards Aralin with a smile. "Aralin, what have you been making with the forge? I'm excited to see what you've come up with."

Aralin looked up in confusion, memory taking a moment to return to the forefront of his thoughts. "Huh? Oh! The sword! Come over and take a look. I've been working on the hilt, crossguard, and pommel while the steel finishes quenching."

Sebhora stood and walked over to the table Aralin had been working at, lifting and inspecting the wooden hilt that he'd been wrapping strips of leather around for a better grip. He smiled broadly at his son, impressed with the dedication to quality he showed despite the urgency of the situation. "I see someone's been practicing in their own time."

Aralin beamed at the praise he'd been given by his father, his features lightening quickly from the prior news. "Mhm! I was actually thinking of making a new sword for the cadet captain before..." Aralin's voice trailed off as he realized that wouldn't be happening. "Anyways, the sword should be done any second now!"

As the last few grains of an hourglass ran out, Aralin grabbed a pair of tongs and heaved with all of his might to pull out a blade long and thick, four feet in length from guard to point. Sebhora whistled softly as his son set the blade on the table, idly scratching his chin. "A bit big for your size, wouldn't you say?"

As Aralin grinned and carried the unfinished blade over to the grindstone, he chuckled and rested one side of the edge over the large stone wheel and began pumping the pedal with his foot. "You're right, even two-handed it's rather big for me. It's a good thing then that I'm not making it for me to use." He responded with a coy smile, staring up at his dad.

With confusion clear on his face, Sebhora opened his mouth to ask a question but was cut off by Chebatli. "We all discussed it, and we've decided that you're our best bet. You test everything you make, which means you have more experience swinging a sword than any of us. Not to mention, you're the only one of us here that the armor actually fits." Chebatli gestured towards the ceremonial armor shimmering softly in the forge's light, the aura of imposing beauty it radiated drawing Sebhora's attention.

The blacksmith sat and contemplated the new role he would be playing in this game of survival, defender as well as everything else. After a few moments he sighed, rubbing his temples with one hand before standing and stretching. The soft popping of dozens of sore joints long spent tensed up echoed through the room as Sebhora began to relax his muscles, limbering himself up and working out any stiffness he could feel. Once he finished, he grabbed a long iron poker and spun it in his hand before adjusting his stance and gripping the handle with both hands.

Sebhora slowed his breathing and closed his eyes, concentrating on remembering each fight he had seen. Slowly he began to go through the motions of swings and techniques, using the imagined sword's weight and momentum to his advantage in whirling strikes and overhead blows. After ten minutes or so, he stopped and rested the poker on the floor. "Ixaroatl, if you could get dinner prepared that would be lovely, you're our best cook by far. Chebatli, if you'd like something to do, cleaning and securing the actual house would be incredibly useful. I'm sure it'd do us all some good to sleep in our own beds tonight, feel some semblance of normalcy. I'll... I'll keep doing this."

Chebatli and Ixaroatl nodded, each going to their separate tasks as Aralin kept to the grindstone and Sebhora walked over to the armor stand. He gently traced his fingers over its smooth surface, reflecting on the months of work that went into creating it, before getting to work. It took Sebhora some time to get the armor on, starting with the chestplate and chausses. Next came the greaves and boots, the long edges of the greaves overlapping the boots and chausses seamlessly. The gauntlets were much the same, reaching up to Sebhora's elbow and leaving barely a gap to be seen. Sebhora twisted and turned, feeling the patches of chainmail which kept the entire suit together shift effortlessly with his movements. Confident that he retained a full range of motion, he lifted the helmet from its rest and placed it over his head. The wide eye holes in the mask-like visor were large enough to grant Sebhora most of his field of view, and he felt barely weighed down by the suit in comparison to the weight of other armors he had tried on.

Picking up the poker once more, he resumed practicing his stance and began to perform his swings while Aralin worked diligently on sharpening the blade behind him. Every now and then, he paused to ask Aralin for advice, relying on his son to relay what he'd learned from the veterans of his cadet squad. After about an hour of being given a crash course on combat and footwork, Sebhora was confident that he could hold his own against a single opponent. Just as he began to take off his armor, Ixaroatl peeked into the forge.

"Dinner is ready, so come up when you're... wow, Sebhora. That looks amazing on you!" She blushed softly at the sight of her husband in shining armor, his hair hanging loose and his body glistening with sweat.

Sebhora smiled and struck a few dramatic poses for his wife, drawing a quiet laugh from her. Once he knew how to get into it, getting out of the suit was much quicker and soon both he and Aralin were heading up the stairs to their home. Ixaroatl quickly shut the door once they were inside, barricading it shut with a collection of heavy boxes and light furniture. Chebatli had cleaned out all of the ash in the home, using one of the bellows from the forge, blowing it out the door and windows with a gust of man-made wind.

Though there was no fire in their dining room to avoid alerting anyone to their presence, Ixaroatl had carried the stew pot in to serve everyone as much as they could eat. Having missed their midday meals and been subjected to a great deal of trauma and stress, there was very little talking for the entirety of the mealtime. Though they were safe for the time being, none wanted to discuss what was happening around them - that would require them to process fully what had so far occurred and to grieve for friends lost, and no one was ready to do that.

Instead they focused on their food, enjoying the newfound relative silence. The drums had stopped with the setting sun, but the barrage had never ceased. Instead it merely slowed down, never allowing the unsheltered Sosians in the city below a moment's rest. A strong ocean wind had blown in from the coastline, sending the massive clouds of smoke hovering high above northbound like a warning to those who followed in Sosias's footsteps. As a result the city was enveloped in a thick oceanic fog, compounded in its thickness by the disturbed layers of ash gently swirling through the air at street level. The moon shone down brightly on the city, the tall obelisks and the Great Pyramid itself jutting through the concealing misty cloud like a strange and otherworldly realm.

Exhausted and ready for sleep, one by one each person finished their food and went to bed. Sebhora was the last to finish, his belly full and his body crying out for rest. Slowly he stood and walked to his room, laying down upon the woven mat that served as a bed beside his wife and fell into a dreamless sleep almost immediately.

Sebhora - Chapter Four

Sebhora was woken with a start some hours later by a distant scream that echoed through the night, sitting up and looking around frantically. He leapt to his feet and ran to the common room, followed by his wife and joined by his son and brother within seconds. Seeing them safe brought a measure of peace to him, but that peace was replaced by fear and anger when he looked outside.

In the city below, a group of Estyrians carrying torches were dragging a woman through a hole in the wall towards the jungle, replaced by another group of two dozen or so who soon entered the city. Scowling in disgust and filled with fury, Sebhora spat on the ground. "Those animals! Dragging off women into the night, harassing already fearful people, it's despicable!"

Chebatli sighed in defeat and rested a hand on his brother's shoulder, trying to get him back inside. "It is, but what are you going to do? Fight them off? You're no hero Sebhora, it's just suicide."

Sebhora's hands clenched into fists as his mind ran at a thousand miles per hour, trying to think of some way to stop the further abuse of his fellow Sosians. Then an idea struck him, and he started down the steps to his forge. "Aralin, how quickly can you get that sword done?"

Surprised by the sudden actions of his father and the drive which filled him, Aralin followed his father down. "I don't know, another twenty minutes to finish sharpening the blade, ten to get the parts fastened in place, give or take a few minutes."

Ixaroatl and Chebatli followed behind, both concerned for what could happen to Sebhora should he leave to try and stop the invaders. As he pushed open the door and made his way towards the armor once more, Aralin started back on the grindstone as the other two ran in behind. Ixaroatl spoke quickly and with no small amount of concern, trying to dissuade Sebhora from his course. "He's right, Seb! Even if you do drive them off, you're only one man. They'll come back with overwhelming numbers, and even if you do save some people you've got nowhere to take them all. Where could you possibly find enough armed-."

She stopped mid-sentence, the realization crashing upon her with the force of a hammer. "The noble district. You're going to take as many people there as you can because it's more defensible, and because that's where the main city guard is based out of. Sebhora, the nobles dislike us common folk! They'll turn you away, and when the Estyrians come marching in they'll use you as a sacrifice to keep them away from the district."

Slipping the chestpiece on and working on getting the legs strapped into place, Sebhora looked up at her with a wide smile. "They normally would, but seeing as Khigstus only knows how many died in the initial attack, I'd be willing to bet they'll take as many able-bodied men and women willing to fight and defend the city as they can. Not to mention the armories are held in that district, so they'll be able to turn every brutalized Sosian into an untrained but well armed and vengeful warrior guided by the will of the Great Protector!"

This stunned both Ixaroatl and Chebatli into silence as the implications of Sebhora's plan took root in their mind, the potential to rise from their calamity with swords drawn not lost on them. Aralin, who hadn't been paying attention, became frustrated with the slow progress of the sharpening and switched from sharpening width-wise to length-wise, doubling down on his efforts. Sebhroa slid the gauntlets on and picked up the remaining pieces of the sword, resting them on the table behind the grindstone as he grabbed a cup of rubbery glue and began to heat it into a more liquid form.

Chebatli crossed his arms and glared at his brother, still unconvinced by Sebhora's idea. "Who's to say they won't just overwhelm you the second that you get close? You're still just one man, they're trained soldiers in a group! Hell, the twisted bastards probably enjoy their killing."

As Aralin finished sliding the pommel onto the sword's tang, using the glue his father had provided to seal it into place as well as the hilt and crossguard, Sebhora picked up the helmet and held it in one hand. He turned a small hourglass on its head, watching the time crawl forwards until the glue dried. "You're right, I'm just a man without any formal training. If I fought them head on, the Estyrians would slaughter me without a second thought."

"But their training won't matter. Their skill won't matter. They won't be fighting a man." Sebhora said quietly, confusing his kin with the cryptic words. Once the time was up and the sword was ready, Sebhora grabbed the hilt with his free hand and slung the sword over his shoulder. Nudging the doorway open with his elbow, he slid the helmet on and stepped into the pale moonlight. Just as fire and sunlight caused the armor to come alive, the moonlight filtered through the armor's amber coating to the highly reflective Mother-Of-Pearl and was redirected outwards, glowing softly with a silvery sheen. The light of the armor greatly shifted and twisted, matching the bleached grayish-white of the ash around his feet - in fact, where the ash ended and Sebhora began was indistinguishable. "They'll be fighting a shadow."

Without a further word, Sebhora ran off with sword in hand down the mountain, his destination the glow amidst the ashen cloud that marked the Estyrian scouting party. The rest of his family were left watching atop the ledge which served as the cave's mouth, unable to do anything but hope and pray for his safe return. They went back up the steps to their home, returning to sleep restless and worried about whether or not Sebhora would return.

The Estyrian scouting party had been past the walls for twenty minutes or so, putting an end to the wounded Sosians they came across with a quick thrust through the heart, when they first heard it: the snapping of burnt wood underfoot. Swords were drawn and torches were raised, the group ready to kill any resistance and, if they were lucky, find some entertainment for the evening. But even with their flickering torchlight shining through the haze, the thick cloud ash obscured their vision to the point of being unable to see anything past a few feet away.

A single man was sent to investigate, and hefting his torch up high he slowly disappeared into the mist. The light of the moon filtered through the cloud enough to make his outline visible, just barely, as he looked around for whoever was trying to sneak past them. The silence was tense, the thick ash coating the ground muffling the sound of footsteps or whispers. The scouting party quickly grew bored, talking amongst themselves as they waited.

WIthout warning the solitary scout's torch was extinguished and a scream pierced the silence. Immediately the scouts snapped to attention, glancing around frantically for any sign of movement. From the direction of the scout, a single figure came sprinting towards them at top speed. Reacting on instinct, the nearest scout cut them down without hesitation. Upon closer inspection, the soldier found that his blade had struck down the very man whose torch had gone out, sent to investigate a few mere minutes earlier.

Their collective blood running cold in realization that whatever was out there was still around, the Estyrian troops drew closer together defensively. A loud crack like clay shattering was heard some distance behind them, and the party spun around with swords drawn. The quiet whoosh of a swinging blade whistled overhead, the tops of several torches falling to the ground and being smothered by the deep ash.

Screams of terror rang out from the startled torchbearers, dropping their useless sticks and whirling around once more only to see the faintest outline of a shadow fading into the fog. Thrown off their balance by the sudden reversal of roles, going from hunters to hunted, the Estyrians huddled together, swords facing outwards. A few minutes passed in, the silence only interrupted by the occasional snapping of a twig or breaking of clay causing the group to collectively shout in fear.

One particularly scared scout turned to the captain, his voice shaking as his eyes darted left and right frantically. "Sir, perhaps we should consider a retreat. Return to camp for now and come back in the daylight, sir."

The captain stared at him in disbelief, suddenly backhanding the scout hard enough to knock him to the ground. "Retreat? From some Sosian scum, sneaking around in the shadows and trying to scare us off? Whoever they are, they're too cowardly to attack us directly, they're not some ghost you fool!" As though to prove a point, the captain walked out of the group into the fog and spun around, his arms raised as he taunted the unknown assailant. "See, I told you. Cowardly Sosian scum."

After a few seconds, the rest of the Estyrians collectively began to laugh at their own foolishness for being so easily frightened. Those laughs were interrupted as a pair of hands and a face materialized from the mist, emotionlessly staring at them as one hand grabbed the captain's arm and twisted until he dropped the sword, and the other clamped down over the captain's extremely remorseful face. A muffled scream was the last thing they heard before the captain was yanked forcefully into the darkness, followed by a wet thunk seconds later.

There was shocked silence for but a moment as the rest of the scouting party stared in disbelief at the empty void where their captain had stood only seconds before. The one still on the ground after being slapped felt something brush his hand, and as he looked to see what it was the man was greeted by the terrified face of his captain's severed head. He began to scream nonsensically, all thoughts of duty and bravery having left his mind long ago as he and a dozen others began running back towards the safety of their warcamp, leaving only a handful left with one torch between them.

The soft crunch of ash behind them caused the remaining scouts to whirl around, freezing in place as they saw the shadow of death itself. An unnatural silhouette of sharp edges and ridged limbs, completed by an emotionless face crowned with menacing spikes. With a shout, the last torchbearer shoved the flame forwards - the specter seemed to come aflame, its ghostly nature hardening into a wrathful demon of vengeance wreathed in dancing fire.

The Estyrians dropped their weapons and fled as fast as their feet could carry them, screaming about demons and shadows in the ashen cloud that were killing them all. Upon hearing of the specter haunting the outer rings, all scouts were withdrawn until the Estyrian's sorcerers could dispel whatever witchcraft was at play.

Sebhora panted softly as he watched the Estyrians flee for their lives, screaming and crying as they went. His hands were shaking as he sat down upon a nearby rock, his eyes red and blurring as he yanked his helmet off. He was overwhelmed with a roiling sea of emotions, and as he buried his head in his hands he began to cry softly. Sebhora had never killed someone before, and though the Estyrians deserved it more than anyone else he still felt the burden of his own actions weighing heavily upon his heart. It took everything Sebhora had to hold himself together until the threat had passed, but now that he had time to think on his actions he began to question if he was any better than the invaders themselves. Suppressing an inwards disgust, he forced himself to regain his composure and don the helmet once more, venturing into the darkness of the night.

It didn't take him long to find a group of survivors closer to the river, twenty or so people banded together for safety in the ruins of a barn. Sebhora took off his helmet as he approached, hands raised high to show his peaceful intent. "Hello! I come in peace!"

The group, startled by the sudden approach of Sebhora, immediately separated into two groups; those who could fight raised spades, hoes, and pitchforks while the others ran and hid within the barn. Sebhora slowed down but kept walking forwards, giving them time to spot him and recognize him as a non-threat. The group seemed to relax a little when they finally managed to make out his silhouette, but didn't lower their weapons quite yet. Then, as Sebhora drew closer, one of the survivors lowered his pitchfork. "Sebhora? Is that you?"

"Yes, it's me! Who am I speaking to?" Sebhora responded, lowering his arms and approaching the group at a normal walking pace. The other people lowered their makeshift weapons and breathed a collective sigh of relief as Sebhora got close enough to be seen with relative clarity, the man who had spoken stepping forwards with a broad smile.

"Well shit, Sebhora, I had hoped you survived! It's me, Bembe! You sold me the nails to construct this very barn with," he said as he gestured to the mostly-intact structure behind them, "and seeing as it's still standing I'd say I made a good choice in sourcing them." Though the barn had obviously received some burns and some structural damage, the fact that most of the walls were still standing seemed a miracle.

With the lot of them now assured that they were safe for the time being, Sebhora and Bembe walked into the barn. Areas had been sectioned off for eating and for sleeping, and a crude map of the city had been drawn on a wall with hundreds of white dots in the outer rings. Sebhora stared at the map in wonder, seeing the effort that went into it - despite its crude appearance, darker splotches on the map seemed to symbolize areas of the most damage to the city. Small white lines ran between the large white dots on the map, connecting the smaller ones to create a large network. "Bembe, what is all of this?"

The farmer chuckled and looked at the map, standing beside Sebhora and staring up at the drawing with him. "It's us. Well," he said as he pointed to one of the smaller dots in the southwestern outer ring, "that one in particular is us. Each dot you see on this map represents a group of survivors, connected by messengers and by the careful work of a few cartographers. Each line is a route we've deemed unlikely to be discovered by the Estyrians, and the entire network stretches across a good quarter of the slums and a little into the trade district. We're hoping to connect all of the survivors soon, maybe plan some way of getting out of this alive."

Sebhora's face brightened with a wide smile as he heard this, staring up at the map in awe of the accomplishment. "By Khigstus, that's incredible. How many people are with us? How many are injured?"

Bembe grimaced, sighing softly as the subject of the number of survivors was brought up. "Well, we can't say for certain, but we can guess based on how many we have and just apply that to the rest of the city. We had, what, nearly half a million people scattered throughout the ring a few days ago? Farms, unskilled laborers, travelers coming to see the approaching festivals, traders, the like. Now, we're guessing maybe three hundred thousand are dead. We're not looking good, Sebhora, they really did us in."

"Even worse, the fires were strongest in the trade district. You couldn't look at the place without having your eyes melted in your sockets if you were too close to the river, the heat was insane." Bembe paused for a moment, forcing himself not to vomit as memories of the event floated to the forefront of his mind. "Similar story. Two days ago, three hundred and fifty thousand people throughout the entire ring. Now, we've got less than half of those who survived, and most of them have severe burns somewhere on their bodies. They've been a big help though, doing most of the math for us."

There was a few minutes of silence as Sebhora simply stood and processed this information, his eyes blankly staring into nothingness as he tried to wrap his head around the fact that half the people in his entire culture were likely dead or dying. The urge to scream, to flee, to retreat into his own mind and just shut down began to creep up on him, and he had to take a seat as nausea settled deep within his gut. Head held low, Sebhora clenched and unclenched his fists over and over again, struggling to keep his breathing steady.

"I have a plan," he said softly after some time had passed. "But to get it to work, I need you to get as many people to the noble's district as possible, as soon as possible. I'm going to head there now, so spread the word as far as you can, okay? The quicker people start moving, the quicker we can get people to safety and maybe, just maybe, take our city back." As soon as he finished talking, Sebhora put the helmet back on and stood, walking out of the barn and in the direction of the noble district with sword in hand.

Bembe turned towards Sebhora to ask a question but stopped, his words stuck in his throat upon seeing the normally cheerful smith becoming such a cold and furious figure. His eyes, the only part of him visible through the mask, were filled with a cold pool of hatred and disgust that seemed to be endless. He simply watched the blacksmith walk into the foggy night, his armor causing him to fade into the mist seamlessly within a few seconds. A chill ran down Bembe's spine as he turned back to the barn, walking back inside.

After a few moments, Bembe called over the nearest man. "Get everyone ready to leave and check if our runners are ready to send a message, we need to let everyone know to move inwards before sunrise. I don't know what Sebhora's plan is, but..." Bembe turned towards the fog that Sebhora had disappeared into, that cold chill returning for a moment as he shuddered. "I'd rather not find out if he was making a request or a demand."

Sebhora - Chapter Five

Sebhora trekked through the mist in haste, following the blackened and corpse-strewn roads until the bridge between districts was once more in front of him. When he'd been here last, the sky was still blue and hope still held sway in his heart. Once more he stopped at the threshold, overwhelmed by the disparity between what the city was like only a day ago, and the murky gray ashen fog which masked the burnt husks before him. There was no contemplation about the future however, only a grim determination to survive for as long as possible and to protect his family. Taking a deep breath to calm his nerves, Sebhora crossed the bridge and entered the embers of destruction.

The first thing he noticed was the heat. Though the fires were gone, the wooden buildings and ruins around him - long since turned to charcoal - still radiated an oppressive heat that thickened the very air. The burnt support beams which held through the inferno still glowed with a soft radiance, dimming and brightening slowly like a swarm of creatures softly breathing. The crumbling timber stood ominously as Sebhora walked down the road, the battered bones of prosperity exposed to the open air by ruination.

The second was the bodies, strewn everywhere and reduced to ash in more than a few places. Bone-thin bodies were curled up in the fetal position, blackened and dessicated beyond recognition. Sebhora had to stop and allow himself to cry halfway through the district when he entered one of the many open market squares, sorrow flooding into him as he gazed at the sight within. In the center of the square was a tall stone obelisk inscribed with central stories of the worship of Khigstus in the form of murals and images. Frozen in place by rigor mortis and by the sheer pressure of the other bodies, upwards of a hundred people were stuck in the poses they died in. They had swarmed the obelisk, desperately clawing over and on top of each other to try and escape the fires around them.

Sebhora ran from that square as fast as he could, eyes locked straight ahead so he wouldn't have to gaze on that shrine to suffering a moment longer. The great quantities of death he had seen in so many varieties was beginning to undermine his resolve, the raging anger he previously felt being slowly replaced with the urge to flee. Sebhora was a kind and peaceful man, ill-equipped for the atrocities against life that were present here. Even the emotional numbness, which had thus far been a saving grace against the traumatic journey, was soon being swallowed up by an abhorrence so strong I nearly made him vomit.

The moon had passed its apex in the sky by the time Sebhora made it through the trade district, beginning the slow journey down to the western horizon. The bridge between districts was a stark contrast between the safety of the noble district, mostly untouched with people clearing the last of the bodies from the street without fear, and the hellscape of the trade district. There were guardsmen on watch standing at the far end of the bridge, four men in dented armor who looked battered and bruised.

Happy to see some semblance of normalcy, Sebhora walked across the bridge quickly and without trying to conceal his footsteps. The four guardsmen snapped to alertness as he emerged from the shadows, weapons raised and clearly surprised to see someone approaching. The rearmost one ran off into the district, shouting something Sebhora couldn't quite make out.

"Halt, or be fired upon!" One of the guardsmen shouted, causing Sebhora to freeze in place and raise his hands above his head. Within seconds the guards who had left returned, accompanied by several others bearing torches and bows. One man stepped forwards from the group, throwing his torch at Sebhora's feet and inadvertently causing the front of his armor to shine orange and red in the light. A few gasps of shock could be heard from the armed men, followed by each archer nocking and drawing their bows. The foremost guard drew his sword and took a step back, grimacing at the sight. "Identify yourself!"

Sebhora slowly removed his helmet before tossing his sword aside, raising his hands once more. "Don't shoot! I'm a Sosian! My name is Sebhora, I'm a blacksmith, and I've come to speak to whoever's in charge. Lord Quetzlipoc, if possible."

The guards seemed to relax somewhat once the sword and helmet had been removed, but not a single man lowered his weapon. The foremost guard narrowed his eyes and stared for a moment, considering his options, before slowly walking up to Sebhora and glancing around him. Once he was satisfied that Sebhora was alone, he raised a hand for the others to see. The rest of the guards warily lowered their weapons, and the foremost guard motioned towards Sebhora. "Pick up your sword, and keep that helmet off. The rest of you, keep watch until I return. I'm going to take him in, and let the lord decide what to do."

With that, the guardsmen resumed their positions either at the foot of the bridge or just out of sight. Sebhora picked up his sword and followed behind the leader of the guards, noticing that his armor stopped shimmering as the torches were snuffed out behind him. The two men walked in silence through the district, giving Sebhora plenty of time to look around. Several large gardens they had passed were dug out for use as mass graves, and within a few minutes life was both visible and active. Nobility and people of the upper classes in general were trying to keep things normal and cheery, but the knowledge of tragedy was thinly hidden behind each smile.

Soon enough, Sebhora and his escort turned off the winding main path onto a large estate ground, polished granite pillars flanking the large oaken doors to its interior. Upon them was inscribed the Quetzal, a brightly colored jungle bird, holding a sword in one talon and a scroll in the other - the symbol of House Quetzlipoc. The doors opened as the approached, two servants heaving on the doors with all their might, and the duo went inside so the doors could be closed behind them.

Sebhroa was instructed to stop and wait outside the room as the guardsmen went in, watching with keen interest as the guard opened the door to the Lord's study. Inside a man in high quality guard armor, likely a commander, stood over a table across from a familiar face: Lord Ritzal Quetzlipoc. A regal man in his mid-thirties with a thinly cut beard and piercing green eyes beneath a head of shoulder-length brown hair, he glanced up towards the door and made eye contact with Sebhora. Then the door was closed, and he was left standing awkwardly in the hallway, waiting to see whether or not he would be permitted an audience.

A few moments passed where nothing happened, the only noises in earshot being servants quietly going about their business and muffled conversations from within the study. Sebhora idly looked around, drumming his fingers upon the side of his helmet, before the door was pulled open hastily. A firm hand on both of their shoulders, Lord Quetzlipoc guided the guard commander and the man who'd brought Sebhora out of the room with such haste he nearly threw them into the hallway. "Yes, we'll continue this conversation at a later date, but at the moment I have a guest and it would be very rude of me to ignore them."

Before they had a chance to respond, the nobleman grabbed Sebhora by the arm and tugged him into the room, still smiling at the commander. "If you don't mind, I'd quite like to be left undisturbed until I call for you. I'll send someone to find you when I'm available, goodbye!" With that, Lord Quetzlipoc quickly shut the door and slid several iron locks shut. He slowly turned around and leaned his back against the door, letting out a low and exasperated groan as he slid to the floor.

Sebhora stood in shock, staring speechlessly at the lord who had pulled him into the study. Of all of the ways he'd imagined the meeting going, this was something he wouldn't have expected in a thousand years. A few seconds passed in silence between the two as Ritzal sat on the floor, Sebhora trying to think of something - anything - to say in this situation. Soon he decided to just go with what came to mind naturally; extending his hand to the patriarch of House Quetzlipoc, he smiled. "Rough day?"

The man simply stared at him for a moment before beginning to laugh, taking Sebhora's hand and rising to his feet. "You've no idea, my friend. I am so happy to see you, Sebhora, I've got so much on my plate and no one to talk about it with who doesn't want the impossible from me. Some are looking to me for guidance and leadership, some want more of the able-bodied people we have guarding the bridges though we're stretched thin enough as is, and the rest of the nobility-bah! A third of them want to surrender, a third of them think we can just march out there and rout the lot of the invading force with the numbers we have now, and a third have just gone into denial! I'm trying to grieve my own losses, and I cannot get a moment's rest." By the time the lord was finished speaking, his face was red and he was slightly out of breath. "You'll... you'll have to forgive my ramblings, I haven't slept since yesterday."

Composing himself, the lord ran a hand through his hair and walked over to the table at the other end of the room, slumping into a chair beside the fireplace. He motioned Sebhora into the chair just across from him with a wave of his hand, breathing deep and calming his agitation. "It's nice to have someone to speak to who I can actually help, without having to consider the ramifications of an entire city's remaining populace with each word. I see you've completed the armor!"

Sebhora nodded and stood in the firelight, allowing the reddish flame to dance and flicker in the amber coating upon his suit. Lord Quetzlipoc leaned forward in his seat, inspecting the designs carved into the metal and the layer of glass-like material which acted as a thick lacquer. Smiling in approval, he gestured towards the helmet Sebhora carried under his arm. "May I?" He said, extending a hand towards the blacksmith.

Sebhora bowed his head and placed the helm in the noble's hands, sitting down and allowing hsi weary legs a moment of rest while the other man gazed in wonder upon the headpiece. Tracing his fingers first over the mask-like faceplate before gliding up to the crown of spikes seated upon the top of the helm, he smiled in both great satisfaction and wonder. "Beautiful work Sebhora, truly beautiful. The way that the armor seems to come alive in the firelight... it's unlike any I have seen before in my life."

Sebhora smiled and bowed his head respectfully once again, this small moment of respite acting as a restorative salve upon the tattered cloth of his mind. "Thank you m'lord, I spent no small amount of time finding the right materials and experimenting with different armor styles to come up with the finished set. As someone who's fought in it, albeit only by a very skewed definition of the term, I can say with surety that it will serve you well. Speaking of which, are you wanting the suit now? It wouldn't trouble me at all to consider this my delivery, unorthodox as it may be."

Lord Quetzlipoc chuckled, handing the helm back and waving his hand dismissively. "No, no, it's served you better than I so far. If we make it through this, I'll ask for it. And once I have it, I'd like to put you on retainer as my personal blacksmith. That means your family could move up here, and experience the benefits and luxuries of living amongst the higher classes of our society. Speaking of which, how are they doing? Do you require aid?"

Sebhora's eyes widened as he was told of the position he might fill should all go well, and he bowed repeatedly in gratitude. "It would be an honor, my lord. And as to your question, my family is doing fine. We were far enough from the main slums to be somewhat free from the bombardments. Though, now that you mention providing aid m'lord... I have come to you with an idea, a proposal which may offer all of us a better chance at living to see the dawn, and the next dawn after that."

Ritzal leaned forwards and steepled his fingers, gazing curiously at the blacksmith. "Oh? Well then, you're an intelligent man. Let's hear this idea, some fresh insight would be of more use than the endless doomsaying of my advisors and commanders."

"Well sir, you and the nobility are having some issues like you mentioned earlier, and it goes without saying that people in the lower classes like myself aren't faring much better. However, it seems to me like these two groups are the answers to each other's problems. For example, you don't have enough men to spare in order to adequately defend the ring and Sosias at large, and the survivors in the outer rings have too many people to shelter safely. What I'm suggesting is that you bring in the survivors from the outer rings, shelter them in the safety of the district. I'm sure that helping hands would be appreciated by the healers, and there'd be no shortage of men and women wanting to fill the role of the guard." Sebhora explained his idea slowly and carefully, watching for any sign that what he was saying wouldn't work on Ritzal's face.

Instead of the hesitation he'd been expecting, Lord Quetzlipoc had leaned forwards with great interest and followed every word. Once Sebhora had finished speaking, he leaned back in his seat and grabbed some papers off of the table beside him, mentally calculating the demand for bodies by the other noble houses and the approximate numbers of the common folk still alive. After a few minutes he scratched his chin and looked at Sebhora with a wild smile, standing up and pushing parchment around to make room. "Sebhora, I must say. If we survive this, I swear to Khigstus himself that I'm going to strong-arm the entirety of Sosian's nobility into elevating you into a minor noble house. I'm... I'm going to get to work on this, and as of right now you don't have the battlefield experience or training to command men, but I promise you that you will should all go well. You should get home, tell your family to sleep easy tonight."

Sebhora stood as well, bowing low once again in respect for the noble before him. As much as he wanted to believe Lord Quetzlipoc, a significant part of him thought that these claims were simply the joyous thoughts of a man given hope. "As you command, m'lord. I should let you know that you'll be receiving the first of the arriving commonfolk soon, I ran into a group of them on the way here and told them to spread the word."

Ritzal chuckled and glanced up at Sebhora, smiling a coy smile. "A man who takes action rather than wasting time, yet another good trait. Be safe, my friend." The lord then returned to his work, grabbing new papers and feather pens with which to put into action the start of a plan. Sebhora's idea wasn't enough on its own to get the city's wounded populace to safety, but in the hands of a capable man with power at his disposal it could blossom into a grand migration inwards.

Senhora then took his leave, picking up the helmet and sword before walking back out into the hall where the two rather irritated guardsmen still stood. He nodded sheepishly at them before walking towards the exit, hearing the lord calling them back inside as he left. The doors of the manor soon opened and once more he was back in the noble district, beginning the journey home by retracing his steps through the winding streets back to the bridge. He shuddered inwardly at the knowledge of what awaited him in that realm of nightmares made solid, but the thought of being able to return to his family gave him the strength to swallow his disgust and keep moving.

It wasn't long before Sebhora found himself back at the bridge, his travel swift and unaccosted by the guardsmen. As he crossed the bridge he paused, recalling the swarm of petrified bodies that he would have to pass yet again if he took the same route, and decided that it would be much better to take a more direct path. He'd seen the great road from his home many times, a wide avenue that cut straight from one end of the district to the other, reserved for people traveling through the district rather than those choosing to peruse the many markets. A few minutes of walking the perimeter of the district soon led him to the wide road he'd been looking for, covered in a layer of ash thicker than he'd seen anywhere else. Sebhora started trekking through the ashen road immediately, not wanting to waste any time on his journey and hoping to bypass the horrors of the district entirely.

The ground crunched beneath his feet as he walked, the crack of snapping timber echoing softly with each step. It was oddly peaceful, the barrage having finally stopped some scant minutes ago. Light was slowly fading into blackness as the moon drifted downwards even further, the pale glow that filtered through the settling ash and rising mist disappearing into the ambient shadows. Sebhora was lost in thought, his mind occupied with visions of newfound hope for the future, when his foot became stuck in something buried beneath the ash. This threw him off balance, nearly causing the blacksmith to trip over entirely.

With a grunt, Sebhora gave his foot a hard tug. He felt the thing trapping his ankle give beneath the ash, watching the thick material shift with the movement. He tugged again, this time with all of his might. His foot came free, and with it came the blackened human rib cage it had somehow gotten stuck in. He wasn't fortunate enough to have the bones of the body or just the torso stuck to his leg; he stared in shock as an entire shriveled corpse, long blackened by the inferno, came free of the ash. He let out a loud scream and shook his leg, the body sent flying by the abrupt motion. It collided with the wall, shattering into fragments from the impact.

Sebhora's heart was beating faster than it ever had before, his breaths were shallow and fast. The terrifying shock of the corpse emerging from the ash had caused his blood to run cold, and he reflexively took a step backwards. He heard a loud crunch as his boot crushed something underfoot, and a glance confirmed that the object crushed was a skull. The cracking of timber beneath the ash along this road had not been timber, but rather the bones of countless people suffocated by the fire and smoke on this very road.

The wide path Sebhora had been walking suddenly felt claustrophobically small, the walls closing in slowly from both sides as horror and revulsion welled up deep within his core. Sebhora took off at a mad dash, wanting - no, needing - desperately to get out of this place. Countless remains were disturbed, each one only adding to Sebhora's mania. Skeletal hands poked out of the ash, trying to grab him as he ran by, and every skull staring at him as he passed glared at him with their hollow eyes.

Eternity seemed to pass as Sebhora scrambled as fast as his legs could carry him, his vision tunneling to mere pinpricks as he left reason behind. Without warning, the road ended and the walls which had been so close to crushing the life out of him seemed to just disappear in the blink of an eye. He stumbled and fell, pain shooting through his torso as he crumpled to the cobbled street in a heap. Gasping for breath, Sebhora yanked off his helmet and inhaled as much air as he could, his heart finally beginning to slow down. His legs and lungs burned from exertion as he lay there in the ash, the thick odor of burnt wood permeating every aspect of his perception. Tears flowed from his eyes in long streams as he began to cry, the feeling of loss in his heart growing to unbearable proportions as he couldn't help but imagine the painful deaths of all those who had fallen in the path. Witnessing death on such a large and cruel scale wasn't something he could ever have prepared for, and it was slowly eating away at his very soul.

After a few minutes, Sebhora forced himself back to his feet and wiped away his tears. He slid his helm back into place as he started walking again, the chirping of distant birds alerting him to the coming arrival of the dawn. He realized with a jolt of fear that if he was caught in the morning light, he would stand out like a beacon to any scout or invading soldier who happened to be looking in his general direction. With no small amount of urgency, Sebhora suppressed his aching and began to run at a manageable pace instead of the manic sprint he'd just finished. It was another straight line home from where he was, across the bridge and through the slums back up to the mountain. Noting with a grim satisfaction that the pockets of life he'd seen passing through had disappeared, traveling to the noble district for safety, he was at the foot of his mountain by the time the sky began to turn pink. He raced up the path to his home, but when he reached the top he froze in place.

Standing by the doorway was Aralin, his bow drawn taut with trembling hands as he aimed it at the unknown figure standing only a dozen feet away. Sebhora slowly removed his helmet, and the second he did, Aralin let out a choked gasp of surprise and let his arms relax. He threw the bow aside and ran towards Sebhora, hugging him tightly as he began to cry both in gratitude and relief that his father was home safe. Sebhora returned the embrace, holding his beloved son as close as he could. Soon they went back inside, Aralin returning to his room as Sebhora took off the armor by the doorway. Soon he climbed back into bed with his sleeping wife, laying down next to her and letting sleep consume him within seconds.

Sebhora - Chapter Six

Wakefulness did not come gently. It did not slowly grow stronger than sleep, nor did it softly shake Sebhora from his slumber. Wakefulness came with a loud roar, a crash, and rumbling from every direction: it came with pain and light and screaming. His eyes snapped open as he sat up, brushing shards of rock from his chest and looking around. Ixaroatl had woken up in a similar state of panic and confusion, grabbing Sebhora's arm reflexively. He barely noticed however, his attention caught on the large portion of the wall which had given way to reveal the outside world.

The drums of war sounded once more, overwhelmingly loud at the Western Gate rather than spread around the city like beforehand. The barrage had finally come to a close, but not before one final volley was launched to ensure the Sosians did not wake peacefully, and not before one boulder had overshot its target. It was nearing midday, and the sheer number of people milling about in the noble district was visible from the city's edge. Banners were raised high throughout the entire middle ring, flying the colors of House Quetzlipoc and some of the other noble houses who'd rallied behind his cause.

Each rooftop was packed with people, the traditional jade-adorned cloth of Sosian archers glistening like a teal wave above the stone. Iron weapons and armor filled the streets with metallic gray, survivors and soldiers alike prepared to fight for their homes. The temple district was similarly filled with commotion, the families of those unable to fight and those who had been wounded gathering there to take shelter from any stray arrows that may be fired towards them.

Sebhora stood and helped his wife to her feet, rushing to check on Aralin and Chebatli. They were already in the common room, scared and still struggling to brush the sleep from their eyes. Chebatli and Sebhora's eyes met, and the same thought seemed to come to them at the same time. WIthout a word Chebatli took Ixaroatl and Aralin, guiding them down to the forge while Sebhora began to put the armor on once more. By the time he finished, the other three had gone down to prepare and to hide. Sebhora joined them soon after, keeping to the shadows of the outcropping above to avoid the sun's glow.

He found them standing in the mouth of the cave, gazing in shock at the shattered fragments of the large wooden barrier which had once sealed the cave mouth shut. A large rock sitting amongst his damaged tools appeared to be the culprit, a piece of stone knocked loose from the impact. Sebhora stood with them, their hearts aching in grief at the violation of this last sanctum of safety. After a few moments, Chebatli found his words.

"It's more open, but still the safest place we've got right now. Come, let's get inside, the sooner we can make a barrier the sooner we can relax a little." Chebatli said as he stepped forwards and began to clear the wood and stone from the workshop floor, motioning for the others to help him. Everyone was soon working hurriedly to get some semblance of protection together, assembling a hasty wall from the pieces they had.

As the wall neared completion, something in the distance caught Sebhora's eye. Turning to look, Sebhora's heart skipped a beat in his chest as the stone in his hand fell to the ground. His family turned to see what was wrong, but soon succumbed to the same paralyzing fear that he had. Across the city, at the Western Gate, the towering door of iron and stone had been torn from their hinges and thrown to the ground. Trampled upon by countless Estyrian boots, a column of armored soldiers two dozen men wide slowly began to make their way through the slums. With the ash settled and the morning mist dissipated, the advantage of low visibility had been lost to the Sosians.

Whistles and shouts echoed through the noble district as the Sosians began to mobilize, hundreds of thousands of angry survivors of the attack baying for blood. Baskets of arrows were carried up to the archers as the bannermen of Lord Quetzlipoc and a dozen other houses made their way to the front lines, rallying the men and women of Sosias to war. When the bannermen reached the district's edge, the tension broke like a dam; dozens of makeshift bridges were lowered so that the Sosians would not be limited by a select few chokepoints, and the swarm of people ran forth in a great tide. Sebhora and his family could only watch with a strange combination of fear and hope as the dull gray of the iron-clad Sosian horde raced through the trade district, the familiar layout of their home emboldening them even further.

The Estyrian column had not yet changed its formation, their sheer numbers enough to keep the column going without an end in sight. Though they were halfway through the district, it seemed there was no end to the orderly rows of invaders pouring from the jungle with each passing second. As the two forces neared the river which separated the rings, the archers on the rooftops fired their bows high, a thick cloud of arrows congealing in the air from many directions as they flew towards their target.

Sebhora broke away from the sight of two great forces nearing their clash, turning to his wife. "Ixa, pack as many things as we can carry and get ready to move. Khigstus willing, we shall stand victorious, but if they don't succeed then I want to be able to leave at a moment's notice. We'll fare better in the jungle than in a doomed city."

She nodded and grabbed Aralin by the arm, the two running off to prepare as Chebatli stepped closer to his brother. They stood in silence as the battle drew ever closer, before Chebatli turned back to the wall. He resumed working on the barrier, seemingly dead set on fortifying the cave even if it wouldn't amount to anything should they have to flee. Sebhora simply stood and watched the city from afar, one hand on his sword and the other clenching into a fist over and over again as he prayed to the Great Protector for salvation.

The great cloud of arrows fell upon the Estyrians with countless thuds against wood, steel, and flesh, the entire head of the proverbial snake being cut off as a fair number were killed by the initial volley. However, their victory was short-lived - the Estyrian column continued their unceasing march, stepping on or over their fallen comrades with shields raised high. They continued marching towards the river until the forefront of the column could see the Sosians rushing forward, a vengeful horde eager for blood with the might of Khigstus at their back.

The Estyrians lowered their shields and spears, bracing themselves to break the Sosian charge upon the wall of bodies and metal. The two armies met at last, the Sosians flooding across the river with their bridges in a swarm, crashing upon the disciplined Estyrian column. Dozens were carried forward by the momentum of the charge, impaled by their own recklessness upon the spear tips of the Estyrians. The soft twanging of bowstrings being released reverberated across the city as another cloud of arrows was released into the sky - however, the

Estyrians were prepared this time, the people just inside the column raising their shields high to block the rain of death. Very few Estyrians were felled by this second volley, but Sosians fell left and right from otherwise atrocious friendly fire.

The Estyrian column was compressed by the assault from all sides, rows of men falling as overwhelming force broke their lines and were either trampled or stabbed repeatedly. Then, as orders finally reached the head of the column from the jungle, the Estyrian force switched tactics. As they blocked volley after volley of arrows, always losing some ultimately replaceable men with each time, the Sosian wave was pushed back by a sudden surge of movement. An unexpected thrust forward by the Estyrian's spears killed the nearest Sosians, and drove the others back a few steps.

This pattern of bracing, attacking, and advancing was how the Estyrians continued their slow march to the city center, pushing the Sosians back to the river. As the bannermen of the noble houses retreated to the trade district, the rest followed and withdrew their makeshift bridges. All that remained was a single stone bridge, a strong chokepoint with the river acting as a natural barrier.

Yet the Estyrian army did not balk at this, merely taking the opportunity to spread out along the open space of the riverbank. With shields raised to block the volleys of arrows which fell upon them every minute or so, rolling their dead forwards into the river as they went, still more soldiers made their way to the front lines. First came squads of men carrying large crossbows, each weapon carved with the head of a snake whose open mouth the bolt would fire from. They hid beneath the shields of their comrades, weaving their way through the ranks with ease.

Next came a far more dangerous handful of people, the weapon which oftentimes gave the Estyrian army the lethal edge it needed in difficult situations. Three robed figures slowly made their way through the central column, soldiers parting left and right to give them a wide berth. Each had their hood concealing their face, and in their hands was held the chain of a spherical, swinging censer which poured thick purple incense smoke in coiling trails upon the ground. The smoke smelled like the cloying odor of desert serpents, and with the quiet hiss-like chanting of the sorcerer-priests accompanying it, it felt like three snakes of smoke and dust were slithering through the ruins.

Accompanying each priest was an escort of five massive warriors, each bare-chested and tattooed with sigils of the Estyrian's serpentine god across their entire torso. Serpentine eyes darted across the area, searching for any perceived threat they could dispatch. When arrows fell, these escorts picked up foot soldiers bodily and used them as shields to protect their priestly wards from being slain. Once, an arrow slipped past the wall of shields held high towards the priest - in a single fluid movement, one of the warriors had cut it from the air and separated the soldier who'd failed to block the arrow from his head.

At the entrance to the open street where the Estyrians had begun to amass, the three sorcerous practitioners parted ways. Two went left and right respectively, situating themselves amongst the crossbow-men, while the third continued forwards until he stood at the foot of the bridge. Seemingly in unison the trio of battle-priests opened their censers further, the purple incense smoke pouring across the ground in thick pools. These battle-priests, while possessing no true magic, were masters of the art of alchemy; this proved to be an equally valuable skill, as they could create the illusion of magic.

Their censers weren't simply an aesthetic choice - the smoke they poured out held a carefully concocted mix of reagents, giving the front lines of the Estyrian forces a healthy dose of numbing agents, strength enhancers, and minor euphorics to increase their battle fervor. The crossbowmen were handed special bolts, filled with a sickly yellow smog. Then the chanting began; from beneath their concealing hoods a low and guttural litany was recited, the language ancient and full of sharp, hissing consonants.

The combination of mind-altering incense and mystical chanting drove the Estyrians into a frenzy, dozens of soldiers tossing aside their shields and howling into the sky, only to be silenced by the next Sosian volley. The river was thick with floating bodies, and the Sosians were shaken by their displays of bloodlust. As seconds passed amidst the sudden uproar, the crossbowmen suddenly raised their weapons for the first time since their arrival. The Sosians took what cover they could, but none landed amongst them. Instead, a small return volley arced high above their heads, spreading wide to cover a large area. The bolts landed amidst the rooftop archers, their fragile payloads shattering and releasing the smoky gas into the air.

It spread quickly, dispersing wide and obscuring vision for all caught within. Then a few among the archers began to cough, followed by a few more, and within but a few moments most of the Sosian archers had begun choking on the very air. Their eyes bulged in their sockets as their tongues swelled and they clawed at their throats, desperate for a breath that would never come. Another alchemical creation, the gas was inert until it touched saliva - then it would coalesce and expand into a thick, sticky substance which sealed the throat entirely.

With their ranged support gone, the Sosians formed up and prepared to hold back the Estyrian assault on the bridge. That army of berserkers did indeed charge - not just over the bridge, but across the river as well. They ran across the floating corpses, each soldier who fell into a watery grave becoming a sturdier stepping stone for the soldier behind them. Their fighting spirits dimmed by their forced retreat, the

Sosians were quickly beginning to be overwhelmed by the sudden tide of murderous invaders in the throes of a battle-frenzy.

The force of sheer numbers the Sosians had employed was turned against them, an undisciplined mass quickly breaking under such pressure. With their singular advantage in melee lost and their archers dying in droves a district away, the Sosians began a harried and bloody retreat. Lord Quetzlipoc and his bannermen did what they could to rally a solid defense against the coming army, but they too began to retreat lest they be trampled beneath the frightened militia members. It was only a matter of minutes before the Estyrians, fighting with inhuman ferocity, began to push into the trade district.

With their feeble resistance shattered, the Sosians seemed to have their momentum reversed as the Estyrians returned their bloodshed twice over. Hope, that fragile banner which has toppled tyrants and allowed people to survive insurmountable odds, was trampled by the invaders and burned away in the conflagration of their zealotry. Without hope, the Sosians in the noble district collapsed the bridge and hid behind barricades of rubble, abandoning their kindred to their dooms as they cowered fearfully. This was the turning point, a last clash between men born of desperation and doomed to fail.

There was naught man could do for the once proud city, merely observe and weep as the undefeated Estyrian forces dealt the killing blow to any resistance. So the Sosians, from the battlefield to the noble district to the Grand Temple itself, begged and prayed to Khigstus for salvation with all their might.

SEBHORA - CHAPTER SEVEN

An Estyrian soldier glanced over the corpse, a woman of fair skin and olive hair - perhaps not even midway through her life. Blood dripped from his curved, serpentine blade onto the ground below as he caught his breath. It was apparent she was a fighter, for it was obvious she tried to fight him back. The battle for the city was going into its second day of the Estyrian-initiated genocide, and there were many more soldiers and civilians lying dead and dying than there were soldiers.

"That's m-my..." A man solemnly spoke out, catching the attention of the Estyrian soldier. They were in the middle of an alleyway littered with dead bodies, both Estyrian and Sosians alike - it appeared the bulk of the battle had transitioned to the nearby districts and the Grand Temple of Khigstus. Without finishing his sentence, he quickly reached over to one of the dead Sosian guards and grabbed the guard's battle ax with his right hand, tightly gripping it. His form was not there, he was not a trained soldier, but he was a man that had just lost his wife and possibly his city - a man with nothing to lose has oftentimes been seen as a man more dangerous than most.

The unknown soldier and the unnamed widow - two men that knew they had to fight. One, simply because he was doing as his orders commanded, the other due to a need for vengeful wrath. The air blew solemnly, carrying with it a faint cacophony of battle and slaughter - the fabled song of iron and flame, steel and fire. The rise and fall of the battle that raged nearby, of which they were surely only a small part. And yet, even amidst the living misery of war and genocide, they could still hear the murmurs of triumph, though whether over other soldiers or their own sacrifice, no one could say.

Their blades clashed, the clang of steel ringing through the air like silver bells. The warrior spun his own sword, the power of both blades seeming to clash and hum in the air. Lashes were slashed, grunts were bellowed out, and the two men found themselves standing before each other, their own blades dropping with traces of the other's blood. Panting and trying to catch their breath, they were tired - and, for a brief second, it was as if they respected the other person just enough to offer a period of rest. However, no rest would come to them.

There was a roar from the distance, one that resounded through their ears like a scream of thunder, before the warring men were briefly distracted by a mighty cough of wind. A heavy mist had come upon the city's battleground, the light of the sun diffused, the sky around them turning dark and gray. The light was so dark it threatened to be black and yet the fog surrounding it was so heavy and dense as to defy any definition of darkness.

Above the Grand Temple, far into the heavens, there it began - lightning arced across the sky as if a hundred thunderstorms were in the area. The bolts began to change from their white and blue hue to crimson and orange, lightning the sky up with a flurry of colors.

And then it stopped.

The city had grown silent, the sounds of battle coming to a momentary pause, as if all eyes were fixated on the shimmering wound that was now in the sky. A strange laughter reached the ears of those within the city, a laughter whose place was not meant for this world. An explosion rocked from the great wound in the sky, and then another loud boom - not much could be seen, for smoke and fire had now surrounded the Grand Temple. And yet, a strange fear came upon the city. A strange fear that seeped itself deep into the hearts of both the Estyrians and Sosians alike. The widow and the soldier had stopped their battle, their war-torn eyes fixated on the spectacle.

It was when the smoke and fire began to settle that the hearts, hopes, and dreams of all those fighting on this day ended. Towering above the ruins of the Grand Temple stood the manifestation of all of those years of war, rage, greed, hate, and disgust that had bred itself across all of Galoholme and Vuros. A body made of maroon steel with specs of molten lava dripping from some cracks, a head adorned by a crown of the golden flakes of Nyel'sal with what appeared to be two warhammers going up on each side of the crown, seven teal eyes that scoured the battlefield, and a massive greatsword that had seven, black hearts that resembled the night-time sky running along the blade. Behold, Khigstus - the Fallen God of Vuros!

Shifting his gaze across the battlefield, the mighty being grinned as he gripped his sword with both hands, bits of molten steel dripping from his hands and onto the ground below. A roar that resounded through the land as a breath from the broken heavens above was followed by the first strike against those that dared be within his pseudo-graceful sight. As his sword slammed into the ground, a shockwave of fire and smoke swept through the city and into the nearby forests with a force stronger than any storm that had hit Vuros. Buildings that had stood the test of time, even from the Age of Vuron, were now crumbled as if they were dust in the wind. A single strike by the god that was their supposed protector had done what even the Estyrians couldn't - brought the city to ruin and more.

The widow and the unnamed soldier simply stood there, glancing at each other at the moment of the attack - fire quickly slithering its way through the alleys like water rushing into a crack. They looked at each other, the last glimpse of their life on Vuros fading away as the flames of an angered god extinguished them in beautiful anguish. With most of the invading army and the Sosians defeated within mere seconds, the Patricidal God was not done. He extended his blade up with just his right hand and extended it towards the forests that surrounded the ruined city. His left hand extended outward, the hearts in the blade began to stir - first with single thumps that quickly escalated to roaring, eldritch screams that continued to build in pitch. The tip of his weapon began to glow an eerie crimson that was littered with what looked like little stars that would otherwise glisten in the night-time sky. A torrent of molten steel, the very steel that comprised his body, erupted from the blade and began to spread over the forests.

Each drop of molten steel made its way into the ground, connecting to a crack or otherwise broken place on the forest floor. With each new impact on the earth, more cracks would open in the ground, spreading across the land as if making their own parallel path to the Grand Temple. The ash and smoke of their passing would spread and cover all of the forest and Sosias. Lit asunder with an unnatural flame, littered with cracks filled with molten steel, what life remained in the forest began their ultimate test of survival. Not done just yet, the deitic being turned around and looked to the ruins that lead into the ocean.

One final blow against the mortal world - a scar that would poison the most precious of commodities on this canvas created by Vuron. Slamming his blade into the ruins of the Grand Temple, the hearts in his blade fluttered and beat with vengeance and determination - and then his final attack came. A whirlwind of fire, brimstone, hate, and steel erupted from his blade, pieces of the shore and even the city beginning to crack away and fall into the sea, a sea littered by Khigstinian steel and the foul energy that had flowed through the Fallen God.

And, just as quick as the god had appeared, he was gone - the rippling wound in the sky now replaced by the sun yet again. However, much had changed in just the few minutes that the god's appearance.

Sebhora stared both in awe and fear as the very sky cracked asunder, a twisted and demonic avatar of his god made manifest. Before he could even ponder what happened to the Great Protector's appearance, Sebhora fell to his knees and clutched his ears in pain as a roar screamed down from the heavens above. He watched through teary eyes as the deity slammed its blade down onto the city, a fiery shockwave tearing through buildings and rendering Sosians and Estyrians alike to dust. The very earth itself rumbled as the destruction tore through Sosias, the mountain trembling despite the distance.

Loose stones shook from above and fell down to the path, cracking upon the ground as Khigstus raised his sword once more. For a moment Sebhora's attention was drawn away from the sight by a shrill scream, his head snapping towards the carved steps up to his home. Ixaroatl knelt beside Aralin, who lay unconscious and bleeding from a wound on his forehead. The sight of his wounded son tore Sebhora from his shock, but he only managed to take a few steps before another scream erupted from the unholy blade of Khigstus. Clutching his ears in agony once more as the sound of otherworldly screaming mixed with the roar of a raging inferno, he turned back to the city and gazed upon the wrath of a god. Sosias and its jungles were enveloped by flame and metal, the very earth rupturing as it spread.

Cracks in the ground spread like lightning, tearing across the ground and spreading rubble in their wake. That same horrid metal which flowed from the blade bubbled up from the cracks and crevices, consuming all that fell within. A large and jagged split ran up the side of the mountain, the smell of brimstone filling the air. Sebhora cried out the names of his wife and son, but his voice was drowned out by the torrential sound. Forcing himself to his feet, he took one staggering step forwards, then another, determination burning in his heart as he continued towards his family.

One final resounding boom echoed through the ruined city of Sosias as the god who had betrayed them slammed his sword into the Grand Temple, soon erupting into an infernal column of whirling fire and hatred. The resulting explosion sent shards of metal and rubble flying in every direction before the avatar of destruction disappeared without a trace. Air rushed in to fill the void left behind by the vanished god, an implosion carrying such force it created its own shockwave. Sebhora was hit by the shockwaves less than a second apart, knocked backwards into the wall and fell unconscious.

He awoke some hours later, his body weak and aching with a dull intensity. Slouched against the wall of rock, he struggled to lift his head and look around. The first thing Sebhora noticed was the large shard of Khigstinian steel piercing his shoulder, going through his shoulder's armor and impaling him to the stone. He grunted and tried to pull himself off of the shar, but the agony it caused sent him back into unconsciousness.

When next Sebhora woke, he was in a feverish state. His body was sweating and the armor felt constrictive, but he was unable to so much as lift his arm to remove his helmet. He slowly turned his head to the left, looking towards where Chebatli had last been. He was greeted by the sight of his brother's corpse, the shattered magma forge burning away everything below his navel as the molten rock slowly consumed his body. He tried to lift his good arm to reach out to Chebatli, his eyes burning as though he was about to cry but never feeling the wet tears running down his face. No matter how hard he tried, he couldn't lift his arm - the sword he'd been carrying had fused to his closed gauntlet, and Sebhora couldn't find the strength to lift it.

Looking dead ahead, the city still burned with scalding flames. Corpses like countless tiny ants littered the streets, and like the vultures they were, the Estyrian soldiers had already begun picking through the wreckage of the civilization. In the distance, the main Estyrian military force was visible slowly moving in towards the flaming city-state, the countless dead Estyrians only a shock force before the main army arrived. Sebhora's heart sank with despair and grief at the futility of the Sosian resistance - they thought they'd have a chance, but the numbers they fought were merely a fraction of the innumerable whole.

Blinking away that crying-like sensation and mustering his strength, he swung his head to the right. Sebhora's heart shattered as he gazed upon the bodies of his wife and son, their bodies blistered and scorched until they were charred black by the fires of the fallen god. Sebhora threw his head back as far as he could and screamed out an anguished, sorrowful wail, the cries of a man who had been broken beyond repair. He wept there until the bliss of unconsciousness overtook him again, his only solace found in the voice.

It was nightfall when Sebhora drifted back to awareness, shaken back to consciousness by the rumbling of the mountain. A large crack had split the rock face above him, slowly dripping that foul molten metal which covered everything in sight. He winced as a slow flow of the burning steel fell upon his helm, heating it painfully as more flowed down to consume him as well. He knew that if he didn't do something he would die entombed in the metal, but the cold apathy which gripped his heart and the weakness of his body resigned him to his fate. He lay still, suffering in his final moments as his entire body was covered in steel.

Though the armor scalded his skin, what truly ended Sebhora was suffocation. With his head encased fully, he choked to death on hot air, his body reflexively shaking and seizing before going limp. When his body finally perished, Sebhora's soul was trapped within that corrupted steel coffin for what felt like an eternity. His soul struggled and thrashed, desperate to join his family in whatever afterlife awaited him but unable to escape the shell of accursed steel.

Eventually he gave in to despair, losing himself in an endless sea of sorrow as time moved on without him. But sorrow is not content to remain forever, and slowly the ocean of grief fermented into an all-consuming rage and resentment towards the world. His soul was twisted and warped by it, his personality slowly subsumed and eventually consumed by that wrath. The man who was once Sebhora desperately clung to the few happy memories of his life, terrified of what awaited him in the darkness. Like all else he had held dear, those memories were destroyed or twisted into a darker version of the truth. A rising anger filled him, flaring as each memory faded to ash and dust.

Soon all that remained were the core memories that had made Sebhora who he was, holding them close to gain some semblance of control. He recalled the adventures his brother had gone on with him when they were boys, before in his very hands that memory fragmented and crumbled to dust. That anger welled up deep inside of him once more, and this time the damaged soul of Sebhora swung at the walls of the Khigstinian shell in rage. From an outside perspective, one could see a chunk of the metal fall away to reveal the finger of a twitching metal gauntlet. That anger felt good for the first time, and he began to pound at the walls of his prison with all of his might.

Behind the tattered soul of Sebhora, another memory - the first time he had kissed his wife - dissipated. He snorted in anger, the rage inside growing as his incorporeal form began to shift and blur slightly. The Khigstinian steel-encased suit shook with each blow, the anger of the being fueled by the corruptive taint of the wrathful god. Another memory - the birth of his son - shattered into non-existence, and the creature roared in rage. It raged against all the wrong done to it, against all the good taken from it, even if it couldn't remember the specifics of what it all was.

A once humanoid form had devolved into a terrifying chimera; hulking limbs which could better turn its wrath into raw force, claws to stab and rend, sharpened fangs to bite and tear. Behind it, the tethers of humanity snapped as corruption took root. Sebhora's first day running his smithy - shattered - his wedding day - broken - Aralin's first steps - utterly destroyed. The armor shook with each blow, its general shape emerging from the metal cocoon as each memory was erased.

The beast of fire and ruin roared in guttural fury as it lifted its arms over its head, humanity all but forgotten. The taint of Khigstus resonated with the anger, the helm's faceplate contorting from calmness into a wrathful grimace. The beast beheld one final vision of hope, memories of the countless meals Sebhora had shared with his family flashing before his eyes. The long nights of laughing, sharing stories, and enjoying the company of his loved ones hovered there, a final chance for redemption and peace open for the monster once called Sebhora. There was not a moment of hesitation as it made its choice.

The abomination, born of a human soul and made into a lesser entity in exchange for raw power, swung its fists downwards with all of its fury and might. The sound of breaking glass echoed through the void as the prison of tainted steel fell away, the last of Sebhora dying a true death as the final memory crumbled to nothing. The thing that remained lunged forwards, and the final coating of thick metal which had encased the armor burst open in an explosive cloud of ash and smoke. The eyes of the mask opened for but a moment, lit by two orbs glowing as red as molten steel.

CHAPTER NINE

PRESENT TIME

There was a loud screeching of rusted metal suddenly moving as the right hand of the suit suddenly shot upwards, grabbing Khonsu's wrist and holding it there in an iron grip. The sudden movement and noise caught the attention of the other six members of the group, who turned to watch in abject horror as the head of the suit slowly lifted upwards to stare at the cook. The once-hollow eyes now held two burning red orbs, floating incandescently just behind the mask as the snarling face of wrath glared directly at Khonsu. "Invader," it hissed through unseen bestial teeth, "trespasser, murderer!"

With a grunt of fear and anger combined, Khonsu grabbed a dagger from his free hand and tried to stab it into the eye of the animated armor. His blow landed, the creature shrieking and thrashing as the tip of the dagger slipped past the eye hole of the mask. The creature howled in surprise and shook with rage, its other hand reaching up to grab the hand which held the dagger. Slowly it fought against Khonsu's strength, pulling his hand away and squeezing his wrist until the bones popped and cracked beneath the pressure. Khonsu cried out in pain as he dropped the dagger, agony burning through his wrist as he lost all feeling in his hand. He thrashed and struggled with all of his strength, trying to free himself from the grip of the creature.

Rather than overcoming it, the struggle only seemed to infuriate and invigorate the monstrous being. Slowly it rose from its seated position to a full height of over seven feet tall, plunging its left hand into the ash and pulling out a greatsword of jagged red metal which it strapped to its back. With a roar of fury it swung Khonsu by the arm against the wall, knocking the breath from the cook and sending him groaning to the ground. While the others were frozen in shock, indecision freezing their bodies in place, the suit reached down and grabbed Khonsu by the throat. It lifted him high off the ground, making sure that the dazed cook could see the wrath burning within its masked face, before it moved its left hand up to Khonsu's head.

The abomination grabbed Khonsu by the skull, placing the sharpened tip of its thumb over his eye before plunging it inwards. Khonsu thrashed and screamed in agony, his body shaking as the creature smiled a hideous smile. It continued to increase the pressure until the sharp cracking of bone could be heard, and soon half of Khonsu's head caved within the palm of the abominable armor's fist. The hostile being dropped the cook's corpse to the ground like a sack of potatoes, raising its hand above its head and allowing the blood to drip down onto the mask. An otherworldly groan of satisfaction rumbled from the armor's mask, less a voice and more the sound of metal being dragged across stone.

The sight of Khonsu's body laying on the ground, half of his head reduced to a bloody mess of flesh and bone shards, shocked Sephis into motion. Drawing his serpentine sword in a blind rage, he raised it above his head and charged at the armor with a scream of rage and grief, the loss of his closest and most dear companion urging him to avenge Khonsu's death. Without stopping or turning to look at him, the creature simply swung its right hand and backhanded Sephis, knocking him to the ground with little effort. Once the blood had stopped dripping from the hand it had used to crush Khonsu's skull, it looked down at the man laying on the ground and chuckled in that same horrific tone. Sephis had rolled over onto his stomach and began to crawl away from the creature when he cried out in pain, the boot of the suit planting itself on his back hard enough to fracture most of his ribs.

As the creature unsheathed its blade and cocked its head to the left, pressing and twisting its foot upon Sephis's back to see what cries of pain it could elicit, Sephis extended a shaking hand towards Commander Zayid. Through the blood that was quickly welling up in his throat and his lungs, he burbled one last word to his comrades. "Run" he gurgled, his eyes widened in terror and agony as the boot upon his back dug in further.

As the creature lowered its sword towards Sephis, Amon turned and began to run down the path without a word. The others however couldn't bear to look away, torn between saving themselves and trying to rescue their friend and comrade. Without a word the beast plunged its blade through Sephis's back, driving it all the way through his torso and twisting it inside. Sephis weakly thrashed and groaned in pain through the blood before going limp after a few seconds, his life taken as quickly and as cruelly as Khonsu's.

Zayid was the first to return to his senses, shaking the others out of their grieving stupor and dragging them down the path as well. They could hear the clinking footsteps of the creature as it slowly approached the edge, staring down at them as they fled. Once they were free of the mountainside, they turned to stare back up at the cave. The monster stared back down at them, its sword raised high in one hand. Sephis's impaled body was still attached to it, blood dripping down the maroon metal in crimson streams.

With a roar of victory and bloodlust it swung its sword towards the group, sending the corpse flying down to them. Sephis's broken and bloodied body impacted the ground with a wet thud, the force of the impact flattening his already shattered form and skidding it across the ash-laden ground in a red smear. The group recoiled from the body, their hearts stricken with terror and compelled to flee from a supernatural sense of predation. It stared and laughed at them, the sound of rending metal twisted into a harsh cackle echoing across the empty landscape of the slums as the second scout group fled without their casualties.

Zayid led the rest of his men back through the trade district in a frenzied sprint, the oppressive aura of despair that the ring seemed to invoke seemingly ineffective against their manic terror. Through courtyards of ashen outlines and roads filled with blackened corpses they ran without a second thought, sights that would otherwise chill the blood and linger on the mind for years to come, disregarded as the five survivors focused on putting as much distance between them and the mountain as possible. Though Zayid ran the hardest and the fastest, consistently staying ahead and creating a trail for the others to follow to safely, he was the one most affected by the losses. He ran through burning eyes and blurred vision, tears streaming down his face at the loss of two of his men. Though they'd all accepted the risks, each man in his scout company was as dear to him as a brother.

Before the sun had reached the height of its journey through the sky they returned to the embassy, bursting through the doors in a heap and collapsing onto the stone floors. The men who'd been standing guard drew swords as soon as the doors had opened, but once they recognized Commander Zayid and the other members of the second group they dropped their weapons to help them inside. Heru and Hathmon looked at eachother with worried expressions as they carried their comrades into the hall, seeing that they'd returned with two less people than they'd left with. The alchemists, who'd heard the commotion, peeked out of their laboratory to see what had happened. Once they saw that a group had returned, they too ran down the stairs to assist them.

The returning second group had been seated at the makeshift benches of rubble arranged into a circle around a fire, drinking water in silence and catching their breath. Every time someone opened their mouth to speak, Zayid raised a hand in their direction and silenced them. Fifteen minutes passed in utter silence, the haunted members of the second group staring into the fire blankly as they recovered physically from the exhausting sprint. By now the seven men who'd stayed behind had realized that Sephis and Khonsu hadn't come back, and Ra-Kep had gathered their things to put in the main hall. The room was somber, filled with an air of grief and tragedy exuded by the five men who'd watched their friends' slaughter.

Eventually Zayid sighed and leaned forwards, putting his face in his hands and letting out a low groan of sorrow. Once he had composed himself, he sat up and wiped the tear stains from his cheeks. "Alright.

That's it. As soon as Mosegi and his group get back, we're getting the hell out of this gods-damned city. This entire place is cursed, and I refuse to spend a minute longer in here than I have to. From this moment onwards, we should consider this entire operation noticed by hostile forces and take the appropriate actions to safeguard ourselves from that thing."

Sahura was the first to ask the burning question which had occupied the scout group's mind since they'd returned, giving a voice to the collective curiosity of the seven men who'd stayed behind. "What happened? What did you see?"

Zayid turned towards Sahura, staring at his left-hand man for a few moments. Contained within his eyes was an emotion that Sahura had never seen, not once in the fourteen years they'd been working together. Zayid's eyes held absolute dread, a fear that ran so deep that thinking about it caused something to recoil deep inside. In a quiet and soft tone of voice, Zayid said the only words that could accurately describe what they'd seen. "A demon rose from the ashes, and it took my men from me."

Silence once again dominated the central hall of the Estyrian embassy as Commander Zayid's words sunk in, the idea of a demon prowling the accursed streets of Sosias striking fear into the hearts of them all. Many chose to begin praying to Stygirius for salvation inwardly, closing their eyes and muttering silent praises to the serpentine god that he might choose to tip the scales of fate in their favor. Unlike the others however, Amon remained grim in his attitude and actions; he did not pray to any god for aid, instead choosing to stare at the fire with a determination and hatred burning in his eyes.

"What if it followed us back?" He said quietly, drawing the attention of everyone in the room. The cold touch of fear ran up the spine of the rest of the scout company as the possibility that the malicious being had followed them came to their awareness.

Zayid stood up a second later, pulling everyone seated to their feet before snuffing out the fire. "He's right, it could have followed us back. And if it didn't, we'd likely be quite easy to find in the city, we're the only living things in the entire blasted place. We can mope later, right now we need to get to work. I want barricades up, I want traps placed. If it comes back to try and finish what it started, I want to make sure that demon has as hard a time as we can give it."

Working together towards the purpose of defending the embassy, the scout camp and the courtyard outside of it was transformed from an impromptu base into a fortress of no small scale. Every breach in the walls of the building itself was packed tightly with rubble and a makeshift mortar to make it as strong as possible, and the rest of the stone pieces were either arranged into walls or used to conceal traps. Tripwires were laid across the courtyard in several places, which would either drop a great number of rocks upon the unfortunate target or activate a blinding explosive the alchemists had cooked up. The windows were sealed or turned into arrow slits, and Nuru had suggested they use the red metal shards they'd collected as arrowheads. He and Ra-Kep had been put to work replacing the arrowheads they had on hand with the shards, keeping them occupied and away from the important work.

It was well past midday by the time that the fortifications had been completed, the members of the scout company sheltering inside and awaiting the return of the first group before moving ahead with any other plans. The day passed slowly without a sign of the beast from before, the horrific roars and screams like twisted metal given speech unheard. Concern for the first group grew more and more as time went on, the sun slowly dipping towards the horizon once more without hide nor hair of the six scouts Mosegi had taken to investigate the ruins of the Grand Temple. Sunlight began to fade as the day moved towards its end, and the hope that the other seven would return slowly began to dwindle amongst the scout company.

It was after nightfall when they heard it, a distant but unmistakably human cry for help beneath the cold glow of the moon. Gathering torches and weapons before they left, all twelve of the scouts at the embassy departed from their fortified camp to find the source of the shouts. They had been following the cries for help inwards along the roads to the Grand Temple when they found Kheres, slowly limping along the path back and covered in blood. Behind him, a trail of crimson-stained ash marked the path which he had walked.

Rushing forward to help their fellow scout, Zayid and the others quickly ran up to him. Kheres collapsed into Zayid's arms as soon as he recognized him, falling unconscious almost immediately. With one of the scout group found, Zayid ordered a retreat back to the camp. There Amon used what knowledge he'd learned from his time spent with Sephis to patch up the wounds that Kheres had suffered, and allowed him to rest before asking the man what had happened. Though none of them wanted to stay in the city another night, Zayid knew that Kheres wouldn't survive the journey back if they left at that moment. So, trusting in their fortifications, the scout company allowed themselves to rest for the moment.

A few hours later, Kheres awoke. It was that odd time between night and day when the moon is setting but the sun hasn't yet risen, when darkness is most prevalent. He sat up in his bedroll, looking around frantically for any sign of danger. He winced as he felt a sharp stinging in his side, looking down to see that a large slash across the right side of his torso had been stitched and bandaged somewhat crudely. "Hello?" He called out, unable to see in the darkness.

Kheres's waking had stirred Commander Zayid back to consciousness, who'd been sitting by the door in case something happened. He struck his dagger against his flint and created sparks which fell upon his torch, the flame flickering to life and illuminating the room as he set it in a wall sconce. In the light, Zayid could see that Kheres' skin was a pale, unhealthy tone. "Good morning, Kheres. Glad to see you're still with us."

Kheres stared at Zayid for a moment, his expression one of shock and gratitude before he broke down into a sobbing mess, tears streaming down his face as he let loose the raw emotions of the last day. Zayid slowly knelt beside him and began to pat his back, his heart aching in empathy for the man. Though Kheres was one of the three troublemakers in his scout company, the trio had always kept a sense of innocent playfulness about them. That feeling was gone from Kheres, replaced with the shell of a man who'd seen unimaginable things.

It was a few minutes before Kheres composed himself, leaning against Zayid for support as he let out all of the emotion he'd suppressed in order to survive. After he finished his sobbing and wiped away his tears, he looked up at Zayid with a faint smile. "Sorry about that Commander, I just... I needed a moment. I'm glad to see you're okay."

"And we're glad to see you're okay too. Do you know what happened to the rest of the group you went with? You're the first person we've seen from Mosegi's group since we returned, some stuff happened I'll tell you about later. We... we lost Sephis and Khonsu, and we're hoping that the first group fared better than we did." Zayid said softly, not wanting to hide the truth from Kheres but also trying not to overwhelm him.

Blinking back tears, Kheres looked downwards and clenched his hands into fists. "No, I'm the only one. I shouldn't even be here, I should have died fighting with them. I would have, if I wasn't such a damn coward."

Zayid cocked his head and rubbed Kheres's back once more, trying to calm the man down. "Why don't you just tell me everything from the start, and we'll figure out what to do from there, okay?"

Kheres nodded and sighed, leaning back against the wall as he brought the memories of the day's beginning to the forefront of his mind. "Alright. So, we left the camp for the Grand Temple..."

CHAPTER TEN

The first group walked through the winding streets on their journey inwards, the cracked pyramid that once stood as a monument to a protective god towering above them even in its ruined state. Mosegi, who was leading this group, made sure to keep Kheres by his side. Though the trio of troublemakers often did get the company into more messes than they would otherwise, Mosegi had seen something in them that the others hadn't. Though their actions seemed to be guided and influenced by chaos for the sake of chaos, Mosegi always found that they escaped with little more than minor cuts and bruises. It was this luck that he had hedged his bets on in the past, and more often than not he'd won those bets seemingly against all odds.

Ani, Nofre, Sabak, and Mharo followed behind at their own pace, as Mosegi trusted them not to wander off like Kheres might. Behind those four was Sarapi, staying a few feet behind the group to act as a rear guard. The six of them had been picked out specifically by Mosegi before the company had split for the day, the stealthiest members of the group by far. Any one of them could disappear into a shadow and go unseen for hours at will, and this was exactly what Mosegi suspected he would need as he neared the center of the ruined city. While no signs of life or movement had been seen thus far, a gut instinct told him that the closer he was to the Grand Temple the more careful he'd need to be.

The tall walls of the stone buildings of the nobles district fell away abruptly as they reached the end of the middle ring, finding themselves at the foot of a bridge that crossed the canal into the temple district. Unlike the previous rings, this layer of Sosias appeared to be purposefully open spaces, a few small spires and bell towers of melted iron and stone either halfway ruined from the heat or fragmented from the calamity poking out of the ground. The ash was thin and sparse here, as though it had chosen to simply move to the outer layers rather than fall upon these grounds. The ground beneath their feet was solid stone, massive blocks of granite wedged so tightly together no seam could be found and so smooth as to feel like a singular surface.

Carved into this stone were countless circles of symbols and religious iconography, often overlapping each other and possessing an obelisk of iron at the center of the largest sites. This district was not of temples, but rather *a* temple; the priesthood of Sosias lived within the pyramid, but an entire ring of the city had been dedicated to doing their holy rituals out in the open for the people to see. Tall monoliths of stone stood upon the blank places, covered in carved murals of the myths and legends of the Great Protector. Twisted heaps of metal lay where glorious braziers once stood, the fires in which offerings to Khigstus could be burned permanently snuffed out.

As with the rest of the city, this district too was scarred in many places. Though the damage seemed unusually minimal here, excepting large impact craters where boulders had seemingly fallen from on high, it was marked by the calamity in other ways. Red metal ran along the grooves in the ground which made up the sacred carvings, and some of the obelisks and monoliths had that same metal running down their surfaces to mar and alter their meanings. With the full scenes of the picturesque monoliths obscured and the writings of worship upon the obelisks warped by heat, images of salvation were transformed into those of a wrathful god and words of praise were twisted into foul curses upon the heavens.

Countless thousands had fled towards this district to escape the fighting and destruction, and their presence was marked to this day. The old and infirm huddled together as mothers swaddled their babes to their chests, trying to use their bodies to shelter their children from the all-consuming flame. When the Grand Temple had been cracked, the terrified masses of unarmed and helpless Sosians had died where they stood. Where those same Sosians had died, their bodies had been scorched inside and out so thoroughly as to leave only ashen husks as the last signs they'd ever existed. Shells of ash and cinder were frozen in place throughout the temple district, the mere outlines of innumerable innocents remaining to mark their deaths.

The group of seven crossed the bridge in utter silence, walking slowly as they took in the sight of the district and its macabre display of lost souls. Mharo paused as he passed the figure of a woman, face downturned towards the babe cradled in her arms. He reached out slowly to simply touch the figure, a sense of unrealness permeating the ring so thoroughly that he needed to touch the ashen woman to believe his eyes. As soon as his fingertip brushed against her cheek in the slightest manner, the figure of the woman and her cradled child crumbled to ash as the delicate balance keeping it together was disturbed. Mharo stepped back with widened eyes, overcome for a moment by a sense of grief and fear.

The group continued onwards in silence, not daring to disturb the district or its deceased inhabitants any longer, until they finally reached the bridge which separated the temple district from the great pyramid itself. The colossal structure loomed overhead, fragments of shattered stone and twisted iron peeling from its surface as they gazed upon it. Yet, despite the great and jagged cut which ran from its apex down to the earth it stood on, its size and presence alone were an intimidating sight. A set of stairs ran from its base to the flat peak of the Grand Temple of Khigstus, as it was on the other three sides, and at the base of the stairs a large rectangular doorway led inside the pyramid rather than upwards onto it. Within the doorway there was only darkness, not a single distant light to be seen nor an open area which light could pour into.

Mosegi turned to the six men under his command for the time being before turning back to the pyramid, appraising his options. "Well, we've made it this far. What do you all think we should do first, ascend the pyramid or enter it? The stairs are going to be an absolute pain to climb, but at least I know we won't get lost if we do that first."

There was silence for a few moments before someone first spoke, Kheres unexpectedly taking a serious tone as he did. "I say we ascend the pyramid. I know the climb will suck, but these ruins have only gotten stranger and stranger the closer to this pyramid we've come. If we get to the top and have a look around, we can survey the area and see what's on the other side of the city. It sure as hell beats walking into a structure as big as this is with no lights and no way to tell if the room is even stable."

Mosegi and the other five scouts turned and stared at Kheres with jaws dropped, shocked upon hearing a coherent opinion from the man. After a few seconds he turned and looked at them all with a confused expression, shrugging at their shock. "What? I'm not *actually* an idiot you know, I just find it funny to make people think I am. I'm one of the most competent scouts in the entire company, I'll have you know."

Mosegi briefly considered clubbing Kheres upside the head and verbally assaulting him for a few minutes for not putting the act away in the various times he'd accidentally started some trouble, but decided to hold off until they were somewhere safe to go off on the man. Instead he simply nodded and let everyone else have their chance to put in their vote on the matter. It took all of thirty seconds for the other five members of the scout company to agree with Kheres's vote, and the decision was made to ascend the Grand Temple.

The group of seven began their trek up the pyramid, ascending the endless steps as they climbed to the peak. Breaks were taken semi-frequently to avoid wearing any single person out too badly, and the length of the climb itself inspired some rather odd conversations. For nearly an hour they debated the physical aptitude of Sosian priests. Mosegi, Sabak, Kheres, and Ani were convinced that the priesthood of the city must have possessed the most muscular calves and thighs on the entire continent in order to have made this climb multiple times a day for years on end; Nofre, Mharo, and Sarapi insisted that they must have been an order of people broken both physically and mentally by the strenuous task of working in and around the Grand Temple.

"Maybe at first they might have been a bit broken down," Ani said as he heaved himself up another step, "but you gotta realize that eventually this becomes an exercise routine. I bet that they could have run from one end of the city to the other without getting tired after a few years of climbing this pyramid!" He stopped for a moment and turned around to look at how far they'd come, the city seeming somewhat small from this great height. They'd almost reached the top, and he was debating staying up at the peak for a few days rather than climbing back down.

Mosegi was at the front of the group dragging themselves up the side of the Grand Temple, and though he couldn't show it every step felt like agony. His calves and thighs burned from climbing up stairs for so long, and the soles of his feet had felt like they'd been worn down to the bone for a solid few minutes now. Raising his head upwards, his eyes widened as he realized just how close they were to the peak. Without a word he took off at a sprint, jumping up steps two at a time as adrenaline coursed through his veins and dulled the pain in his legs. The sounds of six others rapidly following behind him assured Mosegi that they'd all made it, and as soon as he got over the final step he stumbled forwards and lay panting on the smooth stone.

The peak itself was a flat surface, a platform from which the entire city could be looked upon from above. The earth-shattering forces which destroyed the city had split the pyramid in half, including the peak, so Mosegi had to make sure to avoid the open crack when he reached the top. He rolled onto his back and let the sunlight fall onto his face, breathing heavily as his heart rate began to slow. He closed his eyes and simply relished the minor personal victory of making it to the top, the aching of his torso and his legs slowly beginning to fade.

Six other dull thuds echoed around him as the rest of the group fell exhausted to the floor around him, quiet groans of pain becoming the most common sound amongst them as their legs were finally given a rest. The seven of them spent the next half hour lounging in the shadow of a giant iron foot, basking in their achievement as they drank sparsely from their waterskins and let their aching muscles rest. Kheres was the first one back on his feet, swaying slightly as he stood. Leaning against the iron of the broken statue's foot, he slowly walked over to the other end of the Grand Temple and stared out at the city.

Silence passed for a few moments, and every head slowly turned to look at Kheres. The expected shout of victory or witty quip had never came, and instead the young man simply stared out at the sight before him. Mosegi pulled himself to his feet with a groan, limping over to his side to see what the fuss was about. "Alright, what's up Kheres? Cat got your... tongue..."

Mosegi's voice trailed off as he looked out upon the other side of Sosias, his gaze revealing more destruction than he'd imagined possible. Though the city was situated rather close to the ocean, the fact that the far edges of the city had crumbled into the red waters was an utter shock. The jungle peninsula that Sosias had sat on the gates of was shattered and broken, large sections of land seemingly collapsing into unfathomable depths when the cracks in the earth had spread. Water flooded in to fill the gaps, and the ruined lands were covered as the distance between Sosias's southeastern wall and the shore was eliminated. What they'd seen thus far had only been part of the calamity, but this utter reshaping of a part of the world was the key to truly understanding the scale of Sosias's ruination.

The seas themselves had been tainted along with the land, a large area around the coast and along where the peninsula had once been stained a ruby red. The waters were clear there, unnaturally so - one could see to the bottom of the ocean if they stood above the surface, and gaze down at the damaged ocean floor. No life existed in the red waters, no algae or fish or even seaweed. The few sea birds that could be seen flying in the far distance stayed as far away as they could from the corrupted region, only visible as specks of black against the blue sky.

Grimly, Mosegi pulled out his map and a piece of charcoal, roughly blotting out entire sections of the peninsula and the southeastern edge of the city to signify their collapse into the seas. Then he drew a rough outline in the ocean around the peninsula, glancing back towards the red waters to gauge how far they extended from the shore. There seemed to be a murky border between the ocean that was affected and not affected, a few mere feet of dark water separating the blue expanse from the sea of red. He quietly muttered a thanks under his breath to Stygirius, grateful for the blessing that was the containment of the lifeless expanse. Once he was finished, Mosegi rolled up the map and tucked it back into his satchel.

As he looked back down at the city itself, he noticed something interesting. In a cone leading away from the Grand Temple, on the opposite side of the city as the great scar which cut through the rings, an area of the city seemed slightly less worse for wear than the rest. It was as though the Grand Temple had acted as a shield against something, a wave of force which had shaken the city to its foundations. Mosegi's brow furrowed as an idea came to him, a possibility which yesterday had seemed absurd but somehow felt closer to the truth now. He walked over to the other edge of the flat peak of the pyramid, unsheathing his blade and raising it above his head in one hand. Staring at the great scar, that abyss which ran straight from a corner of the Grand Temple to some hundred yards past the ruins of the wall, he swung his sword downwards as though striking at the city.

He stopped as soon as the sword was in front of him, his eyes widening slightly as his suspicion was confirmed. The length of his blade perfectly overlapped with the chasm, and as he sheathed the sword he stumbled backwards a few steps. "It was a blade that did this. I knew it looked like a sword wound, I've seen so many by now, how did I not notice it sooner?" He mumbled to himself, turning to look at the giant iron feet of the broken statue of Khigstus and feeling a chill run down his spine. "How big must have been the creature that wielded such a sword?"

Mosegi's mouth went dry as he continued down that train of thought, but the other six members of the group hadn't been paying attention to what he said. They were still gathered at the southeastern side of the pyramid, staring down at the city and the ocean which had been brought to it. Mharo was pointing towards something below, drawing the attention of his compatriots towards the ground rather than gazing out at the heavily altered coastline. He went over to join the others, curious as to what had caught Mharo's eye.

The group was staring down the side of the pyramid, a large gash running down from the peak to the bottom. Down on the ground, the once-mighty statue of Khigstus lay in ruins; upon its chest a large, scorched dent had buckled inwards, and cracks ran all along its body. The head of the statue had been crushed beneath the immense weight of a boulder, likely the same one which had sent it careening off of the Grand Temple in the first place. Mharo was speaking with an animated intensity, obviously quite interested in how the statue had gotten there.

"This must have came down during the siege. I wonder whether it was at the beginning or the end of the siege, or if it came down during the final confrontation." He pondered out loud, the many possibilities of what had happened obviously on the forefront of Mharo's thoughts.

Sabak sighed and crossed his arms, squinting down at the statue. "First of all, have some respect for the dead. Sosian or Estyrian, they likely had to live through it for their final moments, so stop being so casual about it. Secondly, it couldn't have fallen from the sky, no matter what the circumstances. See how the impact's shaped? That boulder hit it dead in the chest from straight ahead, which means something had to have launched it from the ground and hit it at the peak of its arc."

"It doesn't matter," Mosegi said softly, "either way an avatar was summoned and tainted this entire area. Now, enough standing around and gawking at the city. We have a job to do, and I intend on getting it done." Removing a rather long length of rope from his shoulder and tying one end to a large piece of iron from the statue's foot, Mosegi threw the other end down the crack which led into the Grand Temple's depths. Grabbing it, he pulled with all his strength and found it didn't budge. Satisfied that the knot wouldn't be undone by his body weight, Mosegi approached the edge and looked down into the darkness.

"Prepare yourselves, ready your torches. We're heading into the defiled temple of a fallen god, and everything about that seems like a bad idea. Other than already existing security measures, watch out for malfunctioning mechanisms or instability in the building itself. Any questions?" Mosegi didn't wait for an answer before beginning to climb down, grabbing the rope and lowering himself over the edge before he began to scoot downwards into the abyss.

One by one, the other six followed him down. Nofre was the last to climb down, and before he did he looked around at the city once more. "This is a great view, destruction aside. Here's to hoping I live to see it again." Without hesitation, he grabbed the rope and slid over the edge. A chorus of angry shouts from below told him not to swing the rope like he'd done, and with a chuckle Nofre began to climb down to join them.

CHAPTER
ELEVEN

N ofre reached the bottom and dropped from the last two feet of rope with a thud, landing on his feet as the sound echoed throughout the empty darkness of the large room the scout group was in. He lit his torch before joining the other six scouts, who were all waiting for him at a doorway a dozen feet away. Once the scout group had reunited within the depths of the Grand Temple, Mosegi led the seven further inside. They had no maps to go off of, so unlike the rest of the city they were moving about the great pyramid blindly.

The hallway they'd been walking down was long and wide, a main corridor judging by its large size and the lack of turns on its path. On either side of them, dozens of archways branched off into side chambers or smaller corridors, a network of rooms and tunnels which spread throughout the pyramid like the veins of some vast holy being. Rooms which were used for mundane rituals and corridors that led to sleeping chambers were abundant, yet more rarely grand halls dedicated to a specific rite of the Sosian religion were found. Regardless of the size or importance of the chambers, there was not a single place in the Grand Temple which hadn't been damaged in some way. Large cracks closer to the outer walls of the pyramid let rays of sunlight in, illuminating the floors littered with rubble. Some passageways had collapsed entirely, entire wings of the structure collapsing in on themselves.

In the almost subterranean darkness of the Grand Temple's interior, all sense of time was lost. The scout group had spent at least an hour inside the massive pyramid, but they couldn't be certain as to how much time it'd been since the first hour had passed. What they did know however was that the corridor led deeper into the interior, towards the heart of the religious center of Sosias. Despite their concerns, the length of the corridor had been entirely free from any sort of trap or lethal deterrent to prevent anyone from coming inside. They arrived at a large circular chamber when the corridor ended, a set of spiral stairs leading downwards looping around the perimeter of the room. The bottom was too far below to see, so Mosegi directed the group to descend the staircase.

The walk was long and slow, the staircase unstable in some places and broken in others. Yet there was more to the long descent than simply walking down for an unknown distance, the walls were carved with an intricate mural that seemed to progress a story the further down they went. Kheres was the first to notice it, pointing out the carvings on the walls to the others as they started their walk downwards. With torches raised high, the scouts observed the tale that was the root of the Sosian religion.

The tale began a long time ago, before the Sosian people had even come to the southern peninsula. They had been chased from their home by a foe that they'd seen as monstrous, the carving detailing tiny figures fleeing in terror from a shadowy creature chasing them. They journeyed far for many years, setting up homes and gaining some semblance of their normal lives before their pursuers caught up to them and began the chase again. Eventually the figures of the early

Sosians were trapped upon the southern peninsula, with nowhere else to flee and the looming threat of the dark beast close behind.

The people fell to their knees and began to pray, the human shapes drawn groveling on the ground as wispy lines rose up to the sky. Then a great shining light appeared above the praying Sosians, whose brilliance was bright enough to rival the shining sun. Upon a ray of light a larger-than-life figure walked down to the primitive Sosians, towering far above them as it lifted its sword. The light in the sky disappeared as the mural's focus shifted towards the figure, now recognizable as Khigstus. He battled with the great foe of the Sosians as they sheltered behind him, watching as the dark monster fought against the god to no avail. Eventually Khigstus defeated the enemy, striking the monster dead with his blade.

The people of early Sosias fell to their knees and offered praise to Khigstus, praising him as the Great Protector. Using his blade, he cut a great circular swath of the jungle down, freeing up the land to be settled by the Sosians. The glowing light returned to take Khigstus back to the heavens above, but before he left he granted the people of Sosias a sacred boon: the Khigstinian Codex. It was then that Khigstus withdrew back into the light which had brought him to their salvation, promising to return should Sosias once again face destruction. The people of Sosias then built the great walled city in the jungle, and erected the Grand Temple in his honor. The completion of the pyramid, topped by a massive statue of their god, was the final part of the mural.

Once the scout group found themselves at the bottom, they found only one archway leading onwards. The floor was made of a misty white-blue stone, somewhat translucent and emitting a soft glow. The passageway went in a straight direction for some time before opening up into a massive hall, pillars reaching dozens of feet up to hold a cracked ceiling in place. Pieces of rubble from the broken walls were littered across the floor, and a large crack in the corner of the ceiling had allowed a waterfall of ash to pour inside. Braziers hung from the pillars, now long extinguished, and at the far end of the room a large arched doorway led into a separate chamber. Statues of Khigstus and various figures from Sosian religious myth stood in various states of damage along the walls of the hall, creating a sense that whatever lay on the other side was of great importance.

Mosegi and the others gazed upon the statues for a few minutes, admiring and lamenting the loss of such dedicated artistry. Once they'd had their fill of the large entry hall, the scout group went through the doorway which opened up into a massive dome chamber. The pyramid thus far had been strangely empty in terms of bodies, not a single corpse in any state of ruination or decay to be found, but this room seemed to be full of them. Hundreds of priests lay dead upon the floor in circles around the center of the room, either frozen in prayer or thrashing about as they died. In the center of the room, three men stood upon a highly raised dais surrounding an object obscured from vision.

In the corner of the room where the pyramid had been struck, a hole three feet in diameter had been punched through the ceiling all the way from the outer surface of the Grand Temple to this inner sanctum. Red metal had poured through it slowly, coating a third of the floor in it and encasing many of the priests along with it. The hole was still somewhat open, a gap the size of a human fist allowing sunlight to shine in a single focused ray upon the dais at the center of the room. From the angle at which the sunlight entered the room, it seemed to be nearing midday. Mosegi slowly drew his sword and raised his torch high, a nagging sense in the pit of his stomach advising caution as he advanced. The other six slowly spread out through the room, making sure that no devices were set to kill any unwanted interlopers in the chamber and that the area was otherwise safe.

Slowly he approached the dais, ascending the steps until he stood beside the three men. The two on either side of the pedestal wore more ornate robes than the other priests, a sure sign of higher rank, but the priest in the middle wore flowing robes of red silk inlaid with gold trim. Mosegi knew without a doubt then that this was the Grand Prophet of Sosias, a man whose likeness had been drawn upon many targets in the Estyrian camps a little over a year ago. Inspecting the two men closer, he noticed that the high priests to the Grand Prophet's left and right had seemingly killed themselves with ceremonial daggers, hands clutching the hilts protruding from their stomachs as they lay slumped over the wide pedestal. Yet still the somehow standing corpse of the Grand Prophet blocked his view of what he stood over, and Mosegi gently nudged the body with his sword.

The robed corpse slid backwards and fell to the ground in a clatter, the bones of the Grand Prophet falling to the stones unceremoniously. The resulting noise echoed throughout the hall, loud and constantly repeating as the sound bounced off of the large room behind them. Mosegi winced at this, but turned back towards the pedestal to see a large stone tablet which had ancient inscriptions upon it. His eyes widened as he gazed upon the tablet, taking in the ornate runic etchings which seemed to almost whisper their strange words in his mind. In the center of the pedestal was an indentation for the Khigstinian Codex, an artifact that had caused quite a commotion amongst the nobility when the caravan sent to negotiate peace had returned. He'd never seen an image of it, only knowing the faintest idea of its description from the rumors that spread through hushed lips around solitary campfires, but he knew somehow that this was the same holy relic that was drawn on both the murals and the tablet.

Mosegi sheathed his blade and gingerly took a step forwards, standing in the exact place that the Grand Prophet had stood. His mind was flooded with images of power, wealth, fame, and glory, all things that this knowledge could bring him. Though he hadn't wanted any of these things before, seeing the object that could grant him these boons before him made them seem like the dreams he'd held his entire life. As he slowly reached out to touch the stone tablet, a slight draft blew across his neck from behind. Mosegi's eyes narrowed as he froze in place, realizing that the room behind him had no source of air to create a draft from.

In a single fluid motion Mosegi drew his sword and swung it behind him, turning around as he did. A spear composed of red glass flew from the darkness as Mosegi spun into motion, shattering as his sword cut it from the air. Shards of the glass got stuck in the exposed skin of his arm, stinging as blood slowly began to trickle down. Wincing as he glanced at the glass embedded in his skin, Mosegi threw his torch towards where the spear had come from and raised his sword again. The other six members of the scout group drew their swords as well, turning to face their attacker.

From the ash which had poured into the room a metallic hand burst from below the surface, grabbing onto the solid rock flooring and pulling the body it was attached to out of the ash. A second hand emerged as well, then a snarling metallic face, and finally a full suit of armor had emerged from the layer of ash which could only have been a few inches deep. The strange creature, crouched over on the ground of the great hall, pulled a jagged red greatsword from the ash as well before standing up at its full height. Mosegi took a reflexive step back as the size of the being became apparent, the suit being inhumanly large as it stood at over seven feet in height. Rearing its head back, the abomination let out a terrifying howl before charging at the scout group.

It ran towards the dome chamber on all fours, crossing the distance between itself and the seven scouts with surprising speed before lunging at Mosegi. He dodged under its body as it flew over him, rolling forwards and taking off at a sprint as soon as his feet touched the stone. The others followed wordlessly, defaulting to Mosegi as their leader until they managed to escape or kill their pursuer. The metal suit got up and began to chase them, catching up to the fleeing men quickly. With another screeching howl it swung its sword, catching Nofre in the back of the heel and severing his achilles tendon.

Nofre fell to the ground with a cry of pain, his torch sputtering out as it hit the ground. The other six scouts skidded to a stop, turning around to see what had happened. They were met with the sight of the monstrous creature crouched over Nofre, its glowing red eyes staring directly at them as it slowly drew its blade across his other heel and crippled him. They readied their swords and got ready to fight when Nofre shook his head towards them, motioning weakly for them to leave without him. The beast grabbed Nofre by the neck and lifted him into the air, its eyes still locked onto the group as it held their comrade facing them.

With tears running down his cheeks from the pain and fear combined, Nofre stared directly at Mosegi with widened eyes. "Run," he said in a choked whisper, his voice cut off by the tight grip around his throat, "please..."

Suddenly Nofre began to thrash in the creature's grip, shaking and screaming hoarsely in agony. Within seconds four pointed metal fingers covered in gore pierced through the skin of his chest, the creature having slowly pushed its hand through his entire rib cage. He tried to sputter some final words, but all that came out was a spray of blood as he began to choke on his own fluids. The creature's eyes shifted to Mosegi specifically, locking onto his gaze as it pulled its fingers back into Nofre's chest and grabbed something. Nofre shook with all of his might, his dying brain desperately trying to get free from the creature that had wounded him so, before going limp as the monster crushed his heart in his chest.

As soon as Nofre's body dropped to the floor the six remaining members of the scout group took off again, sprinting towards the stairs that would lead them upwards and away from this creature. It watched them go, raising its blood-soaked hand to its face and letting the blood drip into the open slit of the snarling mouth as it did. As soon as the blood began to drip into the darkness within the suit, the creature's body trembled with energy as the glowing orbs of its eyes blazed brighter and brighter. "Estyrian..." It said with a hiss, cackling loud enough for the sound to echo around the hall and down the corridor before it collapsed into a pile of ash, leaving no trace of its presence other than the brutalized body of Nofre.

Mosegi and his remaining five men ran up the spiraling stairs as fast as their legs could carry them, adrenaline coursing through their veins as their hearts beat faster and harder than ever before. No words were exchanged as they ran, no tears were shed. Their only goal was to get up the stairs and away from the thing that had slaughtered their friend, so that they might live to see another day in his honor. As soon as they made it to the top the six men checked to see if they were being followed; after an extremely stressful minute or two, they felt that they could take a minute to breath. They all slumped to the floor, some leaning against the wall while others sprawled out on the ground.

Most of them were still in shock, but Kheres was handling it the worst. He had curled up into a ball, his eyes held wide open as tears poured from them. He rocked back and forth as he muttered quietly to himself, drawing the attention of Mosegi. The leader of the group slowly walked over to Kheres to hear what he was saying, reaching out to rest a hand on his shoulder.

"We're all gonna die, we're all gonna die, we're all gonna die, we're all gonna die!" Kheres mumbled, his voice getting louder and louder with every step Mosegi took towards him until he was screaming at the top of his lungs. When he felt the hand resting on his shoulder, Kheres threw himself back with a scream of terror and drew his sword, pointing it at the group. "I don't want to die! I don't want to die!"

Mosegi stepped back reflexively, the other members of the group jolted back to reality as they witnessed Kheres's mental break. "Hey, calm down Kheres. It's me, Mosegi. There's no need to be scared, we're all brothers in arms here, right? Just put the sword down, and lets talk for a bit."

Kheres's arms trembled as he looked from Mosegi to the others and back, switching between the two multiple times before he collapsed to his knees. He led the sword drop to the ground as he began to sob fully, his entire body heaving as Mosegi quickly kicked the sword out of Kheres' reach and cautiously leaned in. He reached out once more to rest his hand on his comrade's shoulder, and this time Kheres slumped forwards into his arms as he continued to let the grief and terror flow out of him. They stayed there for a few minutes, Mosegi choking back his own tears as he comforted Kheres.

The rest of the group sat and watched idly as their own emotions rose to the surface, a few beginning to cry softly as the loss of Nofre began to sink in. Though the scout company had social circles within itself, every man who'd been in it except for Amon had served together for at least six years. Nofre's loss was like that of a brother, and it struck each man hard enough to make his resolve to continue fall into question. Once the emotional tension had been drained enough for the group to form up, Mosegi silently stood and wiped the tears from his face.

"We need to focus on getting out of here. Nofre was a good man and he will be missed sorely, but I imagine that if we lost anyone else in here because we didn't do as he said he'd kick our asses in the afterlife. We'll figure out what that thing was later, let's just get back to the rope and get back to the embassy." Mosegi said quietly, helping the five sitting men to their feet and raising his torch again. The remaining six members set off into the darkness, hoping to make it out alive.

CHAPTER TWELVE

M osegi led his men at a cautious pace down the hallway they'd came through on the way in, their torches raised high and weapons drawn. He kept Kheres just behind him, both out of sympathy for the man as well as fear that direct confrontation would make him bolt in a blind panic. In silence they retraced their footsteps, stepping carefully and precisely in order to try and make as little noise as possible. Noon had passed by the time that they reached the chamber which their rope dangled down into, and the mere sight of it invoked a nearly hysterical sense of hope in the men.

Mharo ran ahead of the others, dropping both sword and torch onto the ground as he grabbed the rope with both hands. He leapt up in the air as he began to climb the rope, but rather than going upwards he fell back to the earth with a confused thud. A loud rumbling came from above as more and more of the rope dropped down, the end far above somehow falling as a large slab of stone was apparently yanked free by Mharo's body weight. The slab crashed into the hole in the roof hard, shaking the entire room as dust and shards of brick were sent down upon them in a spray. Mharo scrambled away from the falling debris quickly, narrowly avoiding being struck by a chunk of stone the size of his head.

Mosegi slowly walked past Mharo as he sat on the ground, staring in shock at the pile of rubble where the group's escape route had been only moments prior. What had once been preciously held hope melted into despair as the six scouts realized that they were now trapped, sealed within the pyramid with no knowledge of the way out. Kheres walked forwards until he stood beside Mosegi, looking at the rubble and the fallen rope strewn about in a pile. He took a deep breath and let out a sigh, retrieving Mharo's discarded torch and now slightly battered blade before returning them to the somewhat shaken twin on the floor.

Just as Mosegi was beginning to think of a way to get the men's morale up, a low groaning cackle echoed from the corridor behind them. The sound of metal being dragged across the stone floor accompanied the sound of heavy and methodical footsteps, the source of the cackling slowly following them from the path they'd came from. Kheres began to hyperventilate, his legs trembling as panic began to set in. Without a moment of hesitation Mosegi ran to the far end of the room, searching for another corridor that he and the others could use to flee this nightmarish being. As he approached the far wall, he found a large oaken door that seemed to be wedged shut by rubble.

As Mosegi pounded against the door with his fist, drawing the attention of the other six to help him try and force the door open, the wretched voice of the creature which had emerged from the ash echoed through the large room. "Estyrian scum, tainting the very grounds upon which you walk with your presence. Was your kind's first incursion into these lands not enough?" It spoke with the sharpness of hatred and spite in its tone, almost growling the words as it emerged from the darkness with sword in hand. "Was bathing this city in fire and ruin not good enough?"

"You must have thought us all dead, to send your scavengers to pick the bones of my home clean of anything you consider valuable. You are trespassing on land you yourselves defiled, and now you shall taste the wrath you left festering in your wake!" It roared as it charged at the six men, sprinting across the room as fast as it could.

All six men were trying to pull the door open, getting frantic as the creature grew near. A split second before it unleashed its fury upon them, claws outstretched and blade in hand, Mosegi shouted "Scatter!" The scout group dove out of the way and let the creature's momentum carry it forwards, shattering the door and leaving behind only a cloud of dust and wood shards. As the beast recovered from the stunning impact that had crashed through the door, Mosegi led his men running down the hallway that was now opened as fast as it could. They left the beast fumbling in the darkness, trying to figure out where it was as the dust cloud obscured its vision.

Cackling as it heard the six men rush past it, the creature leaned its head back and howled in sadistic delight. "The hunt begins!" It roared as its eyes glowed brighter, taking off at a sprint behind them on all fours as it began to close the gap, dodging into one of the various doorways on the sides of the corridor. The creature dove into a nearby pile of ash, dissipating into the powder as its immaterial form moved ahead unhindered by walls and doors.

Mosegi and the others were running as fast as their legs could carry them, swords in one hand and torches in the other. They didn't slow to check any of the side rooms as they ran unguided down this new corridor, not having any idea where it led but knowing that what was in front of them couldn't be worse than what was following behind them. Kheres was running ahead of everyone else, all care or worry for anything but survival tossed aside as he pushed his body to its physical limits. From the corners of his vision, he could see shapes moving in the darkness of the room he ran past, things shifting and snarling in the shadows that defied explanation. A voice in the back of his mind told him to slow down a little, to try and pace himself so he could run for longer and so that the others wouldn't be left behind, but the fear driving him forwards silenced it every time.

The monstrous creature burst from one of the side rooms and grabbed Ani, slamming him into the wall. The other five men looked over their shoulders and saw his fate, but knowing that their own lives were at stake they kept running. He screamed as the beast planted its boot firmly on its chest and grabbed his face with its free hand, the clawed fingers of the gauntlet digging into his skin. He continued to scream as the grip got tighter, the claws of the monster digging furrows into the bone of his skull before it pulled away hard with a bloodthirsty roar. Ani's face was separated from his body with a wet tearing sound, the bloody flesh of his face still twitching as his body continued shaking and thrashing, his screams getting weaker and weaker.

The armored abomination flung the face aside and swung its closed fist at Ani's skull, crushing it flat and cracking the stone of the wall behind him before once again it ran on all fours after the remaining members of the scout group. The scout group continued to flee, hoping and praying that the next one to get grabbed wouldn't be them. The sound of the creature got closer and closer before Sarapi cried out in pain, the massive blade of the creature having been thrust through his right thigh. He fell flat on his face, weakly reaching out for help from his comrades before the beast began to stab him in the back. His body convulsed as the sword was shoved through his stomach, suddenly being pulled out and stabbed back in a different spot on his torso. He choked to death on his own blood as his corpse was mangled and mauled by the beast before it left him, leaving a trail of gore behind as it ran off.

The remaining scouts saw a pinprick of bright light in the distance, a literal light at the end of the tunnel. With escape now in sight, the remaining four men ran faster and harder, their muscles tearing as the adrenaline dulled their pain receptors to the point of inactivity. The sound of the grinding metal of the suit behind them had disappeared, and the possibility that they'd lost it in the darkness of the corridor inspired new hope in them all. Finally they arrived at the tunnel's end, opening into a large chamber which had been exposed to the open air. Large pillars which would have held up a now destroyed ceiling, most of which had fallen to the ground, littered what was likely once a grand and luxurious main entrance hall. Standing at the far end of the room, ash swirling around its feet as the jagged red metal of the greatsword glimmered in the sunlight, the dark suit of armor stood waiting for them.

The four remaining scouts froze in place, staring at the creature as it stared back at them. It smiled coyly as it drew a line in the ashes with the tip of its sword, stretching from the base of one pillar to another. "If you can cross this line," it said in a maliciously playful tone of voice, "I will let you live. Let me see what filth like you can do!"

As its voice rose to a crescendo at the end of its sentence, the creature lunged forwards and crossed the distance of the entrance hall in a matter of seconds. The scout group barely had time to react, ducking out of the way and splitting up as it began to hunt them down one by one. Mosegi, Sabak, and Mharo ran straight for the open sunlight just beyond the line that the creature had drawn, leaping over rubble and sliding under fallen pillars as they ran. The creature climbed one of the pillars and stared down at the three men making their way across the room, its metallic face contorting into a hideous grin as it leapt from one pillar to the next with ease. Dropping in from above, it plunged down in front of the three men and knocked them back with the force of its impact, forcing them to engage it in battle.

Drawing their blades, the trio of scouts began to duck and weave around the armored creature, striking and stabbing whenever it had what could be used as a weak spot was exposed. More often than not, the creature parried their blows with ease, striking back at them hard enough to rattle their sword arms to the point of nearly dropping them. It gleefully caught one serpentine sword stabbed towards the back of its neck with its free hand, closing his hand into a fist and breaking the sword with a quick bend of the wrist. It threw the broken piece at another of the scouts, embedding the tip of the blade into Sabak's left shoulder.

As Sabak fell to his knees the monster reared back its foot and kicked him hard in the chest, sending a loud crunch echoing through the room as ribs cracked and he was sent flying back into a large piece of broken pillar. It cackled as it focused on the two others, suddenly going from fighting defensively to attacking with sadistic glee. The sudden flurry of blows from the large blade caught Mosegi and Mharo off balance, the two men barely able to keep pace with dodging the attacks as the creature toyed with them. They had to lose ground in order to stay alive, slowly being pushed away from the light of day and back towards the darkness of the Grand Temple's interior.

Beginning to grow bored of toying with the scouts, the creature lunged forwards towards Mharo without warning and plunged its blade into his stomach. He cried out in agony as the sword went through several vital organs, his body quickly growing weak as he bled profusely from the wound. The creature gleefully began to twist the blade back and forth inside of Mharo's gut, relishing every scream and whimper of pain as he made the scout's last moments agony. It didn't bother defending itself, allowing Mosegi to strike away at its back in futility over and over again as it finished with Mharo.

Mosegi took a few steps back, breathing heavily as it watched the armor stand up straight and casually walk over to the place where Sabak lay unconscious. Quietly muttering an apology to the man under his breath as the beast raised its boot over his head, Mosegi turned and ran towards the sunlight. He heard a wet squish behind him a second later, but by then he'd already almost made it. Four or five steps is all it would take to cross the line which would grant him safety, and that desperate drive to live on pushed his body to its breaking point as he bounded towards the sunlight.

Suddenly Mosegi was frozen in place, a sharp pain going through his abdomen from his lower back to in between the lowest two ribs on his right side. He let out a choking gasp of pain as he felt a lung deflate in his chest, droplets of blood dribbling out of the corner of his mouth. Looking down slowly, his vision grew slightly blurry as he saw the jagged red greatsword of the creature protruding from his chest. "Not... not like... this..." He groaned through pained, gasping breaths, feeling the strength leaving his body as the adrenaline finally began to wear off.

"You're right," said the voice of the beast from behind him, the noise more comparable to cutting steel with a saw than a human voice, "not like this. I want to savor this moment, and I want to make it last." It slowly withdrew the sword from his chest, letting it clatter to the ground as it caught Mosegi's limp body. The creature slowly lowered him to the ground, letting his head loll to the side. Sunlight and freedom had been but an arm's length away, so close yet now impossibly far.

A cold and metallic grip forced Mosegi to stare up at the monster as it kneeled over him, the two glowing red orbs floating in the darkness of the monster's eyes peering into his soul. "I want you to look at me as I kill you. I want you to know that your death is because of the crimes of your people, perpetrated by the only thing that you Estyrians left behind: wrath. I am the fire and the fury which burned this city to the ground, I am the vengeance of the souls that burned along with it. I am the Shadow of the Ash, and I am your doom."

Mosegi had not the strength to speak, merely gurgling quietly as his last few breaths pushed blood up his throat as he breathed raggedly. The Shadow stared into his eyes with that emotionless gaze, its faceplate set in a gruesome smile as it gently thumped Mosegi's chest with its fist. It lifted its hand and let it fall back down onto the scout's chest, this time with slightly more force. Its other hand joined in as the Shadow of the Ash brought both fists down on Mosegi's bloodied torso, the force of impact causing his body to twitch. Over and over it brought its fists down on Mosegi's chest, each time with more force and more strength.

As it did, a low and hoarse growl began to rumble in the Shadow's ephemeral throat, growing in volume and intensity as it began to pound on the slowly dying scout's chest again and again. It eventually grew to an unending roar, never ceasing for even a moment as it needed no breath. It caved in Mosegi's chest entirely, broke every rib of his ribcage as it pounded Mosegi's battered corpse into nothing more than a smear of red paste upon the ground. Once there was nothing recognizable as human left from the waist up of Mosegi, the Shadow of the Ash stopped and simply kneeled there, basking in the utter brutality of its actions and the gore which soaked it.

Kheres, who had hid the moment that the Shadow had charged them and slowly worked his way to the far end of the room, tripped and stumbled as he finally crossed the line. He'd managed to sneak past the Shadow of the Ash, using the others as a distraction to get to safety. It stared at him for a moment before beginning to chuckle, rising to its feet and picking up its blade once more. The blood and various chunks of flesh which stuck to every inch of its armor coated the entire entity red as it walked into the sunlight, glistening with the trophies of its kills as it approached Kheres. He scrambled back in terror, tripping backwards before trying to crawl away desperately as it walked up behind him and planted a boot on his back.

"P-please! You said you'd spare anyone who crossed the line! I did!" Kheres begged, tears pouring down his face as his body heaved in hysterical sobs. With the boot keeping pressure on his back, he couldn't hope to escape from the Shadow of the Ash's clutches. The vengeful demon chuckled as it stood over him, considering its options.

"I did say that, yes. I said nothing about hurting you, though." It sneered as it leaned down, resting its hand at the nape of his neck. Kheres screamed wordlessly as he felt a thin point of pain piercing his skin, slipping below the surface before it stopped. Suddenly it rolled him over bodily, dragging its claws down his torso and raking deep lines into his flesh with a cackle. Kheres screamed and shook, and the Shadow of the Ash watched for a few moments before it removed its boot. "Run back to your nest now, little vermin. Run back to where all of you pests are hiding."

Kheres got up shakily and began running off immediately, the only thought on his mind getting back to safety. With a smile the Shadow of the Ash watched him go until he disappeared from sight, turning around to walk back to the Grand Temple. Once it was inside, the Shadow of the Ash's body dissipated into ash and disappeared, finishing whatever business such a foul being needed to complete. Kheres wandered in a weakened haze through the temple and noble districts until the sun went down, eventually being discovered by the rest of the scout group.

CHAPTER THIRTEEN

During the time it had taken for Kheres to finish his telling of what had happened, the eleven other scouts had awoken and congregated in the room that Kheres and Zayid were in. They listened in silent anguish as they were told of the deaths of their brothers-in-arms, some having to step away as Kheres' voice cracked and broke during the more gruesome moments. Mhuro fell to his knees and began to sob openly on the floor as he realized his brother wouldn't be returning, his body heaving with each ragged breath as the loss shattered him to the core. When Kheres finally finished his reporting of the events, his eyes dull and deadened as the trauma had truly set in, Nuru and Ra-Kep slowly approached their friend and sat beside him. The trio of troublemakers, typically a sight which would bring anxiety to Zayid, seemed diminished in some way; there was no air of playfulness or mischief about them, only one of loss and sympathy.

After a few minutes passed and Zayid had time to mull over what he'd been told, he slowly looked up at Kheres and shifted over to him.

"You said that it did something to your neck, right? Lean forward for me, I want to see what he did."

Nuru and Ra-Kep moved out of the way as Kheres slowly leaned forwards, brushing his hair to the side and revealing the nape of his neck. Zayid leaned in to inspect the place that Kheres had pointed to, and his eyes widened in shock as he saw something protruding from the skin. It appeared to be a thin black needle, extending about half an inch from his nape outwards and of an unknown depth into his flesh. All around it, thin black veins spread out from the needle and branched off in all directions in a three inch radius. Zayid gritted his teeth, turning towards Amon with a grim frown.

"Fetch me Sephis's medical bag, we're going to need the tweezers." He said to the infantryman, watching him go to find the medic kit before turning back to Kheres. "You just stay still now, it seems like it stuck you with something and I don't want you to exert yourself. Try and remember for me, what exactly was the last thing it said to you?"

"Run back to your nest now, little vermin," Kheres mumbled, "run back to where all of you pests are hiding." The thin needle in his neck twitched as he spoke, causing Zayid to recoil slightly from the sight. Suddenly Kheres let out a low groan, his eyes closing tightly as he clenched his hands into fists. The tendril-like veins which were affected by the needle twitched, pulsed, and throbbed before suddenly expanding further into the scout's flesh, causing Kheres to whimper. "It burns..."

Amon came back with the medic bag, handing it to Zayid quickly. The commander dug through it with a single-minded focus, searching for the tweezers until he pulled them out quickly and returned to facing Kheres. "This is probably gonna hurt a hell of a lot, so just try and stay with me. But if you can, do your best to stay still. If it snaps off in half, there's no telling how we'll get it out of you."

Kheres nodded silently, bracing himself for whatever may come. Zayid took a deep breath and leaned over Kheres, gently grabbing the base of the needle with the tweezers while avoiding poking his fingers with the other end. He began to pull, starting off with only a little bit of pressure before increasing the strength which he used to try and extract the needle from Kheres' neck. The man groaned and grunted in pain, his brow furrowing as a horrific sensation of intense burning sprung up as soon as Zayid started to remove the needle. His hands began to shake, his heart beating faster and faster as the pain only increased.

Zayid grunted as he twisted the tweezers, the needle somehow fighting against him as he pulled. The veins began to retract as a tiny bit of the needle left Kheres' skin, more and more of the affected flesh returning to normal as Zayid removed the object. Suddenly Zayid fell backwards as the needle was pulled free in its entirety, holding the strange sliver of dark material up in the light. The entire object was six inches long, but everything that had been below the skin was not a needle like he'd thought. Instead, numerous tiny tendrils whipped around in the open air, thrashing about as they searched for a warm body to implant themselves in. After a few seconds the tendrils went limp, and the strange parasite crumbled to ash.

Once the tendril-needle had been removed, Kheres slumped forward and went completely limp as he lost consciousness. As soon as the parasitic creation crumbled away he sat up straight and drew in a deep breath, his eyes wide and frantically looking around. A healthy color began to return to his skin almost immediately, the energy of the man returning as his bodily infestation was removed. Yet instead of seeming glad that he was no longer under the influence of the parasite, he seemed more aggravated than before. His energy had returned, but it was a manic and highly panicked energy.

"I-I-I could feel it, in the back of my mind." He stuttered as he spoke, his voice shivering with each word as his rattled psyche wrestled with the remnants of the Shadow of the Ash's influence. "It was like it w-was watching me from behind my eyes, waiting. I could hear that voice in my head, whispering in the dark recesses of my skull. I could *feel* its hatred, its hunger..."

Amon turned to him immediately, a hand going to the hilt of his sword. "Wait, you said it was seeing through your eyes? Shit, it let you go on purpose. It used you to lead it right to us!" Pivoting on his heel, Amon turned around and ran towards the doors. The others followed behind him quickly, the sound of steel being unsheathed ringing throughout the hall as they did.

Zayid sighed and got to his feet, walking towards the doorway and mentally preparing himself for a second encounter with the monstrous being that had killed eight of his men. As he crossed the threshold, he paused before turning to look back at Kheres. "You've been through enough. Lock this door, barricade it if you can, and stay silent. If it doesn't know where you are, it might think that we killed you for leading it to us and leave. We'll let you know if we survive."

With that, Commander Zayid shut the door behind him. A few seconds later he heard the deadbolt slide into place with a soft click, getting some satisfaction in knowing that Kheres wasn't too broken to follow orders quite yet. He raised his fingers to his mouth and whistled loudly, getting the attention of the eleven men who'd likely be fighting at his side before beginning to speak. "Listen up! The Shadow of the Ash is almost certainly on its way, seeing as we took out its little parasite. Sahura, Arta, Hathmon, and Heru, I want you four with me in the courtyard. We've trapped that little square to high heaven, and I know that you can dance around them with ease while fighting."

"Nophi, Senuf, I want you to see what you can do from a distance. Throw things from the second floor, prepare anything that you've got on hand. If all else fails, grab that little glass ball from your experiments and throw it at the damn thing, maybe that can kill it. The rest of you, get your bows ready and grab some of those modified arrows Nuru made. Still might not be able to penetrate its armor, but maybe a lucky shot from one of those will put the Shadow out of commission." Zayid shouted to the assembled remnants of his scout company, his voice booming through the hall as orders were given to his men.

With his serpentine sword drawn and held in one hand, a fresh torch blazing brightly in the other, Commander Zayid pushed open the front doors with his shoulder and walked out into the courtyard. Mentally he began to picture all of the traps that had been placed in his head, stepping over tripwires and hopping over pitfalls with ease as he moved around the perimeter of the courtyard and lit braziers they'd place in the corners. Though it would alert the Shadow of the Ash to their location, it would also allow them to see their opponent in the darkness without having to carry a torch in their free hand. Sahura and the three remaining fighters of his company followed him outside, spreading themselves out around the courtyard and readying themselves for battle.

The scout company had barely gotten into place when they heard it, a haunting screech echoing over the rooftops. Zayid raised his sword and adjusted his stance, eyes shifting around the street and the courtyard for any sign of movement. A few seconds passed in tense silence, each man listening closely for whatever minor sound might alert them to the Shadow's presence. A minute passed, then two. Sahura lowered his sword slightly and shifted his weight, unsure of what was happening.

Without warning the Shadow of the Ash leapt from the rooftop across the street from the Estyrian Embassy, falling towards Commander Zayid with its sword raised and a brutal screeching roar from inside the suit. Zayid dodged out of the way, rolling to the side and watching as the Shadow's momentum carried it forwards into the concealed spike pit he'd been standing on the rim of. Tipped with the largest shards of the red metal that the scouts had found, the dozen or so spears pointing upright within pierced through the armor with a loud crash. The Shadow of the Ash howled in pain, thrashing as it tried to free itself from the spikes which it was impaled upon.

Zayid quickly ran up to the rim of the pit and threw in his torch, igniting the oil which the alchemists had coated the spears in. As it thrashed and howled in the fire, Zayid watched on with a grim stare as the Shadow of the Ash slowly stopped struggling. Its howls became weaker and weaker, until finally it seemed to go still. The suit of armor crumbled into ash as the spears of the spike pit burnt themselves out, leaving behind no trace of the murderous spirit. Zayid leaned his head back and took a moment to revel in the act, avenging the deaths of his men and putting down the greatest threat to his company he'd yet faced.

A yelp of alarm snapped Zayid back to attention, causing him to whirl around and grip his blade with both hands. At the far end of the courtyard, the Shadow of the Ash stood with that same gruesome smile on its face. Its body seemed to be smoking slightly, embers rising into the air from gaps in the suit before flickering out of existence. In its right hand it held Sahura off the ground by his neck, the heat of its fingers searing his flesh and causing his third-in-command to gasp and grunt in pain. It cocked its head towards Zayid, the two red orbs of its eyes staring directly at the Commander once again.

"Sorry for leading you on, I just thought it would be quite entertaining to see what you would do if you were actually able to kill me. I was right, though I didn't take you for being a big enough fool to try and kill me with fire." The Shadow of the Ash snorted, a flurry of sparks shooting from its nose as it did. "You have a man tell you of a demon of wrath and vengeance, birthed in the flames of a destroyed city, and the first thought you have is to try burning it? Typical Estyrians, seeking to reduce to ash all of that which you cannot control."

The Shadow of the Ash began to cackle loudly, the sound echoing throughout the noble district as it tightened its grip on Sahura's throat. The man struggled and gasped for air harder than before, his eyes beginning to bulge out of his head. It casually swung Sahura to the right, holding him there as it stepped on a tripwire purposefully. From within a concealed pile of rubble, a tension-loaded spear launched out towards the Shadow of the Ash and impaled Sahura instead. Dropping the man to the ground casually, the Shadow smiled maliciously as it drew its blade. "You and your men have provided adequate entertainment, but I think it's time to remove your taint from this city."

Zayid and the other three charged the Shadow of the Ash, dancing around traps and tripwires as it adjusted its stance and lifted its blade with one hand. From all four sides, the commander and his men struck at the metal suit of the Shadow, striking sparks from the impact of steel against steel. Heat radiated from the wrathful spirit as it swung its blade in sweeping arcs, Arta and Heru sliding through the ash under the blade to avoid being cut while Zayid and Hathmon began to slash and thrust their blade towards the weak points in the armor. With a roar, the Shadow spun around and slammed its sword into the ground where Zayid had been just moments before. The cobblestones of the courtyard cracked under the impact, and with a whistle from Zayid the drawn bows inside the building let loose their arrows while the Shadow's back was turned.

Six feathered shafts soon stuck out of the back of the armor, causing it to roar as the shard-tipped arrows pierced through. A quick slice of its greatsword along its back severed the shaft of the arrows from the tips, and the six arrowheads clattered inside of the armor as it stood back up to its full height. The Shadow swung its free hand towards Heru, sending the six shards of metal flying out from its palm in a flash of motion. He staggered back, wincing as the six arrowheads embedded themselves in his arm and chest. He looked down at the damage for but a moment, but this moment was all it took.

As Heru looked upwards, instead his gaze returned to the Shadow. He saw that it had leapt forwards with sword in hand. He opened his mouth to shout in surprise, but the Shadow of the Ash's thrust drove the sword through his face and out the back of his head. The blade's width severed the skull from the lower jaw and the neck, and as the Shadow of the Ash yanked its blade free from the head of the man, Heru's skull was launched off to the side. It tumbled to the ground in a wet splatter, his eyes still looking around frantically for a few seconds before his face went limp.

Arta cried out in grief-fueled anger as he charged at the Shadow of the Ash, swinging at its back in a fury of blows. The sheer force of the sudden attack caused the entity to become staggered for a moment, knocked off balance by the amount of sudden sword swipes being rained down upon its metal shell. It responded with a violent swing of its right fist, the heated metal fingers clenched together tightly as the Shadow of the Ash struck Arta directly in the sternum. The man stumbled backwards, coughing up a little bit of blood and cradling his stomach as he tried to regain his footing. The Shadow of the

Ash rotated its arms upon its shoulder joints, as though loosening up muscles that were no longer there.

With this momentary break in the melee, the scouts inside took this as an opportunity to let loose another barrage of arrows. From the arrow slits where windows once were, volleys of arrows were fired in quick succession. The Shadow of the Ash was prepared however, dodging backwards into the ash and disappearing below the surface of the gray powder. Hathmon took this opportunity to check on Arta, running over to him and inspecting his wounds. A few ribs had been cracked, but the more concerning injury was the large shape of a fist burnt into his chest, branded onto his flesh by the heat which the Shadow radiated.

The hands of the Shadow burst from the ash and grabbed onto Hathmon's legs, dragging him away as the Shadow slowly rematerialized. Hathmon screamed in pain and clawed at the ground, trying to grab onto something that could stop the Shadow of the Ash from taking him, but it pulled him away from his comrade quicker than he could grasp something. Throwing him bodily against the wall of the courtyard, the Shadow twirled its sword in its hand as it approached the stunned warrior. Zayid burst forwards, ready to risk his life trying to prevent another casualty of the wrathful demon, but stopped when he saw Hathmon shake his head towards him.

The Shadow of the Ash stood above Hathmon, smiling down with that same sadistic glee that it'd held during all of its other kills. As it raised its sword above its head, preparing to plunge it into Hathmon's heart, the scout reached above him and yanked a tripwire with all of his might. The Shadow looked up as it heard a click from above, raising its arms above its head to shelter itself as a day's worth of collected rubble rained down upon it from the rooftop beside the Embassy. Both spirit and scout were buried beneath the stones, the metal armor of the Shadow of the Ash crushed beneath the weight of the falling rocks. Zayid lowered his head, offering a silent prayer for Hathmon's soul.

Zayid and Arta retreated inside, closing the great doors of the Embassy behind them and helping the others barricade it shut with as much furniture and loose rubble they could find. Nuru, Ra-Kep, Mhuro, and Amon stood at the four windows, bows drawn while they watched the pile of rubble. Ash seemed to be slowly flowing towards the pile from all across the courtyard, disappearing into the stones as they waited for the first sign of a metallic limb to poke out from under the pile. Panting heavily with exertion by the time they were done, Zayid wiped sweat from his brow and helped Arta to one of the benches. The warrior was out of commission in his state, so it rested upon the shoulders of the remaining battle-ready members of the scout group.

Zayid waved down the alchemists, who left their posts on the upper floor to convene with the commander. After a few moments of sitting down to let his breathing finally slow, he looked up to them with desperation written clear across his face. "That orb with the gas, will it work? Will it kill it?"

Nophi and Senuf looked to each other for a moment before letting out a pair of sighs, clearly uncomfortable with this suggestion. "It might. It also might not. It will however kill us all if even a tiny bit of it gets inside here, so we need a clear shot to throw it and a way to seal off any outside air from coming in."

Zayid nodded and sighed, motioning for them to go. "I'll have them start stuffing the windows shut now, seal them with wax and all that. Go and get the orb, we'll make sure you have a clear shot." He stood and walked over to the rest of the scouts, relaying the information and helping in the hermetic sealing of the front of the building.

The alchemists retrieved the orb quickly, carefully cradling it as they went back down the stairs. Zayid stood at the last open window, a large tarp beside him along with two lit candles and a bowl of melted wax. They handed the orb to him, and stepped back, covering their faces with their robes reflexively as he turned towards the opening in the wall. Just as predicted, the Shadow of the Ash was slowly crawling out of the pile of rubble which had been dropped on it, rematerializing with a hateful glare. Zayid muttered a quick prayer to Stygirius, asking the serpent god to guide his hand, before rearing his arm back and arcing the glass orb through the window.

The Shadow of the Ash could only watch as the black-stained sphere was flung towards him, the window immediately sealed after its throwing. It shattered at its feet, releasing a foul and thick smoke which seemed to spread far quicker than any natural smoke should. The Shadow reflexively lurched backwards, but stopped once it realized what it was. The corruption of Khigstus, alchemically distilled and activated in gaseous form, had been thrown straight at it. It began to laugh as it walked through the smoke towards one of the lit braziers, the same corruptive energies which had created it enveloping its form.

The Shadow of the Ash shoved its right hand into the fire and extended the other hand towards the smoke, drawing in the power which flowed around it. The fire flowed along its arm, traveling up the metal surface and causing the unholy runes inscribed along its armor to glow with power. The glow traveled from its arm to its torso, until eventually the corrupted magic which bound the spirit to the armor was luminescent. In its left hand, the corruption of Khigstus swirled around its palm, collecting in the metallic gauntlet as the Shadow's will was exerted over it. The fury which animated it, which gave the being of malice its power, materialized as another red crystalline spear which formed in its hand.

As the corruptive smoke was all but absorbed into the Shadow of the Ash and the fire which had birthed its ruinous form heightened the spirit's fury even further, the Shadow of the Ash reared its arm back. With all of its unholy might, the wrathful flames of its hollow soul burgeoning into a blazing inferno of untold hatred, it threw the spear at the great oaken doors of the Estyrian Embassy. Upon impact the spear exploded, shattering the doors into wood chips and creating a cloud of ash and dust which shrouded all vision. Shouts of pain and surprise from inside could be heard clearly as the men were knocked away by the explosion, before those cries too were silenced. Trembling with rage and indignation, the Shadow of the Ash drew its blade and walked inside.

CHAPTER
FOURTEEN

C ommander Zayid woke up some time later, his body weak and aching all over. He could barely open his eyes, but what he did see confused him. He saw blue skies above, the light of the early morning sun barely poking above the horizon as he was slowly moving in a direction he couldn't quite identify. The last thing he could remember was darkness before an infernally bright light, and then nothingness. Gathering his strength, Zayid groaned softly as he lifted his head to see his surroundings. In front of him was Amon, facing away from him as he dragged the commander's weakened body upon a sort of makeshift sled.

Zayid opened his mouth to speak, but all that came out was a dried and nearly silent croaking. He coughed and wheezed for a few moments before trying again, this time with more success. "A... Am on..." He choked out through parched lips, his vision swimming as his strength left him once more. The effort of lifting his head seemed to have drained him already, and he lay limply on the sled.

Upon hearing Zayid's voice, Amon stopped and turned to look at him. He stared at the commander with a scrutinizing look before noticing that his eyes were open, his expression suddenly changing to one of relief. He grabbed one of the waterskins from the side of the sled and brought it to Zayid's lips, gently trickling water into his mouth at a rate the injured man could accept. "I'm glad to see you make it Commander Zayid, I thought I might have lost you for a while there."

Zayid nodded silently, simply focusing on the blessing that was water upon his lips and throat. With hydration came renewed strength in great amounts, and soon he was able to sit up with Amon's assistance. "Amon... What happened? Where are the others?"

Amon's face fell as the subject of what had occurred was brought up, sighing softly as he crouched down to talk to Zayid. "We're the only two left. We thought that the gas had worked for a few minutes, we thought we heard it screaming out there. Looking back on it, the damned thing was probably laughing. After a few minutes of silence, suddenly the front door exploded and knocked most of us on our asses. We had no business fighting that thing in the first place, we should have left without a second thought."

"Everyone except you, Senuf, and myself had been knocked out or mortally wounded, and the second the Shadow came inside the first thing it did was put its blade through his heart. So while it was distracted, I grabbed you and some supplies and ran, carrying you on my back until we were far enough away for me to make the sled. I don't think anyone made it, and if you want to go back to check then you can do it alone." Amon said quietly, clearly at his wits end with the sudden loss of the men he'd spent the past few weeks living with.

Zayid slowly leaned back down onto the sled, letting the utter loss of his closest friends and companions sink in as he laid on the brittle wood. He closed his eyes and sputtered out a soft cough, the aching in his chest and throat from his combined fatigue, injuries, and dehydration catching up to him. As he laid there, the cool air of the morning washing over him and the bright sunlight shining through his eyelids, tears gently began to pour from the corners of his eyes. Grieving for the nineteen friends and brothers he'd lost, Zayid's heart broke as the faces of all the men who he'd never see again flashed before his eyes.

Amon returned to the foot of the sled, sighing softly as he leaned down and grabbed the rope which he'd been using to pull Zayid's sled. Sipping from his own waterskin before sealing it once again and hefting the length of rope over his shoulder, Amon sighed as he began to trudge through the ash once again. With the soft sobbing of the Commander behind him and the thick powdery ash clinging to his legs, the infantryman carried the burden of survival upon his shoulders both figuratively and literally as he dragged the makeshift sled down the roads of Sosias. The quiet thud of heavy footfalls echoed softly through the streets, their path marked by the thick line carved through the ash by the sled's bulky size.

Through the quiet hours of the morning the pair of survivors slowly made their way through the districts of Sosias, crossing the bridge from the noble district into the oppressive silence of the trade district. Commander Zayid's sobbing had faded into a silent despair, the hollow sensation in the pit of his stomach a constant reminder of those who they'd lost. Behind his closed eyes the faces of the nineteen men who he'd come to know as closely as kin floated just out of reach, staring at him with fear in their eyes and crying out wordlessly for him to save them. The petrified bodies and outstretched hands of the yearning dead gently brushed against his arms, the phantom grasps of those who had died under his watch tugging at his very soul. Now that he had gained consciousness and some of his strength, Zayid only moved to lift the water flask to his lips and take small sips every few minutes. However even this was a struggle, an inward battle to convince himself that he deserved to prolong his life and recover from the ordeal.

The sun was nearly at its peak in the sky when Amon slid the rope off of his shoulder with a grunt, dragging the sled by the charred wooden base under a large building which had partially collapsed. In the shade of the overhang Amon sighed as he sat down, his aching legs and shoulders burning softly with the exertion of dragging the sled along for hours on end. Reaching for his own waterskin, he poured the cool liquid down his parched throat with a nigh animalistic thirst, tiny droplets running down his chin as he drank deeply. Once his thirst was slaked, he sealed the container once again and leaned back against the wooden wall with a sigh.

A few minutes passed in silence, Amon panting softly as he gave himself the break he needed and Zayid laying limply upon the sled. Amon stared at the commander in silence, his face composed into a mask of deep thought as he gazed at the man, before he stood without warning. Walking over to the sled, Amon reached under the side of the large door which he'd made the sled out of and tipped it onto its side. Zayid was rolled onto the ground with a thump, groaning as he sat up and glared at Amon.

"What the hell was that for? What did I do to you, huh?" He snapped towards Amon, glaring as he unsteadily rose to his feet. His entire body ached, but it felt good nonetheless to get back on his own two feet.

Amon simply shrugged and returned to his former position, sitting in the shade and leaning back against the wooden wall of the building. "I can't drag you the entire way to Estyria, Commander. You've been awake, you've got water and I'm sure I've got food in one of the bags on the sled. It's time for you to pull yourself together, get off your ass, and keep moving. That's the only way we're gonna get out of here alive."

Zayid felt the urge to let loose all of the anger and frustration that had been building up inside, the grief which had boiled into hatred, when he suddenly stopped and took a moment to actually think on what he was doing. As much as he hated to admit it, he knew that Amon was right. He had to be blunt to break through the shell of apathy he'd built around himself, and it had worked. Slowly his shoulders lowered as the tension in his body fell, and quietly he grumbled as he began to look through the bags for some food. "Fair point, but you're still talking to your commanding officer."

Amon let out a soft chuckle at that, letting his head rest against the wall as he closed his eyes. "I'd say that we're a bit beyond that point, Commander Zayid. We can discuss rank when we get out of this deathtrap of a city, surviving that long should be our priority." He opened one eye a crack as he watched Zayid rooting through the bags, a faint smile spreading across his face as Zayid pulled out a length of the jerky which they'd been subsisting on for the last week. "Hey, pass some of that over here. You're not the only hungry one."

Zayid sat beside Amon with a soft grunt, splitting the dried meat in half and handing Amon his piece. The two men ate in silence, chewing slowly on their jerky and washing it down with the water they had left. Time passed slowly as they rested beneath the overhang of the collapsed building, the sun seemingly hesitant to leave its apex high above. Eventually both of the Estyrian scouts rose and brushed themselves off, Zayid groaning as he stretched out his limbs. Slinging their waterskins and bags over their shoulders, the two set off towards the border of the city at a renewed pace.

Both Zayid and Amon kept quiet and low during their trek through the rest of the trade district, doing their best to avoid making noise and leaving as little a trail as they could manage. Though the Shadow of the Ash had not been seen or heard since the harrowing escape, the threat of the homicidal spirit loomed over them like the darkest of clouds. Despite this need for stealth and quietness, the duo passed the time in the only manner available to them - they kept up a conversation. From sharing stories of their prior service or tales of grandeur about those who they'd lost on the mission, Amon and Zayid warded off the darkness of the district by keeping their thoughts on the good rather than the bad.

When they finally reached the edge of the trade district, arriving at the furrowed riverbed which separated the former slums from the inner city, they stopped abruptly. The distance to the city's edge was great, and with the outer ring of Sosias being a flat plain neither of the two thought crossing it in broad daylight would be a good idea. Finding a building that seemed somewhat structurally intact, Zayid and Amon hunkered down within and set up the barest form of camp while they waited. There was no fire or rest area, no comfort available with their equipment left far behind and the demonic scourge likely still trying to hunt them down. Instead they simply found the room furthest from any doors or windows, a small room which had likely once been a pantry, and judged it the safest place to talk.

Amon sat down on the hard ground, sighing softly as he glanced through the doorway towards the large room which had led into this one. The light of day was still bright against the wall, far too bright to attempt the crossing to safety. As Zayid sat beside him, softly sipping from his waterskin, he slowly looked at the commander with a raised eye. "You know, there's no clean water for a full day's walk, and no water at all until we reach the jungle. Take it easy on that, we're not going to be able to refill it any time soon."

Zayid shrugged in acquiescence as he sealed the waterskin once more, resting it on the ground beside him. "True enough, I suppose. Funny how that works out, we bring enough food to last nearly two dozen men a week without resupply, and we leave with barely enough to survive in less than half that time. Damn this city, and damn the idiots who thought sending us here was a good idea."

Amon chuckled and raised up his hand in a mock toast, miming bumping his glass against Zayid's. "If I had anything to drink that I didn't need to conserve, I'd raise a glass to that. So, what's the first thing you're going to do when you get home? I know for a fact I'm going to get blackout drunk and try to forget this whole thing."

While Amon was quietly laughing to himself about the prospects of getting as drunk as he could, Zayid leaned forwards and sighed. His seriousness was in stark contrast to Amon's joking, a great difference which attracted the infantryman's attention. "Well," Zayid said softly, "the first thing I'm going to do is go to the homes of each of my men's kin and apologize to them for not bringing them home. Once that's done, maybe I'll join you in drinking ourselves to death."

Amon grew quiet for a moment, reflecting on Zayid's words and sighing as he thought of the friends he'd lost. Khonsu and Sephis were on the forefront of his mind, and their loss weighed heavily upon his heart. His mouth grew dry, and he took a slow breath before coughing to clear his throat. "What about your daughter? You said you had one the day before we entered the city, so why not go and see her? I'm certain that after this, after everything this has put you through, she'll have no quarrel with you."

Zayid softly smiled and leaned back against the wall, his eyes watering slightly as he began to think of his daughter. "I suppose it wouldn't be the worst idea to visit her. It's been years, and as much as I think she would be angry at me she wasn't that type of person. I wonder if her mother's kept her grave clean..."

Amon's eyes widened as he stared at Zayid, sympathy tugging at his heartstrings. "I didn't realize... I'm sorry for bringing it up, Zayid,

I wouldn't have if I'd known..." He gently reached out and patted the commander on the shoulder, unsure of what would be the appropriate thing to do in this situation.

Zayid shrugged softly and wiped tears away from the corners of his eyes, his smile wavering at the corners of his mouth. "You're fine, you had no way of knowing. My men certainly wouldn't talk about it behind my back, and I hadn't told you. She died before I entered the military, back when I was just a farmer. Her name was Ayenna, and she was my shining star."

Amon listened intently, his attention riveted on the commander as he spoke of his deceased child. The grief in his voice he knew well by now, the somber tones of loss shared between them tenfold. It wasn't the grief that he was so surprised by however, it was the happiness in his voice which drew Amon's attention so closely. Commander Zayid had both laughed and cried around him, shown both deadly seriousness and a deeply comedic side of himself. But at the mere mention of her name, Zayid seemed to come alive in a way that he'd never have imagined.

"She was a beautiful little girl, with long hair and shining copper eyes. She was always full of joy and energy, laughing at jokes only she understood and singing songs only she could hear. That girl could find wonder in anything, no matter how mundane." Zayid's face was no longer that of a hardened officer, but that of a proud father. His eyes were unfocused, his gaze leading off into the past rather than seeing what was right in front of him.

"She was - is - my pride and joy. She could make me smile in any situation, no matter how dire. I mean, look at me! We have a strange wraith of metal and fire hunting us down and I'm still grinning from ear to ear." Zayid chuckled softly at this, leaning back against the wall and closing his eyes. "I miss her every day, y'know? Every time I wake up I think of her, every time I sleep."

"It's my fault she's gone now. I was younger then, stupid and without my priorities in line. The Festival of the Serpent's Maw came around, and Ayenna wanted to go see the snake they brought out from the temple. She was so excited to see it, I just couldn't tell her no. When we went out to go to the Festival our paths crossed with some of my friends, and we took a detour to get a drink before the show. I asked Ayenna to wait, but as one drink turned into two and then three, I must have lost track of time."

"I don't remember much else of that night, but I know what happened. While I was piss drunk, she wandered off towards the crowd to look for the Festival's grand display. When she managed to get through the crowd enough to see it, she slipped and fell into the snake pit." Zayid's voice cracked as he spoke, and he took a few moments to breathe deeply and compose himself before continuing. "The temple serpent ate her whole."

"I woke up on the floor of the pub, rank with liquor and with Ayenna nowhere to be seen. When I figured out what had happened I wanted the damn thing gutted to see if we could recover her, but the priest dismissed the notion without a second thought. 'Disrespectful to Stygirius' he said. My wife blamed me, rightly so, and took her own life a few months later. That's about when I joined the military, looking for purpose or maybe some sort of redemption. Never found it though, just hardship and further loss." He said softly, his eyes downcast as he finished his recollection.

There was silence in the room for a few moments before Amon patted Zayid on the back once more. He leaned over and wrapped his arm around the commander for a few seconds, providing what comfort he could. "I'm sorry, Zayid." Amon uttered quietly.

Zayid wiped the tears from his eyes and cleared his throat, trying to compose himself. "No, no, you're fine. You've got nothing to apologize for. If anything, I'm the one who should be apologizing. We're out here with our lives on the line, and I'm making you listen to my misfortunes."

Amon's face was set in a blank stare as he stood, looking down at Zayid. "Not for that. For this." Before the commander could respond, Amon struck him in the back of the head with the pommel of his dagger. Zayid slumped over immediately, knocked back into unconsciousness by the blow. With a sigh, Amon sheathed his weapon and began to drag Zayid by the arms out of the room.

Chapter Fifteen

When Zayid next awoke, the first thing he noticed was the throbbing pain at the back of his head. Groggily he tried to reach up to touch the place where it hurt, to assess the damage, but found that he could not. That was when he noticed the second thing: his hands had been tied behind his back and his feet tied together. As adrenaline began pumping through his veins and his perception of the world returned to his fullness, Zayid looked around frantically for anything that could help him understand what had happened. Amon stood over him with dagger in hand, illuminated by the last rays of the fading daylight before the world was plunged into darkness.

"Amon? What the hell are you doing? Cut me loose this instant, that is an order!" He barked, all caution thrown to the wind as he stared up at the infantryman. For the first time since they'd met, Amon's face was an image of pure apathy. His eyes seemed to stare directly into the depths of Zayid's soul with an intensity that made his blood run cold, an assessing gaze which seemed to regard him more as meat than man.

"You are in no position to give orders, Scout Commander Zayid. Even if you were, I can tell you with no uncertainty that you do not hold a station high enough to give me commands." Amon said with a cold, emotionless tone. The sudden shift from a man willing to die for his comrades, the same man he'd seen being so friendly towards his men, into a completely different man entirely had come without warning. His posture, his voice, his very gaze seemed almost predatory in nature.

Zayid's brow furrowed in confusion and anger, the sudden betrayal by a man who he'd just shown his most vulnerable side to invoking a rage within his heart. "What are you talking about? You're an infantryman, unless you've forgotten. If you do not cut me loose, I swear to god that when I get out of these bonds I am going to drag you back to Estyria in shackles myself."

Amon merely chuckled, kneeling over the commander as he idly toyed with the dagger. "You're a smart man, Commander Zayid. I'm certain you can put the pieces together if you just try hard enough. Why would the military high command put some nobody infantryman from a classified incident in your unit for this mission, especially one who shares the details of said incident despite knowing the consequences?"

Zayid glared at Amon as he spoke, briefly considering spitting in his face. "Now that's just a stupid idea in every aspect. The high command would never-..." Zayid's blood ran cold as he came to the realization that Amon had been guiding him to. "High command would never send an infantryman from such a high profile incident out of the country, especially on such an important mission."

Amon's face contorted into a strange, almost gruesome smile - it wasn't that the expression itself was ugly, it was that the smile was almost sadistic in nature. His eyes gleamed as he stared down at the bound man, nodding his head slightly. "Very good! A bit slow at times, but once you have all the evidence in the right light even you can see the truth. I was never part of an infantry group, and I've never even been to Ishtar."

"I am in fact an agent of the Golden Sodality, a name I'm sure you've heard of around your campfire or uttered in hushed conversations. I was sent to make sure that the red steel is a viable resource for harvesting, and one that we can defend from other nations while we mine it. However, now that I know there's an entity here already killing anyone and everyone who enters the city, my work here is done." Amon casually flipped his knife up in the air, watching it arc downwards and catching it mere inches from Zayid's face.

"Before you ask the painfully obvious question, the answer is yes. None of you were going to leave this city alive regardless of what happened, it's simply quite fortunate that the Shadow of the Ash did my job for me. We couldn't have you or your men walking around knowing the truth of what happened here." Amon's gaze was directed up towards the sky, watching the last light of day reflect off the clouds as the sun finally sank below the horizon.

"So why spare me then?" Zayid nearly shouted, the rage towards his betrayal by his own country burning hot in his chest. "You could have left me behind to die, but you didn't. You risked your life to get me out of that building, so why bother saving a dead man?"

Amon clapped his hands excitedly, clearly delighted by both the display of anger and the question itself. "Good thinking! You would have gone far if you weren't useless now. Firstly, I thought the Golden Sodality might have been able to recruit you. Were you a better parent and your daughter still alive, we would have been able to make you do anything we liked with her as leverage." Amon appeared to take a cruel sense of pleasure from the scream of wrathful indignation at that sentence, the full force of Zayid's grieving blasted out for all the world to hear.

"Secondly," Amon said as he casually plunged the dagger into Amon's thigh, "was this. I couldn't be sure just how smart the Shadow of the Ash is, so I decided to play it safe and bring a decoy!" Amon chuckled as he flicked the hilt of the blade, watching the resulting movement make Zayid writhe in agony as he screamed in pain. He spent a few moments further twisting it back and forth, smiling all the while.

Once Amon was satisfied that the screams could be heard from anywhere in the city, he stood and brushed the ash from his legs. "Just keep doing that, I have a theory that pain and anger both act like flares for the specter. I'm going to leave you to give my regards to the Shadow of the Ash, don't bother trying to escape. You wouldn't get far on that leg even if you did. Goodbye, Scout Commander Zayid." Amon stood and began running towards the edge of the city, sprinting under the cover of darkness across the ashen plain of the slums before the moon rose.

Amon had nearly gotten halfway across the slums when he heard the screaming abruptly stop, the last incoherent curses upon his name echoing through the silence of the accursed night as Zayid was silenced permanently. Without breaking his stride Amon looked over his shoulder to see if anything was chasing him, turning back to face ahead when nothing came sprinting out of the trade district. He grunted loudly as he impacted a solid object just as he turned back forwards, falling backwards and clutching his head as he bounded off of the object. Looking up at what he'd run into, Amon's amused expression turned to one of terror as the glowing red orbs of the Shadow of the Ash stared back at him.

"Clever trick with trying to sacrifice your friend as a distraction. A shame it didn't work, wouldn't you agree?" It growled as it stared down at Amon, the wrath in its gaze causing the man to unconsciously shrink back. It took a step forward as Amon tried to scramble backwards, keeping pace with the Golden Sodality agent's pitiful attempts at fleeing. "If there is one thing worse than an invader, it is a traitor. You, foolish Estyrian, are both."

Amon's hand whipped down to his belt, reaching for his dagger as he lunged towards the Shadow. With great speed he flung it at the metal face of the creature as he dove between its legs, taking off at a sprint towards the city's edge in some vain hope of escape. Amon cried out as a hand suddenly burst forth from the ash, a metal gauntlet which grabbed his right ankle and squeezed hard enough to break bone. Falling forwards again, Amon hit the ground hard in a cloud of ash. Even then, he did not give up - as soon as he hit the ground he began crawling away, survival the only thing that mattered.

The Shadow of the Ash scowled at this display, releasing the man's ankle before quickly catching up to the Estyrian still crawling as fast as he could. Rearing back its foot, the Shadow delivered a hard kick to Amon's side, causing him to double over in pain and clutch his stomach. It continued to strike the man with its foot, landing some shots on the ribcage and sending Amon reeling with a kick to the head.

Once Amon was sufficiently dazed and wounded, the Shadow of the Ash leaned down and picked him up by the throat.

The Shadow set him down facing the city and grabbed his head with both hands, forcing him to stare at the ruins of Sosias. "Do you see what your people did? Do you see the atrocities that your foul ilk committed upon these innocents? All of this death and ruin is the sole blame of you, the scum of the earth who inflict their will upon the world without consequence. Do you not feel shame?"

Battered and bruised as he was, Amon stared out at the city on his unsteady feet and smiled softly. "I see nothing but a rat nest, destroyed as the home of all vermin should be. Please, the deaths of innocents? Do you seriously think I care about what happened to this accursed city in this damned jungle? I'd burn it all down again myself given the opportunity."

Amon gasped as suddenly there was a pressure on both sides of his head, squeezing his skull as immense pain suddenly coursed through his entire body. He gritted his teeth and groaned loudly, but refused to scream even if it cost him his life. After a few seconds the pressure abated, the hands no longer pressing on the sides of his head. The experience made his vision swirl and swim, leaving him unsteady and swaying on his feet as he tried to process what he was feeling. He heard a chuckling behind him, followed by two scorched black gauntlets resting their palms over his eyes.

"Perhaps what you need," the Shadow snarled with a cruel laugh, "is a change of perspective." Suddenly the palms of the gauntlets grew hot, and within the darkness of Amon's concealed vision an image began flickering into existence. A soft sizzling could be heard from within the hands of the Shadow of the Ash as little wisps of smoke rose from Amon's face. His body trembled and shook softly as visions were forced upon him, a low groaning soon getting louder as he began to beg for mercy.

Amon's eyes felt like they had been lit on fire as he was transported to the past, seeing a great city burning in unholy fire where ruins only laid mere seconds before. He screamed in terror as the fire washed over him, charring his skin and melting flesh to the bone before it grew back in a mere moment. He gazed upon the true form of a god, the mere sight of the corrupted deity Khigstus in its true avatar instantly burning his eyes in their sockets, only to have those boiling liquids reform into eyes once more. Amon was thrown from perspective to perspective over and over again, dying countless horrific deaths from the perspective of those who had been slaughtered during the fall. Be it by the blade of an Estyrian soldier or entombed in the liquid fire that was molten Khigstinian steel, Amon felt the fear and terror of a thousand different deaths in the span of a few seconds. Throughout it all, the Shadow of the Ash stood in the center of his vision like a demon of fury wreathed in fire, laughing and intensifying every horrific sensation.

The Shadow of the Ash stared down at the man as he screamed his throat raw, the begging quickly having devolved into the incoherent screeching of absolute terror and agony. Amon's body was thrashing in place, his muscles seizing wildly as the phantom experience of having one's very flesh and bone singed to ash occurred over and over again. The sizzling had gotten much, much louder as smoke continued to rise, boiling tears running down his face and leaving burned lines upon his skin. The Shadow reveled in the agony and fear, feeding upon it with frenzied hunger and malice. It kept a careful watch upon Amon's very soul as its spectral tendrils carved the mark of the Shadow of the Ash upon his forehead, cursing him to see these visions forevermore.

With a growl of displeasure it pulled its hands away from Amon's face, watching as the man dropped to the ground like a sack of potatoes and continued to shake uncontrollably. Where his eyes had once been were now scorched empty sockets, burnt black to the very bone with the boiling fluids of his eyes having ran down his face in thick lines. He said no more witty and sadistic quips, merely quivered and seized and wept with his ragged throat. The facial mask of the Shadow of the Ash contorted into an inhuman grin as it crouched down, reaching its hand up to the blinded man's face and grabbing his head. It dragged him to the edge of the city and threw Amon bodily across the ruins of the wall, gazing at him with a hateful glare. "Go now, return to the den of rats which you call a home. Tell your masters that never again will any Estyrian find such mercy here as to spare a man's life. Tell them if they send more people, their sorcerers and alchemists, I shall be waiting for them."

After a few seconds, Amon scrambled to his feet and began blindly wandering off into the wastes, the only thing his hollow eyes could see being the visions of Sosias's fall and a faint light leading him to a final destination. The Shadow watched as he stumbled and fell more than a few times, eventually reaching the jungle in the distance and disappearing from sight. With its infernal gift of unsight, it knew that Amon would be led to Estyria one way or another. What they did with him once they found him was no longer its concern. It turned away from the city's edge and walked back towards the pyramid, sinking back into the ash as it did.

EPILOGUE

THREE MONTHS LATER

I n the heart of Neposet, within the chamber which housed the High Court of Nobles, two hundred members of Estyrian nobility were seated at their crescent table of marble. Their attention was directed towards the man standing in the center of the hall, where each and every member could observe and listen to his words. As a representative from the Golden Sodality, he had the ear of even the Grand Osir, so it was assured that everyone in attendance was paying close attention. Having spent the last hour delivering a report on the Sosian situation, more than a few of the nobility seemed greatly troubled by the news of the lost scouting party. Others seemed more fascinated with the potential wealth a nigh-unbreakable metal could fetch them, or the political maneuverings that the loss of a powerful nation could make possible.

One noble rose from his seat and gained the attention of the Golden Sodality representative, causing the man to stop in his relaying of the information. A thin man with a closely trimmed beard and a flowing golden robe, the representative bowed towards the noble with a coy smile. "Lord Sotep, I take it that you have a question? I would be more than happy to try and provide you with an answer."

Lord Sotep bowed his head before voicing his question. "How is it you came to have this information? If I remember correctly, you said that all members of the scouting party were killed in action. If that is so, how did you gain such a detailed report?"

A thin smile spread across the representative's face. "I am glad you asked, Lord Sotep. An agent of the Golden Sodality was inserted into this group in order to gather information for a more detailed report, and he was the only survivor we have yet found from the jungle. All of this information has come from his private journal and some of his...ramblings. If I may have the court's permission, and the permission of the Grand Osir, I would like to bring forth our source for this information. I would first like to warn the court however that he has been robbed of most of his mental faculties, and refuses to maintain his appearance."

The members of the High Council of Nobles turned to look at the shaded seat which the Grand Osir was seated upon, awaiting his influence. A silent wave of the hand from the Grand Osir was all the approval required, and the representative turned towards the entrance of the hall quickly. He clapped his hands twice, and immediately two guards dragged in a manacled man with a hood over his head. Muffled words too quiet to be heard properly came from beneath the hood as he was set on the ground beside the representative.

With a slight grimace, the Golden Sodality representative removed the hood from the man's head. The High Court of Nobles was soon filled with the reviled gasping of nearly two hundred men as Amon's marred face was revealed to the court, his burnt-out eye sockets weeping a thick brownish fluid. His hair was messy and unkempt, and the burns upon his face had festered into a pattern of boils and pustules.

The only actions of the Grand Osir were his leaning slightly forwards, the silhouette of the Estyrian leader shifting as his attention became more focused on the brutalized man. A length of cloth was wrapped around his head to act as a gag, muffling his otherwise quite vivid ravings.

Tossing the hood aside with some disgust, the Golden Sodality representative turned to look at every member of the High Court. "As you can see, this is why we are so hesitant to encourage further investigations into the ruins of Sosias until we have a method of counteracting the entity known as the Shadow of the Ash. According to this man's ramblings, the scarification and permanent mutilation is what the entity considers mercifully sparing a life. If this is mercy, then I think that the risk of desertion from even our most well-trained soldiers is far too high when they encounter what it considers to be cruelty."

Another noble stood, the look of disgust on his face obvious when his eyes passed over the man. "I also have a question. Seeing as there is no way to easily harvest the red metal, and that the entity can both speak and knowingly blame us for the destruction of Sosias, what are we going to do? If the rest of Galoholme discovers our interest in this super-metal, it may be the event we've been fearing that pushes them to band together against us."

This raised a chorus of concerned nobles standing and beginning to shout, adding their voices to the cacophonous roar that filled the room within seconds. It went on for only a few moments before a single voice rose above the rest in both volume and intensity. "Please, members of the High Court of Nobles, settle down. We have a plan." The voice was that of the Golden Sodality's representative, a surprisingly loud voice when needed from such a frail-looking man.

There was silence in the room for a moment, soon broken by the muffled laughter of the Grand Osir at the rather abrupt hushing of his court. The representative bowed to the Grand Osir with that same thin smile before continuing. "With the permission of the court and the Grand Osir, the Golden Sodality will engage in a campaign of erasing all information on the by-products of Sosias' fate. Not even rumors shall be spread, for we shall hear and silence each voice that shares such words. We would also like to recommend a large-scale blockade of the Khigi Jungle until further notice, to prevent any unfortunate souls from discovering the truth."

Quiet murmuring erupted across the table as the nobles began to deliberate, discussing the pros and cons of the plan. The representative did not bother to look through the myriad faces of the High Council, for none of their opinions truly held any sway over that of the Grand Osir. He watched the Grand Osir's face for any sign of his decision swaying one way or another, hoping to see some glimmer of a tell that would betray his inner thoughts. His eyes locked onto those of Ctesphon Estyrius III, and after a few moments a voice cut through the murmurs like a scythe through grass.

"I approve. Let it be done, and let it be over with. We've already sacked the city, let us focus upon the rewards we did not expect. Keep the operation unheard of while it is being prepared, let not a single voice speak of it outside this chamber for now." The Grand Osir leaned back as he spoke. With the decision made and no opposition from the High Council, the Golden Sodality representative bowed to the Council and Grand Osir alike before clapping his hands. The guards returned to drag away Amon, and the representative followed behind as the High Council of Nobles soon were dismissed as well.